Other Plans

Other Plans

Constance C. Greene

St. Martin's Press
New York

OTHER PLANS. Copyright © 1985 by Constance C. Greene.
For information, write: St. Martin's Press,
175 Fifth Avenue, New York, N.Y. 10010.
Manufactured in the United States of America

Library of Congress Cataloging in Publication Data

Greene, Constance C.
    Other plans.

    I. Title.
PS3557.R37964086 1985   813'.54   85-1716
ISBN 0–312–58958–1

10 9 8 7 6 5 4 3 2

Lines on facing page copyright © 1980 Lenono Music.

Other Plans

Constance C. Greene

St. Martin's Press
New York

OTHER PLANS.
Copyright © 1985 by Constance C. Greene.
For information, write: St. Martin's Press,
175 Fifth Avenue, New York, N.Y. 10010.
Manufactured in the United States of America

Library of Congress Cataloging in Publication Data

Greene, Constance C.
    Other plans.

    I. Title.
PS3557.R37964086 1985   813'.54   85-1716
ISBN 0-312-58958-1

10 9 8 7 6 5 4 3 2

Lines on facing page copyright © 1980 Lenono Music.

Life is what happens to you
while you're busy making other plans.

—John Lennon

Other Plans

1

POLICE RAID MALE STRIP JOINT, the headline said. Crowds of women, the story went, were there to watch men take off their jockstraps. That made him laugh. Sometimes, the story went on, women stuffed money inside the jockstraps, the way men stuffed money into belly dancers' bras, to show their appreciation. That was bringing the old women's lib down to the nitty gritty, he figured. Did the women in those places sit there drinking beer and hollering, "Take it off!" he wondered. Anything was possible.

He cut out the story and filed it away in his file cabinet under *S* for strip. He kept his ideas for gags in that cabinet. A certain amount of organization never hurt. The women in that place the night the police raided it, the paper said, ranged in age from their teens to their mid-fifties. He tried to imagine his mother there, watching guys take off their clothes, maybe even tucking a few bills in some guy's waistband. He knew her. She'd probably slip the poor guy a quarter, which would sink inside his jockstrap like a thin, cold stone. She'd never part with folding money if she could help it.

One of the women in the strip joint was quoted as saying, "My husband would kill me if he knew I was here." Maybe that had been his mother. Out for a night on the town. When she said she was going to a meeting for better day-care centers, she was really turning on at a male strip joint. Another lady, there with her teenage daughter, if you could believe what you read, said her husband thought it was her bowling night.

This was good stuff. He might be able to work it into a routine. For late-night TV. Those guys got away with murder. Anything went, as long as it didn't come on in prime time. (And once in a while, even if it did.) After hours, the air was blue with the gags they dished out. By then the network big-wigs figured the youth of the nation were asleep and beyond contamination. Little did they know.

Another possible gag presented itself:

NOSY NEIGHBOR: What does your son do?
PROUD MOTHER: Oh, he's a stripper.
NEIGHBOR: You mean in a paint store or a body shop?
PROUD MOM: No, he takes off his clothes. Makes good bread, too.

It needed work but definitely had potential. Maybe next time his father gave him the old what-are-your-plans-for-the-future routine, he'd hit him with that. Shake him up some. Well, actually, Dad, I'm thinking of becoming a stripper. That'd really make the old man's hair stand on end.

When he was alone in the house, like now, he liked to turn on the stereo and dance, hands in his pockets, jingling his change. Once, having recently seen an old Fred Astaire movie on TV, he'd leaped over the love seat in the living room (the parlor, as his sister Leslie liked to call it) and hadn't quite made it. The sole casualty had been a crystal vase full of phony dried flowers his mother kept on a low table.

So the dog was, had to be, the fall guy. The world is full of fall guys. The dog did it. His mother bought that one. The dog, God rest him, had since died of old age, brought on, no doubt, by his punishment: K-rations for a week, with no attention paid to his mournful, blameless countenance. If it'd been a Disney movie, the dog would've spoken up, declaring his innocence. Then he, John Hollander, would've had it in spades.

When he thought at all about the future, which he did as

little as possible, he thought he'd become a gag writer. Then work his way up, maybe wind up writing gags for a comedian. Or a conglomerate of comedians. Maybe even help out Woody Allen once in a while. A conglomerate of comedians interested him. Why not. Everything these days was a conglomerate of something. In school he had no difficulty making his friends laugh. In school, he was known as something of a wit.

The telephone rang. He considered not answering, but if it was his mother, which it undoubtedly was, and he didn't answer, she'd call the cops and ask them to check the house. He lifted the receiver.

"John? That you?"

Who the hell did she think it was, the mailman?

"Yeah, Ma."

"I forgot to leave you a note. There's stew on top of the stove. All you have to do is heat it. Add a little water. It might be dry. And chocolate pudding in the refrigerator."

"Okay."

"How'd you do on the test?"

"I'm not sure. We didn't get them back yet."

"Well, get your homework out of the way. We won't be late." He held the receiver away from his ear and made faces at it. Her voice took on an edge, as if she could see him. "Not too much television now. Get the work done first."

"Yeah, Ma." He had a sudden fantasy of a blonde waiting for him just out of his mother's view. Tried to imagine his mother's face if he said, "Buzz off, Ma. I got a lady upstairs so hot for my bod she's got steam coming out of her ears. She's up there right now, lying on my bed with her knees around her neck, waiting for me."

"Did Les call?"

"No, Ma," he said and hung up before she could think of anything more—any more instructions, any more questions.

He wrapped his tie around his neck and pulled it tight, watching in the mirror to see if his face turned blue. Strangulation wasn't his idea of a first-class way to die. Drowning, he'd heard, could be a sensual experience, if you didn't fight it. He wasn't against sensual experiences, but he was too good a swimmer. He could never let himself be sucked under, all those fish making goo-goo eyes at him, sucking on his toes for starters.

Only last week he'd read about a guy who'd been through an extraordinary experience. The guy was swimming, a long way from shore, when the air in his scuba tank ran out and he started to drown. He knew he was drowning. Then, all of a sudden, he was up in the air looking down at himself swimming. He also said he had a panoramic view of the beach, as if he were in a plane. Really weird. Then the guy said this great feeling of peace came over him, like he was in his mother's womb, he said. When you thought about it, sloshing around in the womb left something to be desired. What if you had a case of claustrophobia? What then? There were better, more peaceful places to be than your mother's womb, or any other old womb, for that matter. For Christ's sake.

The story went on to say that the guy was pulled from the water in the nick of time. Due to the fact that some guys fortuitously happened to be walking along the beach at the right moment. If this guy was telling the truth and wasn't some weirdo looking for a shot of free publicity—like he was in the skin diving business and was trying to drum up customers, for instance—it was a one-in-a-million event. Anyway, when they pulled him from the water, he was clinically dead. His lips were black, his heart had stopped. They gave him a fast shot of mouth-to-mouth resuscitation, a little heart massage, and he came back, good as new. The Greeks called it "anabiosis," or reincarnation after death. You had to hand it to the Greeks. They had a word for everything.

That was something to sink your teeth into, being brought back from death. That would be cool. To get that close and come back with all your marbles so you could regale your friends with the story of what it was like to die. You could clean up by writing a book about your experiences, which could be turned into a movie and maybe, the way things were going, a Broadway musical. Death set to music. Maybe they'd sign you up for the lead role and a percentage of the gross. Plus you'd get to write the screenplay. There were all kinds of ways to make a buck, if you thought it through.

A near-death experience, they called it. He wouldn't mind trying one on for size. The ultimate. My God, that'd have women hanging on your every word. They'd go ape. You'd have to beat 'em off with clubs. Better than any sexy after-shave. Anabiosis. That was the kind of thing Keith lost his mind over. As long as you could be sure there'd be somebody to haul you out at the crucial moment, somebody to pump out the old stomach, turn off the gas, give you a shot of CPR. Whatever. That was what made for the happy ending.

He unbuttoned his jacket, took off his shirt and tie. He went to St. Mark's, one of those antedeluvian joints that required full regalia every day. Everything but the vest and watch chain. Day in, day out. Out of touch with reality. That's what his school was. Out of touch, like a lot of people.

He flexed his muscles, stuck out his chest, and studied himself dispassionately in the mirror.

You little wimp. You couldn't fuck an ostrich. Who do you think you are? Woody'd have the thing sewn up by now. Woody was no beauty, but one word out of the side of his mouth and that blonde upstairs, just out of his mother's range finder, would be hard at work right now, cooking up a vat of chicken soup just like Woody's mom used to make. He saw her standing at the stove, bare except for an apron tied around her spelling out CHEF AT WORK in big red letters.

He went out to the kitchen, turned on the light under the stew, and ate the chocolate pudding standing up. When he was little, his mother had always made him clean his plate before she kicked through with the dessert. Every chance he got now, he ate dessert as a first course. When the stew was barely warm, he ate it from the pot. Suppose I was an orphan, he thought, maybe a foster kid, living in some total stranger's house, and they beat me, starved me, held my hand over the pilot light when I wet my bed. He'd read terrible stories about little kids brought to hospitals with mysterious burns or bruises all over their bodies, with broken bones, concussions, venereal diseases, even. Stories about little kids dying and being buried with their teddy bears beside them. It made him almost physically ill to read these stories, but he did anyway. They acted like a magnet, drawing him, holding him. He was repelled but fascinated. He thought he could probably kill a person who committed atrocities upon a defenseless child. He thought he might be capable of murder. Everyone was, he believed. Given the right circumstances, the right degree of provocation, the necessary level of rage or urge for retribution, everyone was capable of murder.

On impulse, he took a bottle of ketchup from the cupboard, shook it well, and spread it around. There was something about his mother's immaculate kitchen floor that asked for it. He pretended he was an artist, Picasso, maybe, an abstract artist, who made his fortune painting in ketchup. Every time the artist made a mistake, he could lick it up. He put some in his palm and smeared it on the gleaming cabinets. It made a powerful artistic statement.

On the other hand, this could be the scene of a murder.

"Looks like a crime's been committed here," he said, pulling at his chin, thinking hard.

"What makes you say that? Ain't no body I can see." Sometimes he knocked himself out.

"This much blood, got to be a body."

"Maybe the dog cut his tail. Labs do that. Bleed a lot. Lot of blood when a Lab cuts his tail."

"Maybe you're right. No body, no crime, right? Might as well clean up the mess and pretend nothing happened, eh?"

Someday he thought he might write a play. Like Woody.

He took a bottle of cleaner from under the sink and went to work with a sponge. When the place was pristine, so pristine that even his mother wouldn't be able to detect a trace of ketchup, he ran hot water into the stew pot and slipped in the dessert dish. Then he went upstairs, hung his shirt and tie and jacket on the back of a chair, and took a leak. He studied himself, wondering if he was normal. Probably not. Probably he was stunted. They said you could tell by the size of a guy's nose how big his pecker was. He thought that was baloney, although his nose did seem to have grown some since he'd turned sixteen. Maybe it was his imagination. But there was no denying it looked bigger. But not his pecker.

Ann Landers said it didn't make any difference what size a guy's pecker was. She printed a letter from a guy who said he was a bachelor in his mid-twenties who'd never had sex. He was embarrassed, he wrote, because he thought his pecker was inadequate. He was afraid of failing, so he didn't try. Old Ann fired back a letter telling the guy to go for it, the size of your pecker (his word, not Ann's), she said, was irrelevant. Let me know how things turn out for you, she wrote. She always liked to know how things turned out. You had to hand it to her. She answered the tough ones head-on. He admired that. He kept a close watch, checked the paper every day to see if the guy wrote back to say, "Thanks, Ann, you saved my life," maybe giving some details, the way people did. Up to now, there'd been no reply. Probably the guy was too busy.

He finished his self-examination and went into his parents' room, made a flying tackle and landed, face down and spread-eagled, in the middle of their bed. For a few minutes he stayed there, breathing in the scent of taffeta. His mother had the hots for taffeta bedspreads. He embraced one of the pillows, crushed it in his powerful arms, felt it go limp. If he wanted, he could have an orgy in this bed. Nobody was stopping him. If he ever did have an orgy, this is where he'd have it. The only thing missing was a mirrored ceiling. And a knowledgeable friend of his, already a freshman at Duke, said satin sheets helped.

He lay there, thinking about the size of peckers, remembering the annual or, when he was very young, the monthly feel job he'd endured, courtesy of old Doc Spear, the goddam pediatrician. That had always been a low spot, the feel job. He closed his eyes, saw his mother solemnly escorting him into the examination room. Even at four or five, he'd resented the doc taking liberties. Taking hold of his pecker and squeezing it like it was a grapefruit the doc was thinking of buying and wanted to make sure was ripe. The doc wore big thick glasses that blotted out his eyes. In that phony jovial voice of his, he'd ask, "How're the waterworks, son?"

I'm not your son so don't call me son, he remembered thinking. The worst part was his mother, standing in the corner, staring at the wall like a dog in a Booth cartoon, studying the doc's medical degree. Pretending she didn't know the liberties the doc was taking with him. Why didn't she just stay outside and read the *National Geographic?*

The day came when he handled that problem. He was nine, in the fourth grade, where the teacher found him obstreperous and inattentive. He and his mother were sitting in the doc's office, twiddling their thumbs, waiting for the summons from the inner sanctum. "You may go in now," the nurse said, and his mother had leaped to her feet as if someone had goosed her.

In a very loud voice, filled with so much authority he'd been astonished by his own boldness, he'd said, "I want to go in by myself." His mother had turned, startled, to see who had spoken. A big fat kid was sitting there, reading a comic, waiting his turn. He could see that kid now, see him perfectly, see how the kid's tight pants were caught up in his crotch. "Bully for you," the kid had said, punching the air with his fist, then ducking down behind his comic. His mother stayed where she was, and he'd gone in alone, walked right in, and hopped up on

the examining table like a pro. That was symbolic, he figured.
A sort of coming of age. From that day forward, when they
went to the doctor's, his mother stayed put.

The telephone beside the bed rang. He leaped off the taffeta bedspread and smoothed it hastily. His mother was giving
her famous double cheek.

"Yes? Who iz?" He used his Hungarian accent to throw
her off course, make her think she had the wrong number.

"John, it's me, Les. How are you?"

"How's it going, Les?" He tried, unsuccessfully, to keep
the pleasure out of his voice. Leslie, in her second year of college, was all of the good things: bright and beautiful and funny
and honest. Les could hold her own anywhere. He figured
she'd grab a magna or summa something when she graduated
and go on to head up a big corporation. Maybe make the
Fortune list of the ten most highly paid women in the country.
He could see her flying her own plane to board meetings,
maybe even making it to the Supreme Court.

"I'll be home next week on my spring break," Leslie said.
He could hear music and laughter in the background. There
always seemed to be music and laughter in the background
when Leslie called. College must be a perpetual party.

"I'm bringing a friend, and I wanted to let Mom know so
she'd have plenty of warning. You know how she is."

"They're not home," he said, lying back on the bed, walking up the wall in his stocking feet. "They're cutting a rug
someplace, probably getting stoned. You know them. Is your
friend male or female?"

"Female. You'll like her, John. She's outrageous."

"How come you didn't call collect?" "Outrageous" was
Leslie's favorite adjective; it could mean anything.

She snorted. "I'm too old for that. And so are you. That's
one of the first signs of independence, John. When you pay for
your own phone calls home. That gives you the edge, sonny,
and don't you forget it. They say, 'My baby's finally growing

up.'" They laughed, and he stored that away in the compartment reserved for bits of wisdom à la Leslie.

"When are you coming? Ma will want to know so she can start cleaning out the refrigerator."

"Probably Sunday. If she wants to know what time, say you don't know. If I say three and we don't get there until five, she'll be pacing. They both will. If there's any change, I'll call, okay?"

"Sure. I'll see you," and he hung up fast, beating her to the punch. He didn't want Les to think he was a pest, hard to shake, the typical kid brother. He also didn't want her to know how much he missed her. When she'd gone away last year he'd had no idea how much he'd miss her. He also hadn't realized how much heat she'd taken off him all those years. With Leslie gone, the full force of his parents' attention was directed at him. They discovered what they'd only suspected: he was goofing off. His teachers complained that his attitude wasn't good, his marks likewise. A set of ground rules had been laid down, calculated to lash him to the mast, stake him to the ground, deprive him of his freedom. Study time, meditation time, outdoor activity time, all were cataloged. No more than ten minutes in the shower and a pox on him if he turned up constipated.

He went to the window and peered out at the big blue globe of light shining from the house across the street. The TV set, holding folks in thrall, like a gigantic fireplace in front of which the family gathered in a ritual of togetherness. In the olden days, before his grandparents had been born, they'd probably blown out the candles and hopped into the sack for lack of anything better to do. Which was why they'd had such big families, he figured. And the kids were put to work hoeing and butchering hogs when they were barely out of diapers. Those days appealed to him. He'd never done a hard day's work. This summer he wanted to land a job working outdoors. Anything that might help to build up some muscle. He'd like to work on a farm, but farms were going out of style. Last year he'd lifted weights. Then he'd strained his back and wasn't able to play football. His father's forearms were bulging and beautiful. When he was little, he remembered stroking them, thinking of his father as a good giant. Now he was taller than his father, to his great delight, but his father still had bigger muscles. How come he hadn't inherited any? At night he did push-ups and checked the "For Sale" ads, looking for one reading, "Slightly used barbells, good condition," but none appeared.

His grandfather, usually a reliable purveyor of bygone customs, had told him that in days of yore, folks had huddled around the radio listening to President Roosevelt. Or, if they were Republicans and hated Roosevelt's guts, they could tune in to Jack Benny or Fred Allen, pretty funny guys in their day. "We made our own fun in those days," his grandfather had said, on one of his infrequent visits. "I guess you do the same, eh, John," and he'd winked. "Times haven't changed that much, I suspect."

He liked to talk to his grandfather. Grandy was a rare bird. A class act, Leslie called him. He wore a Homburg and had a pair of pearl gray spats, which he'd promised to leave to John when he died. "If and when," Grandy had said. "I'm not ready to go yet, John. Not for a long while. There are too many things I haven't done, places I haven't yet seen." Grandy was flamboyant. So was Keith. He, John Hollander, was not.

Call me Walter Mitty.

He turned away from the window, thinking again of Leslie. Boy, if she knew how glad he was that she was coming home. Too bad she was bringing a friend. He would've liked it better if she came alone. When it was just the two of them, she talked to him, really talked. He could ask her anything, tell her anything. Almost anything.

Maybe he'd call Keith. He felt like talking. And Keith was the only person, other than Les, he could talk to without crapping around. Except Keith had said it would be better if he didn't call. Don't call me, I'll call you, Keith had said, laughing because he was dead serious. No telling what might be going on over there. Better leave it alone.

A desire for solitude followed quickly on the heels of wanting to talk. Sometimes it happened that way. He was alone, yet he wanted solitude. Odd. That's when he went to his room. It was a lifesaver, that room. His hideaway, one of the few places where no one could get to him. Safe. Inviolable, that room. He made for it, was halfway there when he remembered his homework. He went back downstairs to get his pile of books.

Walter Mitty indeed!

The room had one window. The solitary pane of wobbly old glass looked out on the lawn that sloped down to the pond. Now, in late February, a thin film of green-black ice usually coated the pond's surface, gleaming enticingly, inviting folks to try it out. Last week there'd been a few days of warm sun, almost shirt-sleeve weather. Last night it had snowed. Winter was capricious in southern Connecticut. Spring came slowly, dragging its muddy feet.

He looked down at the pond, layered now with a dusting of last night's snow that hid the dark ice. That's the boy. One step. That'll do it. Walk slow, careful now. Doesn't even creak. Sound as a dollar. Safe as your own bed. A couple of canards, those. Not to worry.

And the blue-eyed boy was hurled down, down into the terrible iciness that grabs the ankles and won't let go. Three little boys, brothers, drowned last week up in New Hampshire. He watched as they pulled the bodies from the water on the six o'clock news. Three of them. A family. No more trio of stockings hung by the chimney with care. He'd closed his eyes against the sight of their mother's face when she got the news.

The room was nine by twelve. Tacked onto the house by some errant builder nursing a hangover, it was cozy and dark, its smallness appealing. Cobwebs festooned the low ceiling with a proprietary air, swaying in the slightest breeze like a lacy curtain. A bordello-type curtain, or what he imagined a bordello-type curtain to be. When even he couldn't stand the room's ambience, he cleaned, wildly wielding the mop, stiffing up dust balls the size of jumbo eggs. The sofa bed beckoned, last year's castoff from a style-conscious neighbor. He had hauled it, with no little effort, from the Tuesday curbside trash heap before the antique dealers could get wind of it. It was definitely collectible. Thin and threadbare, it resembled nothing so much as a wrestling mat. And about as comfortable. He had dreams of wrestling there, on some hot and windless summer night, the humidity unbearable, the family away for a long weekend. If luck was really on his side, they were caught in a massive holiday traffic jam, delayed for hours. Days, even. His partner on the mat will be soft and enthusiastic, an experienced wrestler.

Two chairs cowered in a corner, leaning against each other for support; their springs rested on the floor. This was the furniture that cluttered the room. The decor suited him. He thought of it as understated elegance.

No one was allowed here except by invitation.

"So this is where you hole up, is it?" His father had to stoop to enter.

"Dad," he heard himself say. And was unable to continue. Dad what? His mother, he knew, was responsible for this visit. "Go talk to him," he could hear her say. "Show him you care. He's your son, after all. Talk to him." His mother had a way with words. It was his father's maiden visit. First and last. They stared at each other, uncomfortable alone together, each waiting for the other to speak. His father's eyes were the first to fall. His father, who thought of himself as fastidious, backed out at last, grossed out by the swaying cobwebs, the dense, fetid atmosphere of the place, an atmosphere that discouraged further intimacy. He thought often of that visit, that moment, wished he could call his father back, run through it again. He would handle it differently. "Sit down, Dad," he would say, "and let's chew the fat. Wait here and I'll get us some grass and we can smoke and let down our hair." His father would raise an eloquent hand, rejecting this plan. Ignoring the gesture, he would reach inside his secret cache and produce some pretty good stuff procured by Keith, and they would light up and everything would be all right between them.

"This stuff is as good as, if not better than," his father would say at last, relaxed, friendly, "any martini I ever had." It was the highest form of compliment his father knew how to pay. A warm rosy glow suffused the room, their faces. Joy crowded their hearts. They were as one.

Now he stood looking out at the willows that ringed the pond, struggling for survival. When spring stirred itself, the willows would be the first to know. And would turn pale yellow overnight in celebration.

In summer an occasional swan, an arrogant, small schooner of a bird, sometimes established residence at the pond, advised of this place's existence, no doubt, by some peripatetic relative with a long memory and a love of quietude. The swan, bad temper well in hand, appetite quickened by the succulent slugs that nestled under the water, was ready to bite the hand that fed it. And often did.

He lay on the sofa bed and fished underneath with a long and dangling arm, looking for a surprise, a book he hadn't read. He had read and reread them all many times. He kept a sizeable supply there, waiting for his attention. These books were his source of joy and wonder. His palliative.

The arm came up with one of J. Thurber's collections. Good. Good. He was in need of a few laughs. Somewhere, recently, he had read that laughter wakes up the mind. He believed this to be true. He settled down to read. And was deep into "The Catbird Seat." Mr. Martin had, in fact, just turned down the street on which Mrs. Ulgine Barrows lives, his pocket heavy with the unfamiliar package of cigarettes, which weighed like a small revolver, when John heard, like Radar in *M*A*S*H*, the family car. Or cars. His mother and father traveled in separate cars as others flew in separate planes. If an accident occurred, there would be someone left to look after the children, they reasoned. A habit started when the children were very young, it persisted, like most habits. Doubtless they would travel in separate cars when the children had flown the nest and were titans of commerce, writers of renown. He had a secret plan: when he was middle-aged, about thirty-five, he planned to find a village named Renown so he could settle there and then, when he died, his obituary could truthfully read "John Hollander, writer of Renown."

Quickly he doused the light. His ear was finely tuned. He hadn't been caught with his light on in ages. He didn't feel like answering any questions or talking to anyone right now.

He sat in the dark listening to himself breathe. Then, silent as a cat, he crawled through the room's opening into his own bedroom, pretending he was a second-story man, or perhaps a rapist, creeping with great cunning and boldness to the bed, prepared to place the chloroform-soaked rag over the mouth and nose of the beauty lying asleep, supine, starkers. Just as he reached out, she opened her eyes, like Snow White, and sighed, "You've come at last."

He made it to the bed, just in time. He heard footsteps coming up the stairs, down the hall, stopping outside his door. He knew they would check on him, see that he hadn't succumbed to crib death or, worse, run off to some gin mill. He wondered if they would ever stop checking on him, and he knew they would not. When he was gray and gnarled, or bald and bulbous, however it went, they would continue to run a bed check on him. As long as they were around. Maybe he'd be one of those sons who continues to live at home well into his dotage. And theirs. The way they did in Ireland. The thought made him want to laugh out loud. But caution prevailed. He saw himself, middle-aged, querulous from dentures and/or irregularity, still having his television time rationed, his work habits overseen. If he ever went on a honeymoon, which was doubtful, they would run a bed check on him from their room next door. Of that he was sure.

Actually, he thought, that wouldn't make a bad skit. Middle-aged gent with extravagantly sexy bride, escorted on honeymoon by doddering parents, who made sure that everything was on the up and up.

The door opened. His eyelids fluttered, but not unduly. He hoped she wouldn't stand there looking at him too long. He rather liked the look of the supine and starkers beauty and was afraid his mother would frighten her off. Timing. In affairs of the flesh, as in most others, timing was all.

The door closed. He lay rigid, waiting for the sound of silence out there.

"He's asleep," he heard his father say. So. It had been his father giving him the old one-two all along, willing those fluttering eyelids to part. His father, the architect. The idea startled him into wakefulness. Long after the house had settled down for the night, creaking and groaning its tired old bones, and the beauty had picked up her marbles and gone, he lay staring at the ceiling. There was something about a dark and quiet house that made for a wakeful night. There was something decidedly unsettling about knowing his father had stood on the threshold of his room, gazing fixedly at him without a by-your-leave. It was hours, or so it seemed, before he stopped thrashing, turning, thwacking at his pillow, which unaccountably had been filled with lumps of coal when he wasn't looking, and slept.

2

When he tottered downstairs the next morning, the brash sun already had the kitchen in its grasp. He kept his eyes at half-mast in an effort to shut out the glare, the brilliant colors in the wallpaper. He had a theory, well-tested, never proven, that if he stayed in a semicomatose state until he reached school, his mind would be better able to cope with what the day held.

His mother, alas, had a theory diametrically opposed to his. Hers was the hot cereal bit. Hot cereal to warm the body, feed the brain, coat the tongue. Resolutely he picked up his spoon and, in full truck-driver crouch, attacked the bowl of lumps she'd set so proudly before him, sending clouds of steam into his face. If she ever turned out a vat of lump-free gruel, she'd feel in some small way she'd let him down.

His mother watched him eat and thought what lovely bones he had. And his head was beautiful. Well-shaped. She loved having him around the house, even though he drove her crazy at times. He needed a new sports coat, she mused. Those sleeves barely covered his elbows.

He looked up, caught her watching him. "Hey, Ma. Quit it. You make me nervous when you stare at me." Her morning face was slick with moisturizer. She moisturized the bejesus out of her face ever since she'd turned forty. Locking the barn door after the horse had been stolen, she called it. Kiss her good-bye in the morning and you slid off the edge of her cheek. Her lashes, palely brown, barely discernible, lay against her face, delicate as the wings of a moth. When she was suited up to meet the world, they were thick and black and lustrous. He liked her morning face better. She seemed to him then to be less a mother, more a friend.

"You're getting army," she said.

"My arms too short to box with God," he said.

"I'll have to see if I can find you a jacket at the Thrift Shop. I'm working there today. I'll look for one."

"Ma," he rolled his eyes. "One request. Lay off the Thrift Shop, okay? Those clothes you bring home from there always smell like cat."

"Anybody call last night?" she asked, ignoring his crack about cat smell. He knew she would buy him a jacket at the Thrift Shop, one whose sleeves grazed his knuckles. She would take it to her little man who would shorten the sleeves at great price.

"Yeah. You did," he said. She gave him a look. "And also my money man—my broker—and a couple of girls hit me with obscene phone calls. That's about it." He washed down some lumps with a swallow of milk laced with coffee and studied the ceiling, trying in vain to remember any more calls.

"John, I can tell from your expression that someone did call. Who was it?"

"Oh yeah. I forgot." He took another swallow and swirled the café au lait around like mouthwash.

"Les called," he said as slowly as he dared.

"I knew it!" she crowed. "What'd she want?"

He shrugged. "Nothing much. Just checking to see how we all were. Said she wanted you to send some chocolate chip cookies." Out of the corner of his eye he saw her push up the sleeves of her bathrobe, an old one of his father's she'd managed to shrink pretty much down to her size.

"John, I haven't got all day." He could hear his father moving around upstairs.

"She said to tell you she's coming next week on her spring break."

"I thought so! Wonderful! When, exactly? Why on earth didn't she let us know beforehand?"

"She did. This is beforehand. She's not coming until Sunday." He took his cereal bowl to the sink and squirted water into it, sending the remaining lumps down the disposal, fleeing for their lives. "She's bringing a friend." He watched his mother's eyes dart around the spotless kitchen, checking for pockets of filth she might've overlooked.

"A friend? Who?"

"She didn't say and I didn't want to pry," he said primly. "All she said was her friend was outrageous." Leslie had brought several young men home her first year at college and they'd been reasonably wimpy, he'd thought. Feckless, his father had called them.

"It must be a girl," his mother said.

"How do you figure?"

"If it was a man she'd say he was interesting or attractive or amusing, but she wouldn't say 'outrageous.' You're sure she didn't say who the friend was? That's not like Les."

"Nope." There was no reason to withhold information from her. Still, he liked doing it, liked being the sole person in the house who knew Leslie's friend was a girl. His father appeared in the doorway.

"Does anyone know where my gray socks are?" His father thrust out one bare foot, giving him a significant stare. His father was paranoid about him stealing his socks. Which he did only when desperate. "I can only find one, John. Did you take any socks from my drawer?"

"Dad," he said, "I wouldn't be caught dead wearing your socks." If only the dog hadn't died. Check the dog. He must've eaten it. Why don't you order an autopsy? Check out the poor bastard's stomach. One sock, hardly chewed, only a little bit slimy. Death due to one chewed sock.

"Henry, I put some clean socks on top of your bureau yesterday," his mother said. "Did you check there?"

"What a strange place to check for clean socks," John whispered as his father limped back upstairs, as if wearing one sock made for some sort of disability.

The telephone rang. His mother, by virtue of superior maneuvering, got to it first.

"Hello? Yes, he's here. He's eating," she said, which wasn't true. "All right." Her voice was irritable. It must be Keith.

"I've got probs here." Keith's voice was low and raspy. "She got herself clobbered last night. Brought some guy home for a nightcap and the guy started throwing things and hollering and some asshole of a neighbor called the cops. I didn't get much sleep."

His mother pointed her ear at the phone as if it were a dowsing rod and she was searching for water. He moved away from her. No good would come of it if she heard what Keith was saying.

"Yeah, that's all right," he said in a phony, bright voice. "I can handle that. Sure, fine."

"What?" said Keith. "Tell Gleason I have an earache. Or herpes. I don't care what you tell him. Tell him I'm on my way to the doctor. If he asks, that is. I don't know when I'll make it to school. Maybe not at all. Front for me, okay? Some day I'll return the favor," and with a ghoulish laugh, Keith hung up.

"What'd he want?" She always knew when something was up. Besides that, she didn't trust Keith.

"He overslept." He busied himself with his stack of books. "Wants me to tell Gleason he'll be a little late."

"I bet." Pursing her lips, she said, "It's a wonder that kid gets to school at all, with his home life."

What did *she* know about Keith's home life?

"I've got to split, Ma. See you," and he grabbed his jacket from its hook on the back of the kitchen door. He almost had it made when his father reappeared and nailed him.

"I'd like to talk to you tonight, John," his father said.

"You find your sock?" He looked pointedly at his father's neat gray ankles.

"Yes. Thank you for your concern." His father didn't like to admit that he couldn't find things.

"Block out your time this evening so you can do your

homework and still fit me in." His father's voice was excessively polite. "It's time we talked about your future, your attitude. Where you're going."

"I'm going to school," he said, smiling to show he wasn't being a smartass.

"You know what I mean, John." His father fiddled with the dial on the TV, looking for his favorite newscaster. With any luck at all there'd be a shot of the president taking off for the weekend, and his father could shoot off his mouth and let off some steam talking to the president, telling him all he ever did was wave to the peasants on his way to his weekend place. There was nothing like the sight of the president, taking off or staying in the capital, to distract his old man. It was magic.

"Just pull yourself together so we can discuss your plans this evening."

Why couldn't he say "tonight" like other guy's fathers?

"I don't have any plans, Dad. I can fit you in." Behind his father's back, he made a face. His mother widened her eyes at him and said, "Get a move on or you'll miss your bus." He knew she'd like it if he kissed her good-bye. But he didn't feel like it. He let the door slam behind him and, as the damp February air filled his lungs, he lifted a finger to the sky to show what his father could do.

Head down, bucking the wind, he trudged to the bus stop. If he timed it right, he and the bus would round the turn together. He enjoyed racing alongside while the kids inside peered out, cheering him on, shouting so the bus driver, who was his friend, would order them all to pipe down. Sometimes, when he raced like that and listened to the sounds of cheering, he pretended he was in the Olympics, on his way to a gold medal. Or imagined himself Jimmy Connors. Or even Chris Evert Lloyd. When it came to winning, he was totally asexual.

This morning, no matter how he dragged his feet, scraping them over the frozen ground, no matter how much he slowed down, he couldn't win. He had to wait even after he reached the bus stop, stamping his feet, watching his breath rise in the cold air.

"So. You're an early bird today, eh?" Gus, the driver, swung open the door to let him in.

"More like the worm." He lurched down the aisle to the back of the bus, hoping for a seat next to someone he didn't know. In his bones rested the knowledge of a bad day coming. Keith calling, his father lining him up for yet another session in which he did all the talking: If he didn't shape up, he'd wind up in a bread line. Or selling apples, à la the Great Depression. If he didn't pull up his socks and get serious, he could forget college. A good college, anyway. He had heard it all a hundred times.

If he'd been able to race the bus, maybe he could've worked off the sweat. As it was, a heavy weight lay on his chest.

His mother's hot cereal?

Perhaps. More likely, the weight of impending doom.

3

"Mr. Hollander, sir? Doctor will see you now." The nurse was plain, sallow-skinned, her small eyes made smaller by blue eye shadow applied with a heavy hand. As Henry followed her down the hall to the doctor's office, he could see her shoulder blades through her uniform. She flattened herself against the office door to allow him room to pass and he noticed a birthmark on her neck, dipping down into her white collar. A birthmark the color of eggplant; aubergine, unsightly. He wondered why it hadn't been removed when she was a child. There was no excuse for leaving something that disfiguring on a girl baby. Or a boy baby, either, for that matter. The doctor stood as he entered. He must look as old as he felt. It was only recently he'd begun feeling tired before the day was half over. Only recently, too, he'd taken to examining his face in the mirror and realized he was beginning to show his age.

"Good morning, Mr. Hollander. Nice day. A bit nippy, but nice." There were the formalities to be gone through. The doctor was alarmingly young. With his chubby cheeks, strawberry-blond hair, and freckled forehead, he looked like a very large child. The doctor's hands, however, were reassuring. They were strong and capable, square-nailed, clean, the hands of a good doctor. Hands were more important in this case, he reasoned, than faces. He sat in the chair indicated by the nurse.

Let's get this over with. If it's my gallbladder, let's just get it out. His brother, Ed, had had his gallbladder out last year, and now there was no stopping him. Ed, not quite two years older than he, jogged and skied, played paddle, all to excess. What was he trying to prove?

So let's get this over with, get it out so I can start feeling myself again.

The nurse smiled around at the room as if she were the hostess at a large cocktail party and wasn't sure if she had enough ice, enough glasses. Presently, she went out on her sponge-rubber soles, gently closing the door behind her.

His stomach growled. He'd gone without breakfast, except for the piece of toast he'd eaten to satisfy Ceil. His stomach had been upset when he went to bed last night, upset when he woke at three. He'd gone into the guest room to read *Pride and Prejudice*. Jane Austen was the greatest soporific he knew. Better than Nyquil. But last night Jane had failed him, and he'd lain awake listening to the house noises, the icy branches of the apple tree scratching at the window, like a cat wanting to be let in. February was his least favorite month. The sounds of the wind hurling itself against the house like a battering ram made him long for spring. In late April and early May he'd be rising at first light, starting the coffee, then dressing in old clothes to go out and check the garden, see if anything had grown during the night when he hadn't been looking. Early morning was the best time of day. No good now, in winter, of course, but a joy beginning the end of April, when daylight saving began. He didn't believe April was the cruelest month. His birthday was in April and, probably because of that, spring was his favorite season. He started checking seed catalogs in January, right after they took down the Christmas tree. Last year he'd ordered salsify because it was difficult to grow, therefore a challenge. Plus it tasted like oysters, another good reason, and arugula because Ceil liked it, and basil because it did such nice things for the Big Boy tomatoes they all loved. Then there were the dahlias and peonies and Oriental poppies for the beds bordering the terrace. Planning the garden always gave him a lift. It was as good as a Caribbean vacation, and much cheaper.

"Now then." The doctor splayed the fingers of both hands on his thighs and leaned forward. "Anything special bothering you?"

It was their first meeting. His regular doctor, a friend of long standing, had given up his practice and moved to Dallas, unable to resist an offer to be chief of staff at a new hospital there. Shorter hours, longer pay, warmer climes, Ben had said, shamefaced, as if he weren't entitled to it. "I feel as if I'm deserting you. But Ann said if I didn't take it, she'd never forgive me. I don't know if you've ever lived with a woman who never forgives, but I know I don't want to try."

So his old friend was gone, and the new young doctor—whose name was Hall—and he eyed each other across the vast expanse of the doctor's desk.

"I haven't been feeling up to par lately," he began, already feeling better and silly at having come. "Just thought maybe you could give me the once-over and find out what's responsible. Maybe some vitamins might do the trick."

"How long has it been since you had a complete physical?"

"About a year and a half. Yes, just about that long. Ben Nilson was my doctor and he's been gone about that long. I haven't bothered to see anyone else. There was no need, really. But my wife's been after me," which wasn't true. He'd told Ceil only that he was tired. "She thought it time for me to have a checkup. You know women." He squashed his hands between his knees. "We heard from several people about you, that you were first-rate." The young doctor inclined his head slightly, acknowledging the compliment. "So I thought I might as well come to you and locate the trouble."

The doctor drew a form toward himself and clicked open his pen. "If you'll just answer a few questions for me," he said. "Mother and father alive?"

"My mother's been dead for almost twenty-five years. She died in her sleep. Hadn't been sick a day. It was a coronary occlusion." He stopped, remembering.

The doctor looked up, waiting.

"My father's hale and hearty," he continued hastily, reassuring the doctor. "He's seventy-three and his mother lived to be almost a hundred. She died a month before her hundredth birthday." Surely that gave him points. "She was a tough old girl," he added irreverently.

"You are . . . how old, Mr. Hollander?" The doctor's voice was stern. He gave his age, noticed a shaving nick on the doctor's chin. Aha. Unsteady hands, eh. That's not good. Watch your step, my lad.

"Do you smoke or drink to excess?" the doctor pursued, frowning, perhaps reading his thoughts.

"A couple of drinks before dinner. Sometimes a couple more at a party. I gave up smoking once or twice. Can't seem to stick to it." His hand dove into his pocket, patting the emptiness there nervously. PLEASE DON'T SMOKE, he'd been told in no uncertain terms by the sign in the doctor's outer office.

"Drink a lot of coffee?"

"Two, three cups a day. None at night, unless we go out to dinner." It seemed to him he was acquitting himself nobly, giving all the right answers. Perhaps he'd get an A when the doctor dismissed him. He listed recent illnesses (a bout with bronchitis in the fall, hepatitis four years ago), and the doctor directed him into the examining room, told him to slip on one of those backward hospital gowns designed to humiliate, and he'd be in to take a blood sample, blood pressure, and so forth. Those gowns freaked him out, as John would say. Decorated by a string of faded numerals, they reminded him of Dachau or Buchenwald. Emaciated arms bearing serial numbers. Gas chambers. He shook his head, feeling slightly fuzzy. He undressed quickly, concerned that the nurse with the birthmark might come in and find him standing naked and afraid. While he waited he studied the doctor's medical credentials hanging on the wall to make sure everything was on the up-and-up. It would be just his luck to get one of those guys who masquerade as doctors with a mail-order diploma.

Presently the doctor returned, whistling under his breath. He wrapped the blood pressure bandage around Henry's arm, pumping vigorously as the cloth tightened. "Not bad, not bad at all," the doctor said approvingly. He felt quite proud that his blood pressure at least hadn't let him down. The doctor then inserted a needle into his vein and they both watched as his blood was sucked out of him and into the tube. Suppose his vein had come up dry. What then?

When this was over, the doctor told him to please lie back on the table. After some prodding and poking (This hurt? How about this?) he was told he could get dressed. "We'll need a urine sample," the doctor said, on his way out to his next patient. "There doesn't seem to be any irregularity. I'll let you know," and he was gone.

It's my *life*, he thought, dressing. You don't have to be so damned casual about it. In the reception room, a jolly, middle-aged nurse said, "Mr. Hollander" in a loud voice, causing several patients to look at him, to his immense dismay. "The lavatory is just to your left. If you wouldn't mind," and she handed him a jar with his name on it. Blushing, he almost ran into the lavatory and closed the door. At his age. Ridiculous. When he'd half filled the bottle, he left it on the shelf, as instructed. The bottle felt warm to his hand. Fresh pee is always hot, he heard his brother tell him over the years. They used to have contests to see which of them would be first to write his name in new-fallen snow with pee. His brother always won. His name was shorter. It was easier to pee ED than it was to pee HENRY. He tried peeing HANK but his brother still won. No one ever called him Hank, either, although when he was fifteen or sixteen, he'd told people that was his name. He was a Henry and there didn't seem to be anything he could do about it.

"Doctor will call," the nurse with the birthmark said in measured tones, writing on a record card. He was glad she hadn't been the one to hand him the empty jar inscribed with his name. She didn't look up at him.

"Can you give me some idea when?"

She raised her head. Her face, her eyes were very still. As if there were no one inside her. He smiled at her tentatively, wanting her to like him.

"He's very busy," she said severely.

He wanted to say, "And so am I." Instead he said, "Of course. I understand," trying to placate her. "Perhaps it would be better if I call him." He felt like a child being chastened for something he hadn't done. If it'd been the jolly nurse, the one in charge of handing out pee bottles, he would've said, "I haven't told my wife I was coming here today. I thought I'd wait until I got a clean bill so I could ease her mind," and the jolly nurse would have smiled at him and said, "I know."

He waited while the nurse with the birthmark scrabbled

around, looking for one of the doctor's cards. She took rather longer than seemed necessary. The set of her thin shoulders signaled anger, hostility. He thanked her when at last she handed him the card with the doctor's number. The urge to say, "Why don't you have that thing taken off your neck?" was very strong. If you did, you might be happier, he thought. He hurried out without looking back, glad it was over. For the time being.

He caught the 10:43 into town, reveling in the almost empty car, the gentle swaying motion as the train rounded a curve, the unaccustomed stillness that should have been calming and wasn't. With his handkerchief he wiped clean a spot on the filthy window so he could see out. Just before the train went into the tunnel at Ninety-sixth Street, he spotted a tattered banner suspended from a window of a tenement, shouting HAPPY 50TH! for the world to see. Did that mean fiftieth birthday or fiftieth anniversary? What a party they'd have within those spotted walls. The cockroaches would never be the same. In two years he would be fifty. He told himself he didn't mind. Fifty was nothing these days. A broth of a boy. When he hit fifty, his father would be seventy-five. His son would be eighteen. It seemed only yesterday when he himself had been eighteen. Tonight, when he got home, he'd call his father, see how he was faring. It had been some time since they'd spoken to each other. They'd never been close. He didn't think his father liked him very much. He knew his father preferred Ed, who was more aggressive, surer of himself. These were qualities his father admired. In people. In sons.

A stern, somewhat rigid man, though possessing a sense of humor, his father had married again six years ago. The new wife, a giddy blonde with a soft, oval body slightly gone to flesh, liked to "go" as she put it. "Going" meant motoring endlessly up and down the West Coast, visiting her many sisters, each one blonder, giddier than she. He'd met the lot when he'd gone there on a business trip two years ago. As it happened,

Ceil hadn't gone with him and, in the end, he was glad. He'd been the hit of the evening, a rare occurrence. They'd passed him from one scented, voluminous embrace to the next, like a giant baby at its christening. They were a pride of perfumed octopi, he'd thought, amused at their abandonment as they almost smothered him in their enthusiasm. While held firmly in the ladylike but nonetheless iron grip of one of the younger sisters whose husband had bolted some time before, he'd caught his father gazing quizzically at him. As their eyes met, they'd unaccountably smiled at each other. His father had lifted his glass in a small salute. To what? To endurance? To reunion? To the absurdities of life? He didn't know what his father had in mind, couldn't even guess. Nonetheless, it had been a shared moment. But one of very few.

That night, standing between the cars of the crowded commuter train on his way home, he thought of that occasion, smiling in recollection. He'd had to work late to clear up some plans he was working on for an apartment building, a condo, really, as they all were these days, on Staten Island, plans he'd put off in order to keep his doctor's appointment. The wind crept down his coat collar, up his trouser legs, and he shivered, wondering if he should try to find a seat. On the other hand, the cold air felt good. Under his coat his hands pressed on his abdomen, much as the doctor's had, probing, exploring. There was nothing there, he felt quite sure. Nothing. He'd call Ed tonight, too, when he got home. Ask how he was feeling. Ask, while he was at it, the symptoms of a gallbladder attack. That would please Ed, who liked nothing better than to discuss the state of his innards.

I am like a character in a John Cheever story, he thought wryly. Cheever's characters were forever traveling back and forth on commuter trains, filled with desire and immortal longings. What would Cheever have made of any of this, of me, of my state of mind? Would it be possible for him to concoct an interesting piece out of such mundane material? Cheever was, always had been, a very clever writer, but even he might find the going tough here. Very slim pickings. He'd read recently that Cheever had died after a long bout with cancer. Three times he'd read the obituary, and felt as if he'd lost a friend.

It wasn't until he got off the train and was fighting his way through the bitter wind, skirting patches of ice in the station parking lot, that he remembered tonight was the night he and John were to talk. The last thing in the world he wanted was that, tonight. But he'd made a point of telling the boy to block out the time, and he had to go through with it. You've got to follow through with kids, as with everything else in life, he'd long ago decided. John was goofing off. It was time he thought seriously of where he was heading, and into what was he heading. How he was going to go about it. Middle-class parents had a tendency to keep their children in cotton batting, keep them young too long, to baby them. His father hadn't babied him, and he had no intention of babying John.

He unlocked his car and got in, resting his head for a minute on the steering wheel, its cold so piercing he felt as if his forehead had been penetrated.

A Cheever character would get back out of the car, methodically lock it, then climb back on the train and ride it to New Haven, to the end of the line. Go then to a bar, pick up a redheaded woman, buy her a drink, talk to her in a somewhat high-blown fashion until she excused herself to go to the ladies' room, from which she never returned. Or the Cheever character might cross over to the southbound side and ride the train back into Grand Central Station and spend the night in an all-night movie eating popcorn while musing on his youth, his mistress, the complexities of life. Or he might sit all night on a station bench, eyeing the derelicts, thinking there but for the grace of God, waiting for his office to open.

But he wasn't a Cheever character, not nearly that interesting. He turned the key in the ignition several times until it caught, put the car in gear, and drove home.

As he turned into the driveway and saw the lights, saw figures moving behind the curtains, he remembered he'd read in the paper that Grand Central was locked after midnight these nights. In an effort to curtail crime, the story said.

4

Keith's voice on the telephone had been calm, matter of fact. His mother was acting up again. But Keith could handle it. He had before.

"I'd ask you over," Keith had said when their friendship was brand new, shining, back in the sixth grade. They'd been scuffling through leaves on their way home from school, planning what to wear on Halloween. "But you probably wouldn't want to come."

"Why?" he'd said, wanting to very much.

"My mother, she, lots of times she drinks."

"That's okay," he'd said, worldly-wise, naive. "So does mine."

"You don't understand." Keith had planted his feet firmly, arms crossed on his chest, color rising in his smooth cheeks. "Sometimes she drinks all day. So when I get home from school she's passed out cold. I never know for sure."

"Oh," he'd said, sorry and embarrassed. He thought of asking about Keith's father and decided against it.

"My mother and father are divorced," Keith had said, reading his mind. "My father's in real estate in Florida. Palm Beach, where all the richies live. He calls every month or so to find out how I'm doing. Once he sent me a plane ticket to fly down over Easter vacation. I was seven. I flew by myself. The stewardess was supposed to look after me but she was too busy putting the moves on some rich, fat guy in a vest. It was fun, we went to the Bath and Tennis every day. I had a cheeseburger and a Coke and strawberry shortcake. Same thing every day, that's what I had. It was cool. If you're in real estate you have to mess around, play a lot of tennis, golf, go fishing with your customers. Get to know people with big bucks. Everyone in Palm Beach has big bucks. I think I might be a highwayman."

It was a minute before he'd realized that Keith meant to be a highwayman on Halloween, not as a career in Palm Beach.

"I've got this big cape my mother gave me and a hat with a feather and a big brim, and she said I can wear a pair of her boots."

"You can wear your mother's boots?" He remembered being incredulous. "My mother would never let me wear hers. She'd be afraid I'd ruin them."

"Oh, she's pretty loose about stuff like that. Even when she's not drinking, she's pretty loose. I might also go as Poseidon. I like to have an alternate plan, in case something gets fouled up." Keith had, apparently, experience with things getting fouled up.

"Poseidon?" He was out of his depth, never having known another Keith. "What's that?"

"You mean 'Who's that?'" Keith had said, his voice tinged with scorn. "He's the ancient Greek god of the sea."

Keith's eyes had more light in them than most people's. They were spooky eyes, he thought, and wished his were the same.

"I could always hang a sign on myself that said 'Poseidon,'" Keith had said, looking at him with contempt. He hadn't recognized it then as contempt. It was only later, after he'd known Keith a while, that he knew contempt for what it was.

"On the other hand, I might go incognito. Let those dopes

figure it out. I'd dye my long johns green and wear flippers and my mask. I bet I'd win a prize."

He'd been astonished by Keith's ingenuity. "How would you walk with flippers on? Wouldn't that be kind of hard? On the flippers, I mean." Practical John. He had learned then, and later, that when Keith was involved with a plan, it didn't do to fool around. Keith's mind blanked out the laughs. He was a single-minded guy.

"I'd take 'em off between stops. No prob." Keith had an answer for everything.

"When she isn't in the bin," Keith had continued, shutting off further discussion of Halloween, "she's all right. She's fun. She lets me do anything I want."

Bin? He ventured, "What bin is she in?"

"The loony bin, dope." Keith's voice indicated everyone knew about the bin except him. "When she's on the sauce, she goes kind of loco and she goes away to dry out. Then, when she gets straightened out, she comes home. She's fucked-up. My father is, too. They're both fucked-up. It's a wonder I'm as normal as I am."

With an effort, he kept his face expressionless. He imagined his mother's face if she could hear the things Keith was saying, the language he was using, and he began to laugh. He couldn't help himself.

"What's so funny?" Keith had turned on him, looking ferocious.

"Nothing. It's just that I never heard anyone say their parents were fucked-up before." He pronounced the word softly.

Keith's eyes worked their color change, and he said, "You ought to get around more."

Why? he wanted to ask, and didn't. He almost said, "I'm only twelve," but Keith was the same age, and look at him. Keith overwhelmed him. He was amazed and dazzled by their friendship, by the artistry of Keith's plans, his mind, his ideas. His life-style. It was like being friends with a king. Everything

Keith said and did was a revelation. Now that he knew they were fucked-up, he was anxious to meet Keith's parents. To get a good look, to see what that meant. At the same time, he was terrified at the prospect. He'd never known anyone who was on the sauce or who had been in the loony bin. He wisely kept these things to himself, mostly to protect his parents from the knowledge that such things went on. And also to protect his friendship with Keith.

Eventually, Keith had said it was all right for him to come home with him. "She's back in AA," Keith had said. "Once she gets back with those guys, she's great. If she gets into trouble, you know, if she can't handle things, she gives 'em a call and, day or night, they talk to her, come over and talk it out. They'll talk all night, if that's what she wants." So one afternoon he'd gone home with Keith. He was very nervous, not sure how he should act when he met Keith's mother. Should he shake her hand and pretend not to notice she was fucked-up? Should he say "Pleased to meet you," or should he just keep his hands in his pockets and smile and say nothing? There was no one he could ask.

But it was all right. She was waiting at the door. "How are you, John? I'm glad to meet you," she said, as if she meant it. "Keith's told me about you. Come in." The place smelled of ammonia and floor polish. A vacuum cleaner stood in the living room.

"I made cookies," she said. "I've been working my buns off all day cleaning and cooking." She laughed and ran her hands through her already tousled dark hair. Her face was nice, he thought, pale but pleasant. She was very thin, and wore blue jeans and a sweater with a cigarette burn smack in the middle of it. She smoked a lot, lighting one cigarette from the butt of the one she still had. She listened hard to everything they said, listened with great intensity, nodding her head in agreement or shaking it slowly from side to side. He couldn't imagine her passed out on the couch when Keith got home from school.

Maybe Keith was putting him on, trying to make his mother seem more unusual than other people's mothers. He didn't really think Keith would do that, but he couldn't be absolutely sure.

Then, out of the blue, she'd said, "John, why don't you stay for supper? I have to go to an AA meeting, and I don't like to leave Keith alone. I'm an alcoholic. Maybe Keith's told you." Her fingers were very long, very thin, like the rest of her. Very nervous. "I'm sure he'd like the company if you could stay. Why don't you call your mother and ask her if it's all right? We're having cube steaks. I'm a whiz at cooking cube steaks." She smiled at him, her lips stretched wide in her lean face, her lipstick smudged in the corners of her mouth. "And all the cookies you can eat."

He hesitated. His mother didn't like him to stay at other people's houses on school nights.

"Mom," Keith sounded weary. "John's got to get going. His mother runs a very tight ship. She wants to know where he is when he's not home." Keith's eyes glittered in that way they had. "Isn't that right, John? Doesn't your mother want to know where you are all the time? She's very strict." Keith's voice lent the word new meaning.

"Not exactly." He defended his mother, although many times he railed against her strictness. But he didn't like the tone in Keith's voice, the way he made her sound like a prison warden. She wasn't like that. "She likes me to check in once in a while," he apologized for his mother.

"Don't let him kid you, Mom. John's mother is a tiger. And he's her cub," Keith had laughed. He hadn't stayed for supper.

Twice Keith had been threatened with expulsion from school because his school fees hadn't been paid. "My mother doesn't get the money from her trust fund until January," he'd explained nonchalantly. "They'll have to wait until then. Gleason knows what's what. He knows she can't pay until then. He'll have to cool it. She pays when she gets the bread. That's what rich people do. They don't pay their bills every month. Only squares do that."

With shame, he thought of the neat pile of bills his father laid on the hall table the first of every month, stamped and tidy, waiting for the mailman. The first of the month was bill-paying day in his family. Once, when his father had been sick with flu, he remembered his mother doing the bills. Nothing but death would stop their inexorable bill paying, he was sure. Another fact to be buried, hidden from Keith's voracious gaze. God, how middle-class his parents were.

"Is your mother rich?" he'd asked.

"Her family has money. That's how she latched onto a trust fund. Her grandfather was loaded. He owned a railroad. He left her and her sisters a bundle. But she can't get her hands on it," Keith had said, grinning. "The way the money was left, the lawyer doles it out, inch by inch. Boy, does my mother hate that lawyer. She claims he's stealing her blind. If she could figure out a way, she'd scrag him good. Sometimes, when things are really tight, when my father doesn't kick through the way he's supposed to, she calls the lawyer and sings the blues. But he always cuts her off at the pass. Nada is what she gets unless the time is right for him to cough up some bucks. That guy's got a heart of stone. Probably a good thing, too. Other-wise, there wouldn't be any dough left. When she drinks, the money disappears."

It was like a soap opera on TV. He'd never known anyone who had a trust fund. There was a world waiting out there of which he knew nothing. A world inhabited by people like Keith. And Keith's mother and father. It excited him and, at the same time, frightened him. He wasn't an adventuresome person. He wished he were, wanted to be exciting and daring. Wanting wasn't enough. Wanting wasn't being.

Keith's mother hadn't looked rich to him. Although what rich people looked like he had no idea, except for what he'd seen in the movies and on TV. He imagined rich people climbing in and out of long black cars driven by chauffeurs. They were constantly suntanned and spoke in foreign tongues, to keep poor people from understanding what they said. A lot of poor people spoke in foreign tongues too, he knew, but they didn't have their own planes and ski at St. Moritz. Rich people dressed differently, too: either shabbily, in old clothes, or elaborately, with diamonds and furs. Like royalty, and like poor people, too, they never carried cash. They used credit cards, or a guy with them shelled out. This interested him. He almost never carried cash either. So they had something in common, he and the very rich.

"Who's this Keith that John talks about all the time?" he'd heard his father say shortly after he and Keith had become friends. He'd been lying on the floor reading the Sunday comics and had discovered, to his immense pleasure, that if he stayed absolutely still, unmoving, they forgot he was there.

"He's new in school," he heard his mother say. "I think the parents are divorced. At any rate, the father doesn't live with them." How did she know that? Not from him. "He lives in Florida," his mother continued. "Palm Beach, Gertie said." Gertie was a gossip, he knew. His father called her a female Walter Winchell. His mother said that, unlike most gossips, her friend Gertie had her facts straight most of the time.

"Palm Beach?" his father said.

"Yes, Palm Beach." His mother rolled the words on her tongue as if tasting something tart and vaguely unpleasant, something she was loath to swallow.

"I've never laid eyes on the mother. But Keith has nice manners," she who was big on manners admitted reluctantly. Still, he detected something in his mother's voice that told him Keith hadn't passed her inspection. How could nice manners be bad? It was important to him that his mother like Keith. He would never let her know how important. She was too critical of his friends, and he wanted her to like Keith.

"He's a good-looking boy," his mother continued. "Almost too good-looking."

Too good-looking for what? he asked himself. He admired Keith's looks, thought him extraordinary in all ways. No one else looked like Keith. He recognized a certain truth in what his mother had said about being too good-looking. And began to notice and take notes.

Girls collected at Keith's approach, voices shrill and strident as they clamored for his attention. They milled about, pushing and shoving one another in mock combat, hoping, no doubt, to fall wounded at Keith's feet; wounded and swooning, in need of mouth-to-mouth resuscitation. If they'd asked Keith for his autograph, he, John Hollander, wouldn't have been surprised. Maybe that was the way it was to walk down the street with Woody. To walk side by side with a luminary whose light obscured other lights. He was not offended by his own lack of notice. When people made a fuss over him, it would be because of a play he'd written, or a great, hilarious film he'd not only directed but also written and starred in. A triple-threat man, not unlike W. Allen.

Last year, a boy two classes ahead of them had called Keith "pretty boy," and then said it again, right there in the hall. Keith had punched out the kid, knocked him down all on his own. John had been at soccer practice and not there to help. Next day, reinforced by two bulky brothers, the older kid had waylaid Keith and jumped him. Three against one. Keith wound up with a purple bruise under his eye and two loose teeth.

"Next time they'd better bring the whole family," was all Keith had said.

"He's very conceited, isn't he, John?" his sister, Leslie, had said after she met Keith for the first time. "I can't stand conceited people."

"No, he's not," he'd defended his friend. "Can he help it if he's handsome and well-built?"

"So are you, sugar," Leslie had cried, pulling him to his feet. She was teaching him to dance disco and it took every ounce of his energy to keep up with her. Leslie was a dancing fool, a madwoman on the dance floor.

"Abandon yourself!" she kept hollering. "Lose your inhibitions! Let yourself go! And for God's sake, John, quit looking at your feet!"

That was his trouble. He was always looking at his feet. The subject of Keith had never come up again.

5

Keith showed up halfway through history class. Walking jauntily up to Mr. Simons's desk, he handed over a note, doubtless written in his mother's handwriting, which he'd become adept at copying. Simons read it without comment, nodded curtly at Keith, the go-ahead for him to park his carcass.

After class, they headed for study hall. "Gleason didn't say anything," he said, containing his curiosity. "I guess he didn't even notice you were among the missing."

"That's my forceful personality," Keith said. "I'm missed immediately. I got things settled down. She's asleep. The doc gave her a shot. Said it should keep her quiet until I get home. He thinks it would be a good idea if she went to her drying-out place again. For a week or two, he says." Keith spoke in a detached way, as if none of this were important.

He wanted to ask what had set Keith's mother off when she'd been doing so well. But he had learned from experience. It was better if Keith volunteered information. One direct question and he'd clam up. Keith would tell when he felt like telling.

"My father's getting married next week," Keith said abruptly. "And you know what?" Keith's voice and face betrayed a rare excitement. "He wants me to be best man. Get that. Best man for my own father! It's my official coming of age, right? Some guys get a new car, some get shares of stock. Me, I get to be my father's best man. How about that?"

An answer was expected of him. "Great," he said, trying to imagine himself as his father's best man. Trying to be enthusiastic. "That's really something."

It was all right. Keith was off and running, as excited as he would ever be. "My father said he's sending a friend's plane for me. An eight-passenger Cessna. Then he asked to speak to my mother. Like an ass, I should've said she was out, in the can, anything. Instead"—Keith's face was suddenly wiped clean of all emotion, as if an eraser had been drawn across it—"instead, I put her on the phone, and that's when the shit hit the fan. She said I couldn't go. She said it was March, exam time, that I couldn't miss school, that the whole thing was ridiculous, out of the question. So then my father said if necessary, he'd come up and personally escort me down to Palm Beach. He'd come to the school and explain the situation to Gleason, who he was sure would understand.

"Then she said, 'You try it, buster. Just you try it,' and they were off on one of their better donnybrooks." Keith stopped walking, faced him. The sky seemed very close, resting on the treetops. Wind slithered slyly, looking for a place to light. Neither of them wore parkas or gloves. He felt like walking, wanted to get inside somewhere it was warm. But Keith hadn't finished his story. He hugged himself, wanting to hear, not wanting to, knowing there would be no happy ending.

"They fight over me like two dogs over a bone." Keith threw wide his arms. "I can't believe it. It's not me they want so much as they want an excuse to hurt each other. That I

know. It's not me. I used to think it was but it's not. I'm the
weapon each one of them uses to get back at the other." They
walked slowly up the steps to the study hall. "The upshot is
they wind up screaming at each other long distance. Expensive
screaming, huh?"

He stayed quiet and tried to look understanding. He was
very cold. And weary, so weary. As if what Keith was saying
had happened to him and not to Keith.

"So then of course she had to have a little drink to calm
herself down." Keith held the door open and he walked into the
study hall, a decrepit, somewhat battered building on the
school grounds. The hall was thinly carpeted, long and narrow
and dark. Four rooms led directly off it, each identically
equipped with Salvation Army furniture. The heating was inadequate, a unifying feature of all buildings at St. Mark's.

"So that was that." Keith ran a finger across his throat.
"One drink is suicide. She can't have one. She's got to have
eight. A minimum of eight. I wonder if my father did that on
purpose. Told her about getting married and wanting me to be
best man, I mean. Just to get her going." Keith looked at him
with glittering eyes.

He turned away, shocked, and said, "He wouldn't do that,
would he?"

"I wouldn't be surprised. You should've seen the guy she
dragged home last night." Keith bounded from one subject to
another with astonishing ease. "His neck was bigger around
than my waist. A regular Dallas Cowboy."

"What happened? Did they arrest the guy or what?"

"He took after one of the cops, and they both tackled him.
Lucky for them he was drunk, or he'd have wiped up the pavement with them. The neighbors had a real show. They were
hanging out of the windows like a circus had come to town."
Keith's voice was full of bitterness. "It'll give those old crones
something to chew over for weeks. Who knows? We might get
evicted." Keith and his mother lived in an apartment whose
walls were thin. Through them could be heard a symphony of

flushing toilets, domestic arguments, TV explosions, gunfire. It was not a place for secrets.

"Those drying-out joints run into big bucks," Keith said. A door opened at the end of the hall. They scuttled into the lavatory. He washed his hands in hot water, trying to warm them, avoiding the sight of his own face in the mirror. He knew better than to offer anything other than his ear and his attention. He'd learned the hard way. The last time this kind of thing had happened, he'd made the mistake of offering advice. Keith had turned tense, his manner chilly. Keith didn't want advice, he wanted someone to unload his troubles on, someone he could trust not to tell. And he was that person. He didn't mind. Keith knew he'd keep his lip buttoned. He and Keith were friends. That was what friends were for.

"I could always knock myself off," he heard Keith say over the sound of running water. "Then she could collect my life insurance and be in fat city for about ten minutes."

"You've got life insurance?" he asked, amazed. "I thought only parents and old people had life insurance."

"My father was in insurance before he got into real estate," Keith said. "He messes around with a lot of different jobs. He gets bored easily. Anyway, for my birthday when I was nine, or maybe ten, he gave me a policy as a present. I'm worth twenty-five thou on the hoof. About right for one good night on the town. Or one good week in the bin." Keith laughed his short, humorless laugh.

As they went out into the hall, the bell rang. Mrs. Arthur was there, clapping her hands, sending her dewlaps dancing.

"Order, boys, order!" she sang out in her gravelly voice. Rumor had it that Mrs. Arthur owed her exalted position as study hall head to the fact she was making it with Mr. Gleason, headmaster of St. Mark's. Mr. Gleason was Dickensian in appearance, his elongated body wrapped in ancient tweeds, his cheeks hollowed by debauchery. He affected a stick while walking about the grounds. His dog even looked like the Hound of the Baskervilles. His arms and legs and nose were all very long and thin; Keith had christened him Spider.

Mr. Gleason was all right, actually. His smile was kind. He carried a perpetual musty odor with him, as if his pockets were filled with long-forgotten possessions in need of an airing. He had one front tooth that protruded just far enough to make closing his mouth all the way an impossibility.

"Keith Madigan!" Mrs. Arthur trilled, herding them into an empty room. "You sit there and you, John, sit on the other side of the room. I have to keep you two apart." Mrs. Arthur twinkled at them. "You're as chatty as a couple of girls." Mrs. Arthur was infatuated with the sound of her own voice. She had been the sixth-grade English teacher, and every once in a while, with her eyes misting over and chest thrust forward, she'd start reciting Robert Browning's "My Last Duchess," no matter that the class had been discussing Rudyard Kipling or even Walt Whitman.

"She had a heart—how shall I say—too soon made glad, too easily impressed," Mrs. Arthur told one and all. "My Last Duchess" was a poem about a crappy old duke describing his late wife whose portrait hung on his castle wall. It was Mrs. Arthur's favorite poem. And, as she emoted, the entire sixth grade—numb and uncomprehending, rosy faces lifted to the fluorescent light like hothouse flowers seeking the sun—was thinking its own thoughts, playing its own games.

This state of affairs, like all good things, did not last. Soon there was a new English teacher, a stiff, bowlegged young man with a bushy mustache that completely hid his mouth, leading to the rumor that he was toothless as a result of a social disease. This no-nonsense young man taught them the parts of speech, the art of diagramming a sentence, and rendered the amazing information that a story should have a beginning, a middle, and an end. This was heavy going compared to what had been dished out prior to this, and they didn't know what to make of it.

All in all, the sixth grade preferred Mrs. Arthur, who had expected nothing more of them than their undivided attention as she gave herself freely to her captive audience. And after a brief spell the young English teacher with the bushy mustache left St. Mark's and became a teller in a bank and eventually rose to the rank of a vice-president, where he was lost forever to the parts of speech and the parsing of sentences.

After study hall ended, he and Keith trudged silently toward the gym. A crust had formed on the snow. Gray and filthy, it crunched dismally under their feet.

"Who's your father marrying?" he asked.

"Some rich, gorgeous dame," Keith drawled. "He doesn't know any other kind. I'll tell you what she looks like." Abruptly, Keith came to a halt. "She's got these gigantic knockers." He gestured extravagantly, outlining the knockers. "And she's a blonde, maybe a redhead, probably in her twenties. She reads the *Wall Street Journal* and the *National Enquirer* and she dresses all in the same color. All pink, all lavender, whatever. And before my father goes out with her, he has a massage and a facial and a manicure and he holds in his stomach and holds up his head so his chins disappear and he dances up a storm. He said she could give Brooke Shields a run for her money." Keith hunched his shoulders down into his sweater. "I didn't even know he knew who Brooke Shields was. Usually he sticks with the golden oldies. He gets the hots over Tuesday Weld, for Christ's sake." Keith kicked savagely at the snow.

"My father and I are having a confrontation tonight," he blurted, not having planned to tell Keith anything about it. He was better at listening to Keith's problems than Keith was at listening to his. "At eight o'clock sharp we square off. He's sitting me down to hand out the same old crap. He wants the skinny on what I'm doing with my life, what my plans are for the future. Christ, you'd think I was pushing forty and still living off him. I'm only a callow youth. I'm only sixteen, Daddy. That's what I'm going to give him."

To his utter dismay, he felt his eyes fill with tears. He drew his shirt sleeve across his face, pretending it was part of the act.

"Tell him to put it on tape," Keith said in a bored voice. "That way, he can play it back when he's in a lecturing mood."

"Oh, I just tune out. I know all the dialogue." He imitated his father. "'John, you've got to pull up your socks. Get your act together. Buckle down. Follow through.' All that."

"Fathers are full of bullshit," Keith said. "Just because they're fathers doesn't mean they've got the answers. Keep that in mind next time he lays you out and stomps on you. They don't know an awful lot more than we do. They just pretend, they fake a lot. One thing about my old man, he doesn't hand me any bullshit. He knows I won't buy it. Besides," Keith smiled a little, "with his track record, how can he let me have it between the eyes?"

Later, on his way home, he thought about what Keith had said. Maybe it was easier dealing with a father who didn't live under the same roof, who you saw once or twice a year. Or when you were best man at his wedding. Maybe it was easier getting along with your father if he was divorced from your mother and lived far away and your mother and father fought over you and tried to get in good with you. He smiled to himself, imagining his father trying to get in good with him. That'd be the day.

He admired his father, wanted to be like him in many ways. But if he ever had a kid of his own, an unlikely possibility, he'd pat the kid once in a while. Not too often. He wouldn't be a pal to his kid, but he'd give him the time of day once in a while. Toss a ball around, kiss him on his birthday, stuff like that. His father almost never touched him. Except in anger, that is. Last year, he'd given his father a book on gardening for Christmas. Exactly the right book, it turned out, and his father's face lit up when he saw it and he'd reached out and for a split second he'd thought his old man was going to hug him.

But his father just said, "Terrific, John, just what I wanted." Even so, he'd felt like a star.

Spare the rod and spoil the child, the adage went. No danger in his house. Both he and Les had had their share of spankings, Les not as many as he. But one of the good things about his sister was she never told on him. And there were plenty of opportunities. He'd taken his father's last pack of cigarettes and he and Jimmy Howard had smoked their little brains out behind the garage and she didn't tell. He'd driven the new car up and down the driveway and broken the taillight. She didn't tell. Lots of things she kept to herself. Les was definitely not a squealer. He loved her for that.

The last time he'd been spanked, he'd prepared for trouble by sticking his arithmetic workbook inside his pants. When his father's hand had landed, whammo, in just the right place, the old man had been cured of spanking him forever.

When he was ten, he'd fallen off his bike and broken his arm. It was a Saturday and his mother was out rolling bandages or something. His father had taken him to the hospital to have the bone set. After, they'd gone home and his father had squeezed him a glass of fresh orange juice and asked him how he felt. He said okay; then his father's arm had, as if by accident, rested on his shoulder. He could still smell his father's sweater. It smelled of burning leaves. Nothing else smelled like burning leaves except burning leaves, which you couldn't do anymore due to pollution. . . .

He had an idea for a TV commercial. Skinny guy, hollow chest, glasses, wispy hair, resembling Woody quite a bit, is raking leaves. All of a sudden girls are coming out of the woodwork, from behind trees, coming up out of manholes, they're everywhere, attacking the guy like Indians going after Custer at Little Big Horn. All on account of the way the guy smells. He rakes a big pile, strikes a match to it, then varoom! the product shot. This would have to be a commercial for an after-shave called, you guessed it, Burning Leaves. If he could just get it past the environmentalists.

If he didn't make it as a gag writer for Woody, he might be able to cut the mustard as a hotshot TV-commercial writer. The world was loaded with opportunities, he figured.

6

"For God's sake, John, sit up straight and stop dropping food all over the tablecloth. Anyone looking at you would think you'd been raised in a cave."

"Henry," Ceil said.

He drew himself up ostentatiously and sat erect. John Hollander, West Point cadet. He carried each mouthful of dinner to his mouth with slow deliberation, chewed every bite twelve times, and washed it all down with precise sips of milk. In the heavy silence of the dining room, he could hear himself swallow.

"Hey, you two." His mother's face was white, her lips pressed into a thin, tense line. "Something interesting must've happened to you today, out there in the world. I crave conversation."

Doggedly, his father ate his mashed potatoes. It was his habit to eat all of one thing before he tackled another.

"Ma," he said brightly, "did you know that Woody's real name is Allen Stewart Konigsburg? And I just read that he shelled out three mil for a house in the Hamptons because he wants to escape the madding crowd. How about that?"

His father looked up and said, "Woody who?"

He considered saying "You don't know who Woody is?" imitating his father's attitude when he, John, didn't know some fact his father found essential to an understanding of world affairs. Instead, he said, "Woody Allen, Father. The greatest comic of the twentieth century. He drives a yellow Rolls and eats oatmeal with butter on it and hangs out at Elaine's."

His father laid down his fork and wiped his mouth. "If you paid as much attention to your schoolwork as you do to some fly-by-night comedian, you might be president some day," he said. "If you'll excuse me, Ceil, I have a telephone call to make. I'll be waiting for you, John. Give me ten minutes."

After his father had gone, he said, "Can you just please let me in on something, Ma? How come he gets away with leaving the table before we're all finished? If I tried that, he'd shoot out both of my knees. What is this, a double-standard-type operation? And what makes him think I want to be president? The guy's cracking up."

His mother rested her head in one hand. "You know something, John? I'm sick of acting as go-between. It's exhausting. I'm running out of steam. Why do you have to fight all the time?"

"Ask him. What's bugging him. He's always on my back. Tell him to lay off. What does he want? I'm not on drugs, I stay out of jail. What does he want? If I knew, maybe I could deliver." His throat felt scratchy, pressure built up behind his nose, a sign of imminent emotion that he knew neither he nor his mother could handle right now. Hastily, he got up and took the plates out to the kitchen.

"Darling," his mother said. He knew she felt bad about the fact that he and his father were always at each other's throats. Give praise where praise is due, he'd heard her say once, but even with his ear laid against the door's crack, that's all he'd been able to hear. They had been talking about him, that much he knew. There was a special tone in both their voices when they talked about him. Then, voice raised, his father had said, "If there's a reason to praise him, I will. I've had no reason."

Bullshit, he muttered. Double bullshit.

"He's young, Henry," his mother had said. "Lay off for a

while. Can't you remember what it was to be young, Henry?"
His father hadn't answered that one. That had been the end of
it. . . .

"He's an ace at handing out flak, Ma, and you know it."
He rinsed the plates and put them in the dishwasher. "He
doesn't give Les flak, but he sure shovels plenty my way."

"It's because you're his son," she said. "He expects a lot
from you, John. He expects the best."

"Hey," he said, "he might not know it, but that's what he's
getting. Every day in every way I'm dishing out my best."

"No, John. That's not so. You just coast. He wants you to
buckle down. You're a coaster. That's what bugs your father."

He contemplated his sneakers and didn't answer. Twenty-
six dollars those mothers had cost six months ago, and already
they looked as if they'd been soaked in acid. He could hear his
father keening when he announced he needed a new pair.
"Twenty-six dollars for sneakers!" he'd wail, clutching his
heart. The old man suffered from a serious time warp. Rip Van
Winkle in a three-piece suit.

"Grace Lerner's niece is visiting her from Seattle," his
mother said casually, changing the subject with a quiet clashing
of gears. A warning gong sounded. Industriously, he scraped a
bit of butter left on his plate onto the butter dish. Waste not,
want not was the family motto.

"Any dessert?" He decided to ignore his mother's ploy.

"There's half a grapefruit," she said vaguely.

"Grapefruit's for breakfast, I thought."

"She's a lovely girl. Very bright. Captain of her lacrosse
team, and Grace says she has a stunning figure."

"Who?" he asked, wide-eyed.

"Grace Lerner's niece," she continued inexorably. When
his mother waxed inexorable, stand back.

"Ma, buzz off. Last time somebody's niece was in town, I
got royally shafted. That girl was the biggest turkey in this
neck of the woods since the Pilgrims landed. Hey," his face lit

up, "I might be able to use that one," and he scribbled furiously on the back of a used envelope.

"That wasn't a niece," his mother said, full of reason. "That was Ann Arnold's goddaughter. And I understand she's blossomed, turned into a beauty."

"Ma, you're not pulling that stuff on me twice," he said. "Anyway, I'm scared of girls who are captains of their lacrosse teams. They tend to have big muscles and lots of libido." He wasn't entirely sure what libido meant, but he knew he was on the right track.

"You're too much, John." One thing was, he could always make her smile.

Behind her back, he practiced a few karate chops, slicing his hand through the air close to her ear, missing her by a hair's breadth. Sometimes he had thoughts of decking his mother and father, tying them up, using nothing but Boy Scout knots, and locking them in a closet until they promised to mend their ways, knuckle under to his demands. He planned, if this fantasy ever came to pass, to release his mother first and hang on to his father until the old man called out in a voice weak from lack of nourishment, "Mercy, mercy, son."

She felt the air stir near her head and half turned, tucked her hair behind her ears nervously, wondering where the draft had come from. Once, when he'd been practicing his karate, he'd connected and knocked her to the kitchen floor. Lucky his father wasn't around for that one.

"Grace asked me if I thought you'd be interested in taking her niece to the movies. I said I'd ask you. Grace said you were the only boy she knew about the right age. She's always liked you, John."

It struck him there were far too many occasions recently when "bullshit" seemed to be the only thing he could think of saying.

"She doesn't even know me, Ma," he said stiffly. Grace Lerner was, in his eye, a slick-haired, fast-talking, know-it-all lady who never gave him the time of day if she could help it.

His mother banged a few pots and pans around. "Of course, I'd pay," she said, steaming full speed ahead. "I'd even spring for a bag of popcorn."

"There ain't that much popcorn in the world, Ma."

"Okay for you. If you don't want to, you don't." She brushed back a strand of hair. She was giving up too easily. Watch it. "I only hope," she continued, looking at her watch, "that you never ask a favor of me. That's all I hope." She tossed a sponge in the sink. "Better see if Dad's through talking to Grandy. Ten minutes are up."

"What is this? What the heck. Are we running some kind of a space shot here? All right, men, synchronize your watches. Ten, nine, eight, lift-off. What the heck."

Dragging his feet, he went through the hall and stood outside his father's study, heard him say, "Yes, John's fine. Leslie too. . . . Well, you know she always does. We expect her home next week on vacation. Ceil sent her love. How's Helen? . . . Hope to see the whole gang again soon. Yes, well, give them all my love. Maybe next time I'll bring Ceil out. Nice to talk to you, Dad. Take care of yourself. . . . All right. You too."

Who writes his dialogue? he wondered. The old man really knew how to toss the old bon mots around. He would've liked to speak to Grandy, but his father had hung up. He cleared his throat to let him know he was there. But his father stood looking down at the telephone, his shoulders slumped and narrow in his neat gray suit, and didn't seem to hear.

He cleared his throat a second time, and his father shook himself, like a dog coming out of water, and looked around.

"Oh, John," he said, as if not quite sure who John was, what he was doing here. "Sit down, will you?"

He sat. "How's Grandy?" he said. "Is he coming to see us?" What he wanted to do was to hitchhike across country, visit his grandfather, maybe go on up to Washington State, Oregon, see something of the country. But they'd never let him. No sense in bringing it up.

"He didn't say anything about a visit. He's fine. His arthritis is acting up, but otherwise he's in fine fettle. Sends his love to you all." His father sat down, took out a cigarette, rolled it between his fingers, looked at it, then put it on the table.

"There's nothing I can say that I haven't said many times, John. Same old stuff. I imagine you're getting tired of hearing it. I know I am." His father smiled, a slight upturning of his lips that, if he hadn't been watching him so closely, he might've missed. The old fight wasn't there.

"Your time could be better spent studying than listening to me. I have to call Ed, find out how he is. You might as well go. Just try to remember I'm not talking because I enjoy the sound of my own voice. If you don't get serious about your school-work, you'll regret it. That's all I had to say. Good night."

His father turned again to the telephone, picked up the receiver, and began to dial. He was dismissed. Without a hassle.

Hardly believing his luck, he stumbled over his feet in his haste to leave—before the old man changed his mind.

"Hey, Ma," he said, a feeling of goodwill toward men flooding him. "How's it going?"

The reading lamp cast long shadows on her, making her seem smaller and older than she was. She raised her head and gave him a blank look, her eyes glazed and far away.

Then, because she looked so sad, so tired, he said, though he hadn't planned to, "How old is this chick, anyway?"

"Chick?" she frowned. Then a smile broke and laugh lines fanned out from her eyes, her mouth. "You'll take her? Oh, John, you are a love! About your age, I should think. Grace will be so pleased."

"I'm not out to please Grace," he said. "But before we get into this any further, we have to draw up an agreement, Ma. Sort of a premarital. Like who gets the TV, who gets the BMW, that kind of junk."

"How about who gets the kids?" she asked.

Sometimes she got pretty big for her britches, he thought.

"If she's under fifteen or over thirty, the deal's off. And I'm not just whistling Dixie, Ma. I mean it. A guy's gotta have standards."

She pushed her glasses back into her hair and laughed. He knew he had her.

"First," he said, ticking off on his fingers, "I need plenty of cash. A tenner for the flicks and another tenner should do it."

"For what?" she asked, highly amused.

He raised his brows. "For the fun later, down at Alfie's. What else?"

Alfie's was a lively gin mill down by the station that had a certain cachet due to the frequency with which its regulars got themselves juiced up and, in a strong feeling of camaraderie, had been known to put fists through windows and pound heads on floors. Not an ounce of malice was involved. In the morning, they were all friends again.

He'd never been inside Alfie's, but he and Keith had often hung around outside, breathing the delicious smells of stale beer and perspiration Alfie's exuded, speaking to them of manhood, sophistication, and, best of all, debauchery.

"How'd it go with Dad?" she asked, crossing her arms on her book. "Did you part friends?"

"I'll need some ones, too, Ma, in case this girl has a sweet tooth and has to have a box of Reese's Pieces. And we'll need at least two bags of popcorn. A minimum of two."

"Why don't I just write you a blank check?"

"Ma, I'll say one thing for you. When the chips are down, you give in gracefully." He patted her on the head. "Dad's getting as soft as a grape. He was talking to Grandy, and when he hung up he told me to get lost. I'm home free, no bruises, no nothing. How about that?"

"Oh, John." She snapped off the light. He thought it was because she didn't want him to see she was crying. He saw the tears and wondered what was going on for her.

Taking the stairs two at a time, he shouted out a country-western song about a man whose wife had left him with all the kids while she went off in a pickup truck with a jailbird to find the big time in Natchez. John always knew words to songs like that, and sang them at the top of his lungs. They sounded better that way, he said.

John could hear his father still on the phone, talking to Uncle Ed. For lack of anything better to do, he listened in on the extension.

"The pain was agonizing," Uncle Ed was saying. "No one who hasn't had gallstones, Henry, can possibly know what real pain is. Like hot pokers. Labor pains. When I described the pain to Marge, she said, 'That sounds exactly like the pains I had with Susan.' And that's when I decided to call the doc. You better get yourself checked out, Henry. You're no spring chicken, you know."

Very quietly John hung up. So his father thought he might have gallbladder problems. No wonder he'd been testy lately. He thought of calling Keith, but decided that could wait. To celebrate his good fortune, he did his history assignment. Then, with all those dates swirling around in his head, he lay on his bed thinking of ways to screw his mother out of a couple more bucks. If he was going to go into the gigolo business, feed Grace Lerner's nerdy niece full of expensive munchies, she'd have to pay for first-class accommodations. His time was valuable.

Long after John had gone up to his room, long after Henry, his face gray with fatigue, had said he thought he'd turn in, she sat there quietly, thinking about how things had turned out, thinking about John, about Henry. About the way they were always at each other's throats. John's face, when he said, "Dad's getting soft as a grape," had been suffused with joy. It made her very unhappy that they didn't get on, which Henry knew. But still he pursued his tack, so stiff, so unyielding when it came to John. They had spoken of it many times, always at her instigation. Invariably, Henry turned away, unwilling to say more than that John must be made to understand he couldn't goof off for the rest of his life. "He is very irresponsible, Ceil," Henry had said through stiff lips.

"You're too hard on him. You never give him a break. If you must be so severe, then treat Leslie with the same severity. It's not fair the way you single him out for constant criticism."

"Leslie doesn't need it the way he does; she's disciplined, she's tough on herself, she's motivated, Ceil."

Through clenched teeth she said, "I hate that word. Find another one."

"Whether or not you like the word, it's important to be motivated. I worry about him. He's so . . . so feckless, I guess is the best word. He's always clowning. He's an escapist, Ceil."

"And you? I suppose you were all business, all buttoned-down, chairman-of-the-board dedication when you were his age, is that it?"

"No, of course not. But my father was stern with me, and I think it's the way to be with John. It's the only way I know. I want him to grow up to be a responsible person, a good man. And right now, he's as soft as a grape, to coin one of his phrases."

"He's got good stuff in him," she said. "In a few years, he'll be a man and you'll see. I just hope it won't be too late for you and him to be friends. At the rate you're going, you're going to destroy any chance you have. Your relationship will be too far gone."

"Ah, Ceil." He tried to embrace her and she would have none of it.

John, at six, had come to her and asked, "Would you give up your life for your child?" He'd put one finger on her arm, the way he did when he wanted her full attention. He was getting over the measles and the two of them, trapped in the house, watched a great deal of television.

"Why do you want to know?" she'd said, shaken by his question, by the intensity with which he'd asked it.

"It was on television. There was a fireman who said the lady had gone back into her house to find her child and the flames engulfed her. What's 'engulfed' mean?"

"It means to swallow up," she said.

"Then the flames swallowed her up." He took that in. "Does that mean she got burned up?" he asked.

"Yes," she said.

"Well, they found her child was already out of the burning house so the lady didn't even need to go back. But the fireman said she gave her life for her child. So I wondered if you would do that for me."

He waited, finger still on her arm. She chose her words carefully, knowing he needed reassurance, if not comfort.

"I hope so," she said. "Yes, I would."

"How about Leslie?"

"Yes, Leslie, too."

"That's what I figured," he said. He seemed relieved. "That's exactly what I figured." A few minutes later, she heard him upstairs, making warlike sounds as he moved his myriad little plastic men through battle maneuvers.

Something about John's face tonight had brought that back to her. She took a crumpled tissue from her sleeve and blew her nose. Then she reread the chapter she'd been finishing when John came with his news of being let off the hook. Even after reading it a second time, she still couldn't remember what she'd read. She turned off the light and, feeling her way in the dark, made her way up the stairs to bed.

7

Henry was a genuine romantic. He became Ceil's friend before
he became her lover. But before that, they had almost become
enemies.

They worked together in the office of the architect who
eventually took Henry on as a junior partner. Ceil had a way of
holding her head, thick hair swinging, a way of walking, as if
she owned the world, that got to him. When he first laid eyes
on her, his breathing actually grew labored and his chest hurt,
like a man in the throes of a heart attack. He suggested they
have lunch at the drugstore around the corner; they would go
Dutch, he said, and have a BLT, which the drugstore did su-
perbly, and a chocolate float.

Sorry, she was busy. That day and the next. The whole
week, in fact. It wasn't so much the Dutch bit as it was his
presumption that she'd be free on such short notice. Henry
lunched instead with a frivolous blonde whose brother was a
friend from college. Henry paid the check.

Henry was a Yale man, a fact he did nothing to either
conceal or belabor. Yale turned out to be a drawback, as far as
Ceil was concerned. Oh, he was debonaire; rangy, square-
jawed, with neat fingernails and beautiful manners. Every time
they stepped off a curb, his hand cupped her elbow; doors were
opened for her as if it were second nature for him to open
doors. If she had been a smoker, she knew he'd have lighted
every cigarette for her. But she thought him a snob, not realiz-
ing until much later that his ways were his own and had nothing at all to do with snobbishness. Gradually, she began to like,
rather than resent, the fact that Henry had done well at Yale
and was on the fast track at the firm where they worked. She
herself had quit a mediocre college after two years, eager to get
on with the business of life. Well, that was her somewhat high-

minded reason. The real reason she'd quit was that she hated to
study, despised taking exams. Years later, the mother of two
almost-grown children, she still occasionally dreamed of being
alone in a large, echoing hall, bent over her paper, chewing on a
pencil, knowing she had none of the answers. She woke from
these dreams of failure with her heart pounding.

An only child, Ceil longed for siblings. Her friends were
always telling tales of being sent away from the table for horsing around, or for excessive burping. One girl she knew had
four brothers and, adding insult to injury, fifteen cousins of
both sexes.

Ceil felt her life was impoverished by the endless quiet
dinners, murmured conversations, Jell-O for dessert. She
yearned for a long, loud, crowded table, passing great dishes of
peas and carrots and potatoes up and down, fighting over who
would get the outside piece or the second joint. She had never
been sent from the dinner table. How she had wished for someone to misbehave with.

Ceil's mother and father were both teachers; serious, dedi-
cated, no-nonsense people who tithed to their church, drove an
eight-year-old car, and never played cards for money. Her
mother favored dresses of flowered rayon or nylon, bought a
size too large to allow for added poundage when it came, as it
surely would. Her father wore brown trousers and a jacket of
greenish tweed or, on special occasions, a navy blue suit that
she knew would last him all his days. They were wonderful
people. She loved them with all her heart. They, in turn, wor-
shiped her and, though they tried to conceal the fact, never
quite got over the fact that they'd produced her. Her mother,
who was not otherwise given to jesting, used to say that the
gypsies must have brought her, for she bore no resemblance to
them, or to anyone else in either of their families. They, the
least vain of people, had one vanity, and her name was Ceil.
Long-legged, narrow-waisted, with a luminous complexion, she
was not beautiful but she had something.

Henry had asked for her hand in the old-fashioned way. She had warned her parents what they could expect after the roast beef and Yorkshire pudding had been dealt with. Despite this preparation, her father had done something terribly discomfiting to her.

"I don't know," her father kept saying, stalking around the living room with his hands locked behind his back. "I just don't know."

Finally, she'd said, "Don't know what, Daddy?" feeling tears of exasperation building behind her eyes. She hadn't been absolutely positive that she wanted to marry Henry until her father kept up his litany of "I don't knows." Then, in a flash, she knew that Henry was the man for her.

"They're talking about a draft," Ceil's father warned. "Things don't look good in Southeast Asia, not good at all." It was just before the outbreak of Vietnam.

"Henry's too old to be drafted," Ceil said. "Much too old." Henry was twenty-nine.

Ceil had never actually slept with a man before Henry. There'd been plenty of jockeying in back seats, on beach blankets, lots of flashing skin, unlikely bulges. But no actual skin-to-skin stuff. When the real thing came along, the act of making love leisurely came as a surprise. It was both what it was cracked up to be, and not. Henry was tender and considerate, when what it turned out she was looking for was Tarzan. Or Don Quixote.

As a girl, Ceil had been an avid reader of sex manuals. She and her friends spent many a Saturday afternoon circling the right stores, hesitating, darting in and out, reluctant to be the first inside. They giggled over the pictures, memorizing the page numbers of particularly revelatory ones. There was even a section devoted to describing ways to drive men wild with your lips, your tongue, even your teeth. One of Ceil's friends, whose father was a dentist, went crazy over the teeth section, which was maddeningly silent on the question of her braces.

An older girl, with violet eyes and breasts of startling dimensions, boasted a penchant for vodka and older men with mustaches, and had connections in Manhattan and Paris, if you could believe everything she said. She whispered to Ceil that she, personally, knew of more than one hundred ways to perform oral sex.

Oral sex? You mean kissing? Ceil said. Oh no, the purple-eyed siren said, opening the book. That wasn't what she meant. This is what she meant.

The memory of those sex manuals went with Ceil to her marriage bed. But Henry, after a few sorties resulting in a week-long crick in his neck, called it quits and returned to his conservative ways.

Then, on their first Christmas, Henry bought Ceil a red-lace teddy, cut high on the thighs and low on the chest. He presented it to her somewhat shamefacedly, not wanting her to take his present amiss. Ceil, delighted by what she took to be an unleashing of Henry's hitherto rather restrained sexuality, threw her arms around him and pushed them both toward the couch, the nearest thing to hand. But Henry consulted his watch and said, "If we're going to be at your parents' house by noon, we better get going, Ceil."

All right for him. After Christmas dinner, they went home and Ceil oiled and scented herself and put on her teddy. Henry, in the meantime, went out for an evening stroll. She waited for the sound of his key. When it came, she threw open the apartment door and stood with her fingers laced behind her head.

"For God's sake, Ceil!" Henry slammed the door as if something fierce had followed him home and was even now snapping at his heels. "She might see you!" "She" was Mrs. Romero, their plump and affable neighbor across the hall. Mrs. Romero borrowed sugar and gin indiscriminately and liked to keep her finger on their pulse.

"How do you like it?" Ceil turned this way and that, a

perfect lingerie model. "Don't I look terrific?" She meant to say "Doesn't it look terrific?" complimenting both herself and Henry's taste. A Freudian slip; the best, the only kind.

"You l-l-look fine," Henry said, stuttering a bit, as he'd done as a child. "Better put something on over that or you'll take cold."

Ceil stomped to the bedroom, gritting her teeth, talking to herself. "What did he give it to me for?" she muttered in a loud voice. "What the heck did he pay all that money for if he didn't want me to wear the damned thing?" She went to the closet and put on her old sneakers and a long gray sweater of Henry's riddled with moth holes over her teddy.

"Okay, mister," she said, coming back to him, "my price is five for a half hour, ten for ten minutes. What'll it be?"

Henry patted his pockets, came up with two ones. "It's all I have," he said. "What will that get me?" He smiled his lovely quiet smile and the shivering started up.

"The works," she said.

Nobody ever really levels with you as to what the first baby really looks like. Fresh from the womb, Leslie was a shock. She had a full head of wild black hair and a high and raging voice that scared them both. "She's an anarchist," Henry said, trying to smile. "A beautiful anarchist."

"She's pretty ugly," Ceil said. "If I'd known she was going to look like that, I never would've had her." She burst into tears at this unaccountable sentiment, and Henry patted her shoulder to comfort her, though he felt in need of comforting himself. "She's not ugly," he said. "Don't say that, Ceil. She's beautiful."

Leslie's livid umbilical cord refused to heal properly and fall off. It was still dangling there, staring up from her tiny middle like an angry eye when they brought her home from the hospital. Leslie would never have a pretty belly button, Ceil mourned. Never be able to wear a bikini. Oh, take her back, please. Bring me a pretty one.

She decided she was an unnatural mother. Deeply ashamed of herself, she never told anyone. Not even Henry.

That first year, the croup kettle kept the apartment as moist and warm as a tropical paradise. The darling wallpaper they'd hung in the nursery began peeling away from the walls. Leslie didn't need much sleep. The dark hair fell out and was replaced by a strawberry blonde fuzz. Orange, Henry called it. He said he'd always wanted a daughter with orange hair and now he had one. Leslie smiled a lot when things pleased her, and the high, raging voice turned to quite presentable imitations of human speech.

When John arrived, Henry's aunt arrived to inspect the male heir. She brought a silver porringer, and after a good look at the new baby, she said, "Give that one a good cigar and a good book and he'll be all set." John was a proper baby, all right. He looked as if he belonged. John also had colic and scowled a lot. "So would you," Ceil's mother said, "if you had a constant tummy ache." She had a point.

Ceil was astounded, after a while, at her own competence. So was Henry, with hers as well as his own. He got so he could diaper a baby so tightly its eyes bulged, his diapers like tourniquets, while hers sagged perilously low, skimming the ground at times. She got into the habit of tucking her babies under her arm like an oversized football, and trotting about the house with them that way, their little faces hanging down, laughing at her shoes, while she, the ball carrier, was certain, at least for the time being, of having the upper hand.

But it seemed, sometimes, as if they would never again have any time to call their own. Three years, it turned out, wasn't enough time between babies. Even she, who had wanted a crowd of babies, admitted that. No sooner was one toilet-trained than another was standing there, soggy, petulant, fists digging into eyes, smelling higher than a kite. The old ammonia kid, Henry called each in turn.

One day, pushing John in his stroller, watching Leslie on one of the park swings, a woman she'd spoken to—a former nanny, the woman had told her, indicating Buckingham Palace was a decided possibility—said to her, "Oh my, I don't envy you bedtime. Two suppers, two baths, all that lot."

And Ceil had laughed and said, "I wouldn't dream of giving them separate baths. Just throw them both in the tub. They love it. They have a marvelous time playing together."

"A boy and a girl together in the tub?" The woman pulled up her coat collar and rose to leave. Depravity was everywhere.

Their bow legs straightened, their cheeks grew round and rosy. They were so trusting. "Sometimes they look at me," Henry said, "and I can tell from their eyes that they think I can do anything. It scares the hell out of me."

If they were going to have any more children, Ceil said, they should have them now. John was two, Leslie five. It was time to think of having another baby.

"We can't afford any more," Henry said. "Not with the cost of college. And shoes. And everything else. Let's stick with the two we've got."

Leslie developed a talent for playing second base and for boys. Leslie soon grew famous for falling in love. Usually with someone unsuitable. A large, looming football player, going through the motions of repeating his senior year in high school, became the apple of her eye. "He's so darling!" Leslie would say. Even when the boy was arrested for drug possession and assaulting a policeman, Leslie was unmovable. Leslie knew it all. When Ceil tried to instruct her in the vagaries of sex, Leslie kept saying, "I know, Mother. I know," with an attitude of boredom that alarmed Ceil.

At nine, John had been bounced off the school bus so often they called him Bouncer. The bus driver back then, a stout woman in her forties, buttonholed Ceil in the produce department of the A & P one day and held her captive for a full twenty minutes while she recounted John's proclivity for taking center stage. "He makes 'em laugh, see," the bus driver kept saying. "That's his trouble, he likes the attention so he makes 'em laugh."

And still did.

Never marry a man who's a good dancer. Another of Ceil's mother's truisms. Good dancers are liable to be bad husbands.

Well, Henry liked to dance, all right, but not with her. With himself. Sometimes, after a party, they'd come home and he'd turn on the stereo, put both hands in his pockets, and cruise around the living room, eyes at half-mast, smiling foolishly, as if he were at his junior prom, dressed in a frilled shirt and a rented tux, sporting a red carnation in his buttonhole. Later, when the children came, he'd take them for a spin, cradling them against his chest as he led them in an intricate pattern of mad swirls and whirls and dips he'd never have essayed with a full-size partner. Their little faces, looking at her over his shoulder, were wreathed in gummy smiles and their tiny heads bobbed in time to Benny Goodman or Artie Shaw.

Just look at him, she'd think pridefully. What does my mother know.

8

Henry was already in bed, lying with his hands behind his head, when Ceil came into their room. He watched her as she undressed and went to the bathroom to wash her face and brush her teeth. She slipped under the covers, thinking about what her life might have been if she hadn't married, hadn't had children.

"Who else but Marge would liken a gallbladder attack to labor pains?" Henry said.

Ceil made noncommital noises from her side of the bed. She and Marge were oil and water. Always had been. Lucky they lived so far apart.

"I'm glad I called Dad. It's been too long. I should call him more often." I can't afford to let that slide, he thought. Dad's getting on. I must remember to check in with him once a week.

"What did he have to say?" Ceil was already half asleep.

"He sounded old, Ceil. His voice sounded old. At first, anyway. After we started talking, he pepped up and sounded like his old self. Like his young self, I should say." He smiled over at her. She'd burrowed under the covers so that only the top of her head showed. He folded back her side of the blanket neatly so she'd have plenty of air. He liked doing things for her, taking care of her. He loved her profile, the clarity of her features, the quiet way she slept. Even in sleep she was composed. It was her profile, in fact, that had decided him. There's always some one thing. In his case, she'd told him, it had been the nape of his neck. He'd never thought of the nape of the neck as a sexual thing, as the Japanese were said to do. But from there on, he'd seen to it the barber trimmed his hair very carefully.

He envied Ceil the ease with which she fell asleep. It sometimes took him as much as a couple of hours to drop off. He wouldn't take sleeping pills, pills of any kind. They were anathema to him. Good health ran in his family. Except for his mother. She'd died in her sleep, without warning. Of a coronary occlusion. She hadn't been ill. The family, his father especially, had been devastated, inconsolable. They'd had letters of condolence from total strangers. His father had answered each one by hand; the only glee in his life became the adding up of the vast numbers of letters that had poured in. He'd kept a notebook filled with the names and addresses of the people who'd cared enough to write, and he kept up a correspondence with some of them even after they moved away.

Once, after a late party and a lot to drink, his father had confided to him that Helen, his new wife, had forced him into marriage. "I know you think it's ungentlemanly of me to say," his father had said, "but it's true. I wouldn't be telling you this, of course, if I hadn't had too much gin. Just wanted you to know. For the record, that is. Helen said she'd never be able to hold up her head in her family if I didn't make an honest woman out of her. Maybe it's just as well. She's all right, Helen. I'm not entirely happy, but I'm better off than I'd be living alone. Helen tries hard. Cooks special things for me. She's not your mother, but then, who is?"

It was the most intimate conversation they'd ever had.

After his mother's death, his father had begun to drink rather heavily. Now he'd cut down. Helen was a Christian Scientist and didn't touch a drop. A good thing, too. God knows she didn't need any stimulants. She and her sisters were what he thought of as Southern California vivacious. Everything on them moved: hands, feet, eyes, lashes, mouths. They reminded him of battery-operated dolls. He was amazed at their fortitude. After all the energy they spent on golf, shopping, theatergoing, talking, it was a wonder to him they were still operating after five P.M. It boggled his mind to contemplate what they might've been up to if they'd been drinkers.

He got into bed and opened a library book, a tale of a disintegrating marriage, a dissatisfied thirty-three-year-old housewife, bored with her husband and children, her life, who decides to strike out and try life on her own. Have an affair. The affair, he'd discovered, was obligatory in these novels.

He put the book aside and looked over at Ceil. She'd thrown one arm outside the covers, her hand curved slightly, as if expecting something rare and beautiful to be placed in it. She had lovely arms, slender and rounded, her almost translucent skin golden even at this time of the year. Leslie had inherited her mother's skin, for which she could be grateful. He leaned over and touched one of his wife's fingers, the warmth of it reassuring. A running nightmare troubled him: that one day he would wake to find her cold beside him, rigor mortis having already set in. That was the way it had happened to his father.

After his mother's funeral, when everyone had gone and there was nothing left to do but open some windows to rid the room of the overpowering scent of death, to get on with whatever was left, his father told him how it had been.

"I was stunned," he'd said. "I thought it was a bad joke, that I was being punished for something I hadn't done. She was gone, gone into the night, without warning. Something should have warned me. How can you love someone that long, share a bed, a life, and not know when the soul leaves the body? I should have known. We were like one being. How could I not know? Maybe I could have done something. Mouth-to-mouth resuscitation, anything. I lay next to her all night and I didn't know she'd stopped breathing." And his father had put his head in his hands and cried; long, shuddering sobs that went out to the corners of the room, filled his ears long after his father had sunk into a restless sleep. No one could have done anything to prevent his mother's death. He eventually convinced his father of this, he and the doctor together. It happens this way sometimes, the doctor had said. And it was terrible beyond belief, for everyone except the person who has died. It was the way anyone would choose to die. Don't cry for the dead, Ceil's mother said. Cry for the living.

At last he turned off the light and stretched out full length, hands crossed on his chest. He thought, this is the way I will lie in my coffin. Not long ago, Ceil had surprised and amused him by saying, "I like the *idea* of cremation. It's just that I can't get over the thought that it might hurt."

He turned on his side and thought of his children. I am too tough on John, he thought. Ceil's right. I'm not that way with Leslie. But she's different. Les will work things out to her satisfaction, make a success of her life, whatever she chooses to do. And make some man, men, maybe, very happy. He knew he had to fight smugness where Leslie was concerned. John was the one who troubled him. Tonight, when he'd called off their talk, John's face had been transfigured and joyful, so joyful it had cut to his heart and he'd thought, God, how he must hate me. How he must dread our encounters. I must let up on him. Then, immediately, he'd thought, no, I must not. He will be a man soon, and a man has a tough row to hoe. He was old-fashioned enough to think a man's lot was tougher than a woman's, even though he knew it made Ceil angry.

"Women are supposed to hold the family together," Ceil had said once when they argued about the new roles of women. "The whole climate of the house is supposed to hang on the woman. That's man's way of getting off the hook, if you ask me. Men can do any damn thing they please, but as long as they bring home the bacon, that absolves them of further responsibility."

"Dad's not like that," John had cut in, defending him.

"No, he's not, and it's a good thing," Ceil went on, impatient at being interrupted. "With all the marvelous things they do in the medical profession these days—in vitro babies, heart implants, all that—it is my fervent wish they get it together enough to enable a man to become pregnant and have a child. Not," she'd said, her voice dry and sardonic, "not that I envision men lining up to be the first one to try. Men know when they've got a good thing going. They see pregnant women, they know all about labor pains and water breaking and all that inelegant part of childbirth. They wouldn't touch it with a ten-foot pole." He'd laughed at her then to alleviate the tension, but he knew she felt very strongly on the subject. She'd been a little cool to him afterwards, for a while.

"Let him know you love him, Henry," she'd said earlier that evening. "There's nothing wrong with that. Is there?"

"He knows I do," he'd said.

"No, I don't think he does. Show him. Put your arms around him. Kiss him, even." At the look on his face, she laughed, a short, clipped sound, without humor.

"There's nothing wrong with kissing your son. You used to. Just because your father doesn't go in for kissing doesn't mean it's bad. European men kiss one another. No one thinks any less of them. Try it some time."

"He'd think I'd gone crazy," he'd answered, imagining John's face if, out of the blue, he kissed him. But now, lying in the dark, he wasn't so sure. My father wasn't affectionate, he thought, and I didn't suffer feelings of rejection. I don't think I did. People didn't dwell on things like rejection when I was a boy. My father was reserved. There's too damn much dissection today, too much pulling apart and examining of relationships. Even the word "relationship" had turned into a buzzword. Nothing is simple anymore. If it ever was. Take those fool how-to books. How To Make Love. How To Make Your Kid A Winner. How To Get Pregnant. It was ludicrous. Only this morning he'd read a story about a woman who was suing her lover because he refused to impregnate her. She agreed to drop the suit if he agreed to artificial insemination, using his sperm. If that didn't say something about the world today, he didn't know what did. Diamonds used to be a girl's best friend. Now it appeared sperm was.

Next to him, Ceil murmured in her sleep.

"No," she said, her voice gutteral, unfamiliar. "No, no." He tugged at one corner of her pillow. She shifted position and breathed deeply once more. When they'd first married, he'd been frightened at the intensity of Ceil's cries as she lay sleeping. When he spoke to her about them, seeking the cause, she'd said simply, "I have nightmares, Henry, I always have had. I can't stop just because I married you," and he'd said, "Why not? I'm here to watch over you. You don't have to worry anymore." She'd just given him a look. Her nightmares had continued and when he asked what they were about, although he knew she thought his questions unnecessary, she felt he was prying, she always said she couldn't remember.

"How about you?" she'd demanded. "How come you don't ever tell me about your dreams?" Startled, he'd said, "I don't ever dream," which was true. And she'd said, "That's because you have no conscience." Maybe that was true. He didn't think it was, but maybe she'd hit on something vital in his character.

Just before he'd asked Ceil to marry him, he and his father had lunch together. It seemed a proper formality. That and asking Ceil's father for her hand. He believed in going through the motions. His father had taken the news by saying, "It's a tremendous responsibility, Henry. A wife and family. Hard work, too. A lot of forgiveness is involved. And pain, as well as joy. Families inflict wounds. A family is the most complex entity I know of. Very complex. Can't even begin to tell you. It's something you have to learn for yourself. If the family's strong, there's nothing stronger. I advise you to think long and hard before you settle into the role of a family man." And he had. Two whole weeks he'd thought over what his father had said. In the end, Ceil's golden arms, her walk, the way she held her head, had ensnared him. Theirs had been, still was, a splendid love affair. Those were the words he gave to it in the deep night. A splendid love affair. He would want as much for his children, for each of them to know a marriage like his and Ceil's.

Sleet and freezing rain slapped and tickled the windowpanes. Tomorrow would be a mess getting to the station. As he began the long slide into sleep, he thought with satisfaction that the back of February was almost broken. March heralded spring.

9

"How do you suppose they manage to make macaroni and cheese taste like live worms?" Keith poked a fork at him, just missing his nose. "It must be Gleason's grandmother's ancient recipe."

He chewed absentmindedly. "I read in the paper that people in some parts of the South eat dirt," he said. "They dig it up and put it in paper bags and take it home. It isn't just because they're poor, they like the taste."

"Crazy." Gloomily, Keith contemplated the ceiling of the dining hall, adorned with an intricate pattern of grease spots put there by expert practitioners of the ancient art of slinging butter pats. Margarine pats, to be exact.

Outside, snow swirled, thick, wet flakes that hugged the ground and disappeared the second they hit. With any luck at all, the storm would continue through the day and night, and tomorrow the intrepid students would be free to wallow in the snow drifts, cut loose from school due to hazardous driving conditions.

"When're you going to Florida?" he asked, peeling an orange. He managed to do it so the skin fell away from the fruit in one unbroken arc. It was one of his talents.

Keith's jaws worked on the macaroni as if he'd landed a piece of underdone wild boar. He drank half a glass of milk without answering.

"When's the wedding?" he asked, thinking Keith hadn't heard.

When Keith finally looked at him, his eyes were hard and slick, without expression; a doll's eyes, filled with the strange light that meant Keith had slid away from where he was to a place no one else could go.

"It's off."

"Oh." He felt bad, he should've known better than to ask. Did that mean Keith wasn't going to be best man? Or did it mean the wedding had been canceled?

"My old man got the cold toe."

"What?"

"Yeah." Leisurely, Keith put both arms over his head and stretched. "He chickened out. Called the whole thing off." Keith pronounced each word slowly, distinctly, clipping off the ends like a tailor biting off threads. "In other words, he couldn't go through with it. He skipped town. Sent his intended a telegram saying he'd had a change of heart. Or maybe he told her he'd just discovered there was insanity in the family. Or that he had herpes. Or leprosy. My father has a vivid imagination. No telling what ruse he used to get out of it.

"Or it's possible," Keith continued in a bitter voice, "he delivered the unkindest cut of all. Maybe he told her he was filing for bankruptcy. Nothing like bankruptcy to put the kibosh on love. He sent me a telegram, too. He always sends telegrams when he freaks out. He hasn't got the guts to call. Said he was going to South America for a while. Probably going to dabble in real estate there. Or maybe life insurance. They must sell a lot of life insurance down there. All those terrorists, knocking people off like pigeons. Leave the wife and kiddies well-fixed when you're blown away, amigo." Keith bit off the end of his fingernail in one piece, like the orange skin, and spit it out on the floor.

"You should've heard my mother," he said. "She laughed like a hyena. She doesn't want him, but she doesn't want anyone else to have him. I think she feels better if she knows he's not happy. She's not happy, so she wants him to be miserable, too." Keith threw out his hands, palms up. "Probably if she landed some rich dude, if she got married again or something, she wouldn't give a shit about my father. She might even wish him well, who knows?"

"Oh," was all he could think of to say. He thought briefly

of telling Keith about his upcoming date with Grace Lerner's niece, just to lighten the atmosphere. And decided against it. Keith didn't have a lot of dates, but when he did, they weren't blind. Maybe that was because Keith's mother didn't have friends who had nieces.

"I want you to tell me something off the top of your head." Keith pushed away his plate and put his elbows on the table. "Which do you think would be easier, to commit murder or commit suicide?"

"What kind of question is that?" he said, his voice rising. They stared at each other with a fierce intensity, as if a fight between them was imminent. "How do I know?" Several guys at the next table looked over at them curiously.

"Just off the top of your head. Come on." Keith leaned toward him, speaking softly now. "Don't think about it. Give me your gut reaction. Which would be easier?"

"Oh, that's different. Which would be easier. Why didn't you say so in the first place?" he asked sarcastically. "Well, that's a cinch. Suicide. Because then you wouldn't be around to suffer the consequences. You're out of it. Man, are you ever out of it." He treated it as a joke, although he knew Keith hadn't meant it as such.

"If you commit murder," he said, "you probably never sleep very well ever again. Ever. That's the way I figure it."

Keith nodded, well pleased with this answer. "That's an interesting reason for not committing murder."

There were times when he knew he bored Keith, but this wasn't one of them.

He elaborated. "You'd close your eyes," and he closed his for maximum effect, "and you'd see the person you killed. Big eyes staring at you, always staring. And everywhere would be blood. Vats of blood. You have any idea how much blood the human body contains?"

"Open your eyes," Keith snapped.

He opened them, not having realized they were still

closed. He felt a sudden exhilaration. For once he, not Keith, was in control. "The human body has the most incredible amount of blood. Gallons, probably. I've forgotten how much." He was improvising now, watching Keith's face. "If you're gonna kill somebody with a gun, aim for the stomach. A stomach wound is pretty nearly always fatal. Besides, the guy might be wearing one of those bulletproof vests."

That might make a good macabre routine. Guy in bulletproof vest, looks a little like Woody, wouldn't hurt a flea, involved in shoot-out. Up and down fire escapes he goes, blind alleys, subway platforms, train thundering down the tracks. Don't hesitate to borrow from Hitchcock or any of the other pros. Subway platforms were always ominous. Guys in black suits, black hats in pursuit of Woody-like hero. Who turns out to be an expert dodger of bullets, an expert ducker of flying lead. A wimpy Dick Tracy type, impervious to flying lead and fear. Nothing can touch him on account of his bulletproof vest, which his girl friend just gave him for his birthday. In that vest he's Superman. Then, when it's all over and the bad guys are oozing all over the pavement, the wimpy hero counts all the creeps he's erased, scratches his chest triumphantly, and discovers he's not wearing his vest after all. He left it home on the kitchen table. He faints. Fade out. Laughter.

If only he had his pencil and paper handy. Some of his best ideas popped up when he least expected them.

"Last night on TV I saw a picture of a cop who got his, even with one of those vests on," Keith said in a challenging voice. "They've got a new kind of bullet designed to penetrate the bulletproof vest."

This was turning into some kind of a contest.

"Yeah, well, maybe it was a second. Flawed. They save lives. Why do you think cops wear 'em? They're very expensive. I've read plenty of stories telling about how some cop gets shot in the chest and if it wasn't for that old vest, whammo." He socked one fist into his hand to illustrate, but Keith, having had enough, made for the door, walking fast. Typical. Keith had posed the question: which would be easier, murder or suicide. Keith had a thing about stuff like that, especially suicide. Every time he heard about some kid knocking himself off, Keith would draw an X in the air and say, "Another one bites the dust." Now he was suddenly losing interest.

John took giant steps to catch up. Keith wasn't getting off that easy.

"There's always a knife," he said into Keith's ear.

Abruptly, Keith stopped, turned. They almost bumped heads. "Yeah," Keith agreed, that peculiar light in his eyes, "if I was going to kill myself, I'd probably OD on pills, plus booze. That way you're out of it. No pain, no nothing. The people who hang themselves really do me in. Or the ones who drive into a concrete abutment. Crazy." He kneaded his forehead with two fingers. "You take a gun. Very impersonal. Never even get near the guy. But with a knife, you gotta be up close, right? You can feel the knife go in. Those Manson cats used knives. They got sexual kicks out of knifing those poor bastards. In and out, in and out." Keith's cheeks were crimson. "Even the pregnant one. They nailed her and the baby. In and out. There's a sex thing you don't get with a gun that a knife gives you. A gun, you aim it, boom, that's it."

"Keith! Keith Madigan!" They both jumped. It was Mrs. Arthur. "Mr. Gleason would like to see you. In his office, please."

"God. What now." Keith sloped off in the direction of Gleason's office. And he stood alone in the deserted hall, goose bumps climbing up his arms, the back of his neck, thinking about a sexual thing with a knife. Yeah, he could see that. Come to think of it, he'd never heard of anyone committing suicide with a knife. Maybe it wasn't possible. He drove his clenched fist against his heart, pretending it held a knife. It could be done. Wonder why nobody did it. Too messy, maybe. If suicides thought about mess. Probably by the time they got

to the point of doing the job, mess was the thing furthest from
their minds.

His first year at St. Mark's, the president of the senior
class had killed himself. John had been too young to have
known the guy, but everybody said he had everything going for
him: good looks, a good mind, good athlete. What else was
there? But in the middle of March, during a snowstorm, the kid
climbed a water tower over a hundred feet high and jumped.
He landed in the soft snow, which turned out to be not nearly
soft enough. Everyone was shocked out of their skulls. They
kept it as quiet as they could so little twerps like him and Keith
wouldn't wise up. Mrs. Arthur had worn dark glasses for days
afterwards. Probably she had dished out the Last Duchess to
that kid so many times that she'd pushed him over the edge.
Even the city papers had sent reporters to town. Pictures of the
school, the town, the guy's house, were everywhere. His parents, poor bastards, were on television. At the funeral. They
always get people when their defenses are down, when they
don't know what they're doing. Psychiatrists were dragged in to
give their opinions as to why he'd done it. The TV nightly

"Did you ever suspect he'd do such a thing?"

"Absolutely not. He was a fine boy, never in any trouble.
They were a fine family, went to church every Sunday." How
to make the kid's minister or priest or rabbi feel like a real winner, right?

The kid had left a note that naturally was kept secret. And
later, some columnist wrote a piece about teenage suicide,
which was beginning to rival AIDS as the topic of the day.
Among the salient facts he learned was that March was the favorite month for suicide and that more seventeen-year-old
males committed suicide than any other age group. The senior
class president was a seventeen-year-old male and he had
jumped in March.

Nobody knew what caused the kid to knock himself off
and, as far as he knew, nobody ever found out. A memorial

fund in the kid's name was set up at the school, and for a while contributions poured in. Then the dead kid's family moved away, leaving no forwarding address, and the donations stopped before there was enough money for a full scholarship.

He'd wondered off and on about the suicide note. Not so much about what it said, although he was interested in that, but what the family did with it after they'd finished reading it. And after they'd finished crying, which he figured they'd eventually have to do, once they'd emptied the old tear ducts and tried to see out of their swollen eyes and read every word one more time until they knew them all by heart, what then did they do with the note? Tear it into a thousand pieces and flush it down the toilet? Or did they hide it somewhere, in a drawer or a trunk or even in a safety deposit box in a bank? Or did they maybe bury it in the back yard under the apple tree in a shoe box with 10D written on it, his size, and take out the box now and then to study the words further for clues? Did they take it from wherever they'd hidden it on the anniversary of the kid's death every year and look it over and ask themselves for the zillionth time, Why? And did the words lose their power to hurt after a while? It might be better to burn a note like that, to destroy it rather than torture themselves with endless rereadings. But if they did that, there was always the added torture of thinking that if the suicide note had been studied carefully one more time, it might reveal the reasons the kid had for doing such a terrible thing. It might in some way absolve them of guilt.

He shuddered and hugged himself, suddenly freezing, wishing he'd worn his heavy sweater. The hall was frigid. The school was cutting back, trying to conserve energy, they said. The heat was turned down as far as if would go without being shut off. Mrs. Arthur wore a sweater over her sweater these days. And, when he thought no one was looking, old Gleason rubbed his pale hands together and tucked them up his sleeves for body warmth.

"Healthy, that's what this temperature is, healthy, my boy," Gleason sang out when some novice complained of chilblains. "You'll find you have far fewer colds this winter, Ferguson. Far fewer colds, my boy, because your system will be better able to handle the cold," raising his voice over the sound of poor skinny blue little Ferguson coughing his brains out as his breath fogged the wintry air.

10

Grace Lerner's niece met him at the door. Before he lowered his eyes, in the misplaced hope that this would make him less visible, he saw she had rosy cheeks, a broad face, and big boobs.

"Come on in," she told him, throwing wide the door. How'd she know he wasn't the Boston Strangler? She didn't exactly collar him, but she gave the impression she might. Silhouetted against the light he saw old Grace herself hovering in the background, making little mating noises as she sucked on a cheroot, expelling smoke madly behind her hand so as not to contaminate any nonsmokers in the crowd.

He stared down at his sneakers and wondered if it was too late to run.

"Come on in," the niece said again. Put a menu in her hand and she'd be a natural for a hostess job at HoJo's. I want my mother, said a small voice within him. If I get my hands on my mother, I'll throttle her.

"John!" Grace Lerner cried, striding toward him purposefully. Who else did she think he was. She touches me, he vowed, she lays a hand on me and it's curtains. If ever his karate training was going to come in handy, this was the time. The three of them stood under the merciless glare of the overhead light. Without raising his head he knew that if someone were to run a muscle contest here, now, this minute, he'd lose, hands down. The thought depressed him immeasurably. He opened his mouth to say something disarming, something like "I just found out I have leprosy," stealing Keith's father's line, but all that came out was a little squawk. Like a chicken before the farmer comes at it, ax in hand.

"Grace, this is John Hollander. About whom you've heard me speak." Old Grace was really putting on the dog tonight. The whoms were really flying. His collar felt tight. He wondered if he'd zipped his fly.

"Your name's Grace, too?" he whispered.

"They named me after Auntie Grace because they hoped I'd look like her." The two ladies smirked at each other. It was one of those family anecdotes that should've been shot down the first time it was sent up.

"Well," he shuffled his feet, "we better get going." Young Grace mucked about in her Bean boots, hoisting her down coat in the air suggestively, wanting help.

"You have your key, dear? Uncle Larry and I have a dinner date," old Grace tossed out, hinting that the house would be empty, the young folks free to come in, make some Ovaltine, get to know each other.

"You sure you'll be warm enough?" He waited in his corner while young Grace suited herself up in enough clothing to outfit a family of five. If they arrived late at the movie, the picture would have started, the lights would be dim. No one would recognize him. On the other hand, as he observed young Grace donning her outerwear, tying her scarf up under her eyes, pulling down her knitted hat to meet her eyebrows, then turning up her coat collar to keep out drafts, he figured people might mistake her for a luminary in disguise. His spirits lifted.

They set out. The night was warmer than the day had been. Young Grace was going to work herself up a good glow before she got where she was going. The sky was very black, a small, moaning wind their only companion.

"We're walking?" she said in surprise.

"Yeah, I'm in training for track."

"How old are you, anyway?" she asked, suspicious.

"What's your last name?" he countered, setting a brisk pace.

"I asked you first." They were two tiny tots, playing together for the first time.

"Seventeen," he lied.

"So am I. I'm going to be a chemical engineer." He felt her pause, expecting a reaction. Maybe in Seattle they dropped like flies at this announcement.

"My father's a chemical engineer, and my brother is into music, so when I told my parents I wanted to be a chemical engineer, my father cried."

"Your father cried?" he said, incredulous.

"Yes. He was so happy. Haven't you ever seen your father cry?" He felt her peering at him in the darkness.

He snorted. "The only reason my father might cry is if I got arrested on a drug charge or kicked out of school. Then he'd cry tears of rage. He's been expecting something like that to happen ever since I hit first grade."

"You don't get along with your parents? My mother and father are my best friends." Her voice was solemn, and smug.

He turned to her. "Man, who do you talk to about your sex life, then?" She looked straight ahead and speeded up. As a track star, he had to keep up with her or lose everything.

"My father's not my pal, he's my father," he panted, catching up. "You can't be both. If you have a father for a friend, you don't need an enemy."

"I don't think that's very nice."

"You want me to take you home?"

"Don't be silly," she said, deciding apparently to forgive him. "What do you want to be then?"

He thought of telling her he was into heavy metal and S-M but he figured they might not have S-M in the Pacific Northwest and it would require too much explaining. Anyway, he'd offended her enough for one evening.

"Yeah, well, I'm going to be a writer for Woody Allen." Let her chew on that one. Out of the corner of his eye he saw her retreat into her coat collar. Coming from Seattle, maybe she thought Woody was a logger. "This movie we're seeing is rated PG," he said. "But I hear it's plenty raunchy. The producers figured if they gave it a PG instead of an R it'd make a trillion instead of a billion." She stomped alongside, offering no comment.

To break the conversational logjam, he said, "So what's Seattle got going for it?"

"Plenty."

"What besides fog?"

She stroked her cheek. "Fog's good for the complexion. Seattle girls are famous for their English-type complexions. Are you in love?" she shot at him.

"Sure." He didn't break his stride. "With three femmes. I'm only having a relationship with two of them, though. Two is all I can handle at one time."

She sucked in her breath. "Are you paying?"

"For what?"

"For the movies. Aunt Grace gave me money in case this was going to be Dutch. Out home we go Dutch lots of times. Plenty of women's libbers pay their own way. I don't care. I'm not that much of a women's libber, although I do believe in equal pay for equal work." She said it as if she'd invented it.

"My mother's footing the bill," he said crassly. "On account of she's a buddy of your aunt's. My mother's loaded. She has a trust fund," he improvised. "She hands me a couple of C-notes a week, sometimes more. Depending on the market." He was having a good time lying to her. He was a pretty good liar when the scenario called for it.

She tucked her arm cosily in his and he reminded himself, too late, that the mere mention of money frequently acted as an aphrodisiac. Another of Keith's nuggets. He stepped up his pace, hoping to shake her off.

"Two," he panted at the box office, "on the aisle."

The girl in the ticket booth didn't look up at him. "Aisle seats are all taken," she said, "and no smoking anywhere in the theater. Plus," she raised her head, "the management frowns on making out except during intermission." He felt himself blush.

"Don't mess with the big girls, sonny," the ticket puncher whispered in a friendly way. Actually, John thought, he might like her. Maybe next time he'd ask her to the flicks. On her night off. If she could break away from her husband and three kids waiting at home in front of the TV.

"Quiet please, the show's already started." The pimply usher had obviously let his uniform get to him.

"Wait here until I get some popcorn," he said.

"None for me. It's too fattening. I'm on a diet." Terrific. He bought two bags, one for him, the other for him, too. Giant popcorn pigout tonight.

They settled into their seats. He clutched one bag of popcorn between his knees for safekeeping and dove into the other. This wasn't all bad. A free movie and two bags of free popcorn. So she looked like the Elephant Man done up for a turn in the park. There were worse things. He slid down in his seat. The popcorn was delicious; crunchy, hot. Nice and greasy, the way he liked it. He polished off the first bag while watching some dame dressed in a slip, showing lots of *belle poitrine*, being worked around the head and shoulders by old Burt, who was behaving in his usual lovable fashion. The dame screamed now and then, but you could tell she had the hots for Burt's bod and it was just a question of where and when.

He dipped into the second bag and touched bare flesh. Young Grace was trolling in there already. Her hand moved with admirable skill, as if it had had plenty of practice. She was light-fingered and sharp-toothed, he realized with dismay, listening to her chomping away.

"I thought you said you didn't eat popcorn!" he hissed at last, unable to contain himself. The man in front turned a furious profile aad said, "Shhhhh!" spraying spit indiscriminately.

"I don't," young Grace whispered back, wrist deep in butter and salt.

What could he say. Old Burt scored a couple more points, the popcorn disappeared, and the next thing he knew the show was over. The lights went on. Music swelled as they rolled out the interminable list of credits. He slid lower in the seat. He needn't have. There was no one there he knew.

Once more out into the night they went.

"I'm thirsty," young Grace announced.

No wonder. All that salt would give a horse a thirst.

"How about if we get a soda or something?" she said. "My treat."

A modern woman, after all.

"We could go to Alfie's," he suggested. "It's this really raunchy joint down by the tracks. Full of weirdos. Around this time of night they usually start punching each other out." She looked interested. Very.

Belatedly, he realized he'd painted a too-attractive picture. "You wouldn't like it," he said hastily. "We better head for home. Every once in a while, the cops raid Alfie's." He wagged his head and assumed a lugubrious expression. "Your aunt and uncle would never let you go out with me again if I had you in there when there was trouble."

That last was genius, pure and simple.

"The local blab publishes a list of the people who're in the joint when it's raided. It could get very embarrassing."

Young Grace didn't demur. Instead, she became somewhat

kittenish and snuggled under his arm for protection as a mastiff bared its teeth at them.

"There you go, Chester," he showed off, roughing up Chester's coat. The dog was a friend from paper-route days. "How's it going, Chester? Don't take any wooden bones, okay?" Chester practically rolled over and played dead. When they hit the Lerners' house, young Grace said again that her aunt and uncle wouldn't be home from their party until late, and that there was plenty of beer in the fridge.

He hated beer. And he hated this part, the after-the-ball-is-over part. He was never sure of what to do or how to go about doing it, and tonight he had a real live one. He knew lust when he saw it. This girl, woman, from Seattle lusted after him. A first. She looked as if she'd been around the track once or twice and, although he was disinclined to make it with femmes who outweighed him, he was tempted. If the truth must out, most of them outweighed him. He hoped, with time and good nutrition, he would come up in the standings.

He'd have to be crazy not to go ahead, to pass up such a chance to develop his technique, never mind his libido. And wondered how long it would take to fumble through the layers of clothing to get at the boobs. Suppose the Lerners caught him in flagrante delicto? Old Grace was the kind who'd publish the banns in church next Sunday if she found him fooling around.

"Here." Young Grace handed him the front door key. "You do it. It always gets stuck when I try."

Under cover of darkness he flashed his teeth at her to show he understood, and set to work on the door. Under his skilled fingers it swung open, creaking and groaning, a regular Dark Shadows type door. He half expected a couple of bats to fly out.

"A piece of cake," he said, giving back the key. In a trice she had him in a hammerlock. "They won't be home for hours," she whistled into his ear. He allowed himself to be conducted inside. Without relaxing her grip, she shut the door with her foot. He admired her dexterity. Then, like a plumber's helper, she attached herself to his neck and began drawing blood.

A light touch seemed indicated.

"I knew her before she was a virgin," he mumbled, quoting Groucho, anxious to bring a smile to her lips to distract them from the havoc they were wreaking on his neck.

Grace, however, threw him from her as if he'd suddenly broken wind. He fell against a table, sending magazines flying.

"What's *that* supposed to mean?" she said.

"It was just a funny," he said weakly, running a furtive hand over his shoulder, exploring it for possible dislocation. One false move now and she could pull out a Saturday night special and blow him away. "I didn't mean anything," he said. "I was only fooling around."

Drawing herself up to her full height, she began throwing off garments, one by one, à la Gypsy Rose Lee. She caught him full in the eye with one of her heavy ski gloves, bruising his eyeball, perhaps permanently.

"All I did was ask you in for a beer," she said icily. "You Easterners are all oversexed. It's a known fact."

"Where'd you hear that?" It was the first interesting thing she'd said all night. "I never heard that. Maybe you're right."

She made a sudden move and he flinched, thinking she was going to take him by the scruff of the neck and throw him out. No matter what he said from here on in, it would be wrong.

"I'm sorry," he said, though for what? He didn't know what he'd done that he should apologize for, but an apology seemed to be in order.

She pointed to the door. "You have no couth," she said.

"That's what my mother says." He went in the direction she indicated. Once outside, teetering on the top step, he listened as she shot bolts, slid locks, and, in all probability, turned on the burglar alarm, if they had one. He walked across the frozen turf and stood on the sidewalk watching as young

Grace plastered her nose against a window, watching him. When he blew her a kiss, she thumbed her nose at him and doused the lights.

He loped homeward through the night, which had turned starry, not completely displeased with the way things had turned out. He'd probably regret it in the morning. But he didn't care how big the boobs were if there was no sense of humor behind them.

By morning, the hickey she'd given him glowed back at him in the mirror. It was a beauty, worthy of having its portrait painted by Andy Warhol. How could he keep it in viable shape until Monday morning for locker-room show and tell? Pack it in dry ice, maybe. Plenty of times he'd stood by while guys had exhibited hickeys that paled beside this one. Now it would be his turn.

You sex maniac, you, he told his image fondly. There's nothing you can't do, Hollander. You can do it all. Smiling, scratching his hairless chest, he bounded down the stairs to the kitchen.

His mother was banging around, flicking her dishcloth like a waitress on the night shift at a diner, anxious for the last customer to leave.

"John," she said. No hello, no nothing. "I've got some errands I'd like you to run for me today. The cleaners, the—"

"Hey, Ma. I need some grunts before I tackle the world." He opened the refrigerator and took out the orange juice, along with a package of day-old doughnuts, his mother's specialty. He hadn't had a fresh doughnut in years. They were bad for your teeth, too soft, too spongy, she said. When you sank your teeth into a day-older, you really had something. Besides, they were cheaper.

"It's time you had a decent haircut," she looked at him with narrowed eyes. "With Les coming home."

"Give me a break, Ma. I just got up. Les likes me with long hair. She told me she did. Don't you want to hear about last night? The orgy, I mean." He couldn't believe he'd said that. All he'd wanted to do was cheer her up a little. During the night deep lines seemed to have formed on either side of her mouth, aging her.

"What on earth is that thing on your neck?" She put out an exploring finger and he backed off. "That's my hickey," he said. "I'm guarding it with my life."

"Your hickey?"

"Yeah. Grace Lerner's niece hung it on me. I resisted. I swear I did, Ma. She attacked me. I might've lost my head. Not to mention my you-know-what." He rolled his eyes at her.

She sat down at last, shaking her head, laughing. "Don't you know it's not considered gallant to kiss and tell?"

"I didn't lay a hand on her. If she says I did, she lies."

"Did you have fun? Is she pretty?"

He yawned, an exaggerated, simulated yawn. "Let's just say it was a one-night stand, all right? Where's Dad?"

She got up and began flicking her dishcloth again. "John, I just hope you behaved like a gentleman. He's gone to have some blood tests taken."

"How come?" His family were strictly steer-clear-of-doctors types.

"He thinks he might have a low-grade virus." His mother had a thing about doctors and hospitals. "I do wish Leslie had said exactly when she was coming."

"She said Sunday. How exact do you want?"

"You know something?" His mother wove her fingers together. "I wish she were coming alone. I get so little chance to talk to her. When she leaves, I always think of lots of things I wanted to ask her. There never seems to be enough time."

"I know," he said.

"I've got a hair appointment at ten, John. Will you be a good boy and vacuum the guest room while I'm gone?"

"What for?"

She looked surprised. "Why, for Leslie's guest, of course."

11

The hospital was at the top of a hill. He parked his car and walked slowly toward the massive granite pile, wondering what urban planner would consciously put a place of healing in such a spot. A hospital should be built on flat land surrounded by rolling green hills. Or perhaps a prairie or, lacking a prairie, a plain filled with flowers and trees, sweet-smelling, cooled by a shallow stream. Birds would swoop overhead, mostly blue-birds, the birds of happiness. A hospital should be welcoming in its aspect, beckoning the lame, the halt, and the blind to enter. Abandon hope, never.

An ambulance, siren shrieking, sped up the hill and pulled into the emergency entrance. Another ambulance, quiet as a mouse, drove down the hill aimlessly. I hope I never have to go in one of those things. They scare the hell out of me, he thought. He always averted his head when an ambulance screamed by him, just as he did when a hearse passed.

He passed through the revolving doors into the lobby. He hadn't been here since the last time with John. About six years ago, that was. He remembered how brave John had been. He hadn't made a peep, not even when the doctor had set the bro-ken bone. It had almost finished him when the kid hadn't made a sound. He'd expected all sorts of crying and carrying on. It made things harder, somehow, when they were heroic.

The hospital walls were painted green. An unwritten law states that all hospital walls must be painted a particularly bilious shade of green, peculiar to hospitals the world over. He went to the desk, gave his name, his doctor's name. The nurse checked a list, chewing on a pencil as she did so. That doesn't look sanitary, he thought.

"Oh yes, Mr. Hollander," she said in a sprightly manner. "Doctor said we could expect you." She was young, not much older than Leslie. Blonde and quite homely. Where were all the pretty nurses hiding? The television screen was crowded with pretty nurses. He hadn't seen one since this business started.

"Down the hall." The nurse half rose from her chair, pointing in the direction he was to take. "It's room one-sixty-seven, Mr. Hollander. I'd take you but I can't leave here, we're short today. Turn left, go as far as you can, then turn right. You can't miss it. Room one-sixty-seven." She repeated the room number. Maybe she caught some indication of what he thought of as his approaching senility. He did find it difficult to concentrate lately. Only last week, when Burrell had been showing him the plans for a building the firm had contracted to do, asking him for his ideas, his attention had wandered so noticeably that Burrell, not a patient man at best, had said something sarcastic about snapping out of his daydream and focusing on the matter at hand. That was bad. One lapse was excusable. Two was cause for concern.

He followed directions. Unaccountably, when he made the final turn and had gone as far as he could go, the walls suddenly became yellow, bright yellow, one of his favorites. A good omen. The nurse had given him perfect directions, and he had remembered them. He knocked.

"Come in, please." They were expecting him. He felt like a character in a Kafka novel.

It was 9:20 A.M. A Saturday. Ordinarily, he would be having a third cup of coffee, a weekend indulgence, reading the paper, enjoying the feeling of freedom a Saturday always brought. He liked Saturdays, the open feel of them. He could do anything he chose to do on a Saturday. This was a holdover from childhood, he knew. On his way to the hospital he had stopped at the library to return some books and was surprised, indignant, really, to learn the library didn't open until ten. In a month or two, his golfing pals would be after him to play a round or two. He was terrible at the game, and he played only for the camaraderie. Still, there was nothing nicer on a shining green day than to be out there, swinging, walking, swinging again, just trying not to make a damn fool of himself. Except to garden. This weekend Leslie would be home. That had been his first thought after waking. His heart grew lighter thinking of his daughter's imminent arrival. Once more, they would be a complete family. He knew she was bringing a friend and dismissed the thought from mind, the way he did most thoughts that didn't meet with his approval. There would be the four of them again. It had seemed to him for some time that when any one of them was absent, there was a hole. An empty feeling. He recognized the absurdity of this, since it was only a matter of a few years before he and Ceil would be alone, childless, as alone as when they were first married. But with a difference.

In recent weeks, apprehension had been his constant companion, walking side by side, holding him in its delicate, unbreakable grip. Apprehension of what, he didn't know. It was only when the four of them were together that he breathed easier. As if by having them all in his sights, he could keep them safe forever. His father had been right; a family is a tremendous responsibility.

"Mr. Hollander, we're ready for you now." They have asked him questions, so many questions, the answers to which they solemnly record. He donned another backward hospital gown, looking down at his skinny white shanks with distaste, hating the indignity of a physical examination.

The X-ray technician was a burly black man wearing several gold chains and a heavy gold ID bracelet. Surreptitiously, he checked the man's earlobes and was relieved to see they weren't pierced.

"Bring your chin up, please. Chest a little to the left. Very good. Good. All right now, take a deep breath, please, and hold it. . . . Terrific." The man showed magnificent teeth when he smiled. "Okay, relax now. We'll have you out of here in no time. Plenty of time for your big Saturday night bash, right?" The man winked at him, sliding plates in and out of his machine with dexterity. He would wink back if he could, but he'd never mastered the art. He simply wasn't able to. As a boy he'd spent considerable time in front of the mirror, practicing winking. He'd heard girls liked it if you winked at them, that it was a sexual come-on, but he had only managed to look as if he had a tic.

The man continued to smile, probably thinking of something that had happened to him on his way here this morning. Some funny incident he'd tell his wife when he got home.

"Okay, now if you don't mind, let's try for one or two more, just to be on the safe side, all right? That's good, very good." They regarded each other fondly, two old friends. He felt like a child again, having his picture taken. It had been a long time since he'd had so many compliments on his behavior.

The technician, through at last, packed up and went away, without even a glance. It had been an act, the whole thing. The smiles, the bonhomie, all faked. He felt a tremendous sense of disappointment.

The nurse took several more blood samples. He wondered if he could still function, they'd already taken so much. Nobody told him anything. If he were inclined toward paranoia, he might think there was a conspiracy against him. When he asked a random question, their faces seemed, literally, to close in on themselves, like flowers drawing in their petals when night came. In an effort to be helpful, he said, "I think it might be my gallbladder." This was met with such blank hostility that he stopped in mid-sentence, embarrassed and confused.

Maybe it's an ulcer. He kept this thought to himself, not wanting to further offend them. I wouldn't mind a bland diet, he thought. I could handle cottage cheese and yogurt.

They gave him a glass of orange juice and told him the doctor would be along soon. The nurse's eyes and hair were the color of horse chestnuts. He had once been in love with a girl whose hair had been the same color. The nurse wore glasses. His love had had eyes of a glittering green. He would have liked to linger, to talk to the nurse; thought her face kind, although, again, she wasn't pretty. But this was not to be. She was brisk, busy, probably a fine nurse, but she had no time for him. The minutes stretched into an hour. A doctor is not to be hurried, a doctor is not to be detained. A doctor's time is sacrosanct. He too was eager to be gone, and he considered, in a moment of uncharacteristic daring, just putting on his clothes and walking out. Let them come after him if they wanted. The moment of daring passed.

This afternoon he planned to shop. He liked to shop, although it wasn't considered masculine, he knew. But he enjoyed marketing, liked pushing the cart, buying things they didn't really need. Ceil had told him he reminded her of the children when they were little, loading stuff in when she wasn't looking, so many things that sometimes, when she reached the checkout counter, she didn't have enough money to pay for it all. He had a tendency to buy pastry brushes, capers, anchovies, herring in cream sauce. Snails. In a supermarket he was overcome by desire and greed, finding the most improbable things irresistible. Like a man in love, he acted with abandon.

When he'd about given up, the doctor appeared. "Ah there, Mr. Hollander, they've taken good care of you, have they?" The doctor, smelling of Listerine, pressed and poked him, not expecting an answer. The doctor's face was carved of granite, revealing nothing. He wondered if doctors took a course in making their faces immobile, if they had to pass the course before they got their medical degrees.

"I imagine you're anxious to be off this fine day," the doctor said. "We'll let you go now. I'll have the nurse call when we get the results."

He sat up. "When will that be?"

"I shouldn't think much before Tuesday." The doctor washed his hands at a tiny sink.

"Not before then?" he said in such a desolate voice that the doctor relaxed his stiff demeanor and smiled.

"We'll try for late Monday, Mr. Hollander. I can't promise anything but we'll try. We have your office number?"

"I may be out of the office Monday," he said. "Suppose I call you instead? Would that do?" Then, "Doctor, do you have any ideas what it might be? Do you think it might be an ulcer? Or gallstones? My brother had his gallbladder out and his symptoms sound much like mine."

"I wouldn't hazard a guess, Mr. Hollander." The doctor reached out to touch his wrist. He thought that a kind thing to do, felt reassured by the doctor's touch.

"We won't know anything until we get those pictures. Then we'll have something to go on." The doctor looked at his watch. "I'm sorry," he said, "I'm late for my next patient. Have a nice weekend," and the doctor flapped a hand in farewell.

He dressed hastily, fearful that they'd come in, find him still there, and decide to take more X-rays, more blood. He escaped into the afternoon, the cold, thin light of February on the wane. February was his least favorite month. Nothing good ever happened in February, he thought. Still, he felt a sense of jubilation as he skimmed out the revolving door and headed for his car. He felt as if he'd been released from a long illness, a hospital bed he'd been occupying for several months, at least, and told to go home and never come back. He climbed into his car and, tires squealing, drove back down the hill.

On impulse, he stopped at a florist to buy Ceil some roses. "Would you like me to go with you?" she'd asked, when he told her he had to go to the hospital for some blood tests. He had said no, it's nothing. He wanted to go alone. It was one of the few times in their marriage he didn't want her with him. Instead of roses, he chose a cyclamen plant. They were so beautiful and did well when planted outside in a shady spot. He took his time choosing between a pink and a white one, settling on pink. The florist, a dour man with a large wart nestling by his nose, wrapped yards of thin gauzy green paper around the plant, as if it were Valentine's Day.

"When *is* Valentine's Day?" he said. The florist looked at him and said, "You missed it" in a flat voice, shaking his head, as if to say, "What kind of man are you, to miss Valentine's Day? What kind of a sweetheart are you, anyway?"

"Oh, sorry," he said, smiling at the man. The florist, tiny black eyes pinpoints of hostility, stared back. He carried the plant out to the car and put it on the floor so it would be safe, and drove home sedately, cautiously, wondering where his earlier feeling of elation had gone.

12

When Leslie arrived at last, it was almost anticlimactic. His mother had finished the crossword puzzle and was gnashing her teeth over the double crostic. His father, weary of peering out, checking the sky for snow, the road for cars, his watch for the correct time, had taken to muttering.

"They should be here by now. If they left right after breakfast, and didn't run into any trouble, they should be here by now."

"Henry, please. Don't drive them every inch of the way. You know that drives me crazy," his mother begged. His father habitually sounded a mental starting gun for Leslie's probable departure time, then followed her as she made her way homeward, indicating on his map the routes he thought she should take, places to be avoided, clogged bridges, weather conditions, spots where the cops were known to be extra vigilant. He didn't miss a trick. He turned on the radio for the weather report, turned on the TV news to learn of incipient blizzards. Reports of a tornado wouldn't have surprised him. He expected the worst, muttering under his breath, pacing.

"They might've stopped for lunch, I suppose." His father's voice was filled with doubt. "God knows there isn't a decent restaurant anywhere along the way. If they were smart, they'd pack sandwiches, a thermos of coffee. Save money, too." He clocked them as they stopped for gas, gave them a brief hiatus for visits to the rest room. There was always the chance, though he gave it short shrift, that they'd had a flat. Leslie could change a flat tire. He'd taught her himself. But would there be enough air in the spare? Another possibility: a drunk driver going the wrong way down the highway. Or crossing the divider, a head-on collision. These things he did not say aloud.

As if he were playing Parcheesi, he moved them toward home, step by careful step.

"Henry, you wear me out. I'm exhausted and I haven't done a thing all day. I'm going up to take a bath."

His father looked hurt. "All I want, Ceil, is for them to get home safely. I haven't done anything to tire you out." His mother piled the Sunday papers into a neat stack and said nothing. "Guess I'll go for a walk, get some air," his father said, looking at both of them expectantly. No one urged him not to go. Reluctantly, he followed through, the sound of his feet crunching forlornly on the frozen ground as he went down the path to the street.

He was alone at last, smelling the leg of lamb roasting in the oven, his mother's bath salts sifting through the bathroom door, slithering its way down the stairs. He had just settled in with an old Bogart movie on TV when he heard a car, heard a horn blasting, then the front door banged open and Leslie yelled, "I'm home!"

He leaped up, then made himself sit back down, stay put, so she'd have to come and find him.

"John!" She grabbed him and held on, kissing him fiercely on both cheeks, her face cold against his.

"Come on in, Emma!" she shouted, throwing off her jacket, her cap, her muffler, stepping out of her boots so she could feel her feet solid on the floor and know she was really home.

"I don't believe it!" she said joyously. "I thought I'd never make it. Come on in, Emma!" she shouted again. John stood watching her, smiling, trying to look disinterested, as if she came home every day.

Leslie made another run at him. "Aren't you glad I'm home? Why aren't you delirious with joy, you toad!" She rubbed her face against his and cried, "Oh John, you need a shave! I can't believe it! You actually need a shave. Imagine that, Emma. He needs a shave." He frowned at her, telling her to cool it. "Emma, this is my brother, John. John, Emma Kendel."

"I already figured out this was John," Emma said. "Hello, John." She held out her hand, which was small and cold and full of bones. He took it in his and bowed slightly, as he'd seen his father do. She was tall, almost as tall as he. She stood very straight and the gestures she made were slow and languid, as if she'd just awakened and wasn't sure where she was. She wore a fur jacket, and had a woolen hat perched precariously on the side of her head. Her hair was long and dark and shiny. As he watched her covertly, she shook some strands away from her face and smiled at him.

She's shy, he thought, entranced. Her gray eyes were set wide in her face, and her mouth was full and very red. She was good-looking in an offbeat way, he decided, trying to keep calm. She wasn't quite as good-looking as Leslie, though. But almost.

"Where are they?" Leslie cried, running into the kitchen, then back to where he and Emma stood, regarding each other silently. "Mom and Dad. Where are they?"

"Dad's been pacing all afternoon," he said. "Finally, he drove Ma nuts and she's taking a bath and he's off and running outside to clear his lungs, get a little exercise."

They heard the front door open. "Leslie! Is that you?"

"He must've been hiding down at the end of the street, planning to ambush you," he said of his father. Emma laughed, exposing small, pointed teeth.

"Daddy!" Leslie hurtled into her father's arms, almost knocking him over. He held her for a minute. John stubbed his sneaker on the rug, felt Emma looking at him.

"Are you all *right?*" Leslie cried, as she always did when she'd been away. She held her father off and looked hard at him.

"Are you really all *right*, Daddy?"

"Don't I look all right?" he said. "What kept you? I thought you'd lost your way."

How come he never hugs *me?* he thought.

"Daddy, this is my friend, Emma Kendel. Whoops, sorry!" Leslie cried. "Emma, this is my father. Ladies first, right? Mother!" Leslie discarded her father and leaped upon her mother, who arrived, pink and flushed from her bath, tying her robe around herself.

"Leslie, cut it out! I can't breathe!" she cried, and Leslie let her go. "The minute I got in the tub, I heard you come in. Your father's been like a wild man. He clocked you coming through the toll booths, coming across the bridge, then while you had a hamburger and went to the ladies'. You know him. Hello, I'm Leslie's mother. You must be Emma." She held out her hand. "We're delighted to have you."

"I'm sorry. I get so excited when I first get home I don't know whether I'm coming or going. Emma, forgive me. Mother and Daddy, this is Emma Kendel. How's that?" Leslie said, beaming. "Formal enough for you?"

They were not a demonstrative family. But when Leslie was among them, the atmosphere became charged. Emotion was rampant. She had that effect on them all. Being male and sixteen, he fought it. But eventually, he succumbed. Overnight, they became kissers, huggers, criers, laughers. Everything in the extreme. When Les left, taking herself and her electric charge back to college with her, they collapsed. His mother and father went to bed early for a week, recovering from his sister's impact. They craved sleep. He would've loved it if she'd stay longer, another week, providing lights and action.

"I'm so glad to see you all I can hardly *stand* it!" Leslie spoke in exclamation points. "Emma, I didn't mean to leave you standing there. Let's take our stuff upstairs and get you settled in."

Emma spoke. "John," she said directly to him, "why don't you show me where I'm to bed down and let Les talk to your parents. How would that be?" She gave him another of her pointy-toothed smiles and he fielded it as if it were folding money, astonished at the ease with which Emma seemed to have taken charge.

"That's a good idea. Show Emma to her room, why don't you, John." His mother's face was bland. His father's arm was around Les, who was looking up at him, saying something.

"Sure," he agreed. "Put her in the guest room, Ma?"

"Whatever suits Emma." His mother's smile belied the light in her eye. Her voice had a decided edge. "There are clean sheets on all the beds."

He took Emma's suitcase from her and led the way. "I'm not accustomed to such service," she said, following him into the guest room. She had put on dark glasses and taken off her jacket, he saw, and underneath it had on striped overalls over a thick white sweater that matched her hat. He laid her suitcase on the luggage rack and twitched at the Venetian blinds, straightened the curtains, the way he'd seen the bellhop do the only time he'd ever stayed in a hotel. His parents had taken him to Montreal after dropping Leslie off at college her freshman year. He'd had his own room, his own TV, and had carefully made his bed before going down to breakfast. When he'd told them that on the way home, his mother and father had had a good laugh. The maid must've thought he'd slept in the bathtub.

Emma sat on the side of the bed and took off her boots. She wiggled her toes. "Did you know that feet are an erogenous zone?" she said. And because he hadn't any idea what "erogenous zone" meant, he said, "Where'd you get those?" pointing to her boots, which were made of snakeskin the color of red wine. He would gladly have given a year's growth to possess such a pair.

"Oklahoma City. My hometown. They're custom-made. If you want," she rubbed one foot against the side of her leg, her eyes laughing at him, "I can get you a pair when I go home. All you have to do is trace the outline of your foot on a piece of paper, and they can make them for you from that. They turn out really well. A couple of my friends have ordered them that way."

He ran his hands over the rough skin, reveling in the smell of them. "My budget can't stand that kind of outlay right now."

"Try them on, why don't you?" She leaned back on the bed, supporting herself on her elbows. Her breasts stood up small and neat under the overalls. He flushed as she caught his eye and laughed.

"They wouldn't fit me anyway," he said.

"You never know," she said. "I have big feet. What size are yours?"

"Ten."

"Oh well, I guess you're right. Mine are eight." She pulled her elbows out from under her and lay flat, gazing at the ceiling. "I think I'll take a bath. How would that be?"

"Sure," he said, feeling slightly light-headed. "I'll turn on the light so you don't fall in the can," he said, thinking he should have said "toilet."

She laughed. "You're funny," she said.

Wait'll I really take off, he thought. I'm not even trying.

Emma went to her suitcase. "Are you expecting people for dinner or anything?" she said, holding up an extraordinary garment against herself for inspection. "I mean, is this all right to wear, do you think?" It looked to him like a jumpsuit made of variegated-colored suede patches.

"Far out," he said. "Is that custom-made, too?"

"I can't bear cheap things," she said.

"Anything goes around here," he told her in a too-hearty voice. He edged toward the door. "If you want, I'll show you where the bathroom is."

"Where's your room?" she asked, right behind him. He pointed. "Down at the end of the hall. I keep the door closed so my mother won't freak out when she gets a load of the mess."

"Let's see," she coaxed. He took her down the hall and opened her door a crack so she could look in. "The pits," she said, nodding. "The absolute pits." Fired up by her approval, he took her on a tour.

"This is the master bedroom where the master sleeps," he said with a theatrical flourish. If his mother came up now and caught him showing her bedroom to Emma, she'd skin him alive.

"When I was little," Emma said, "I used to bounce up and down on my parents' bed and imagine them making love there. I used to listen at their door, too. Did you ever do that?" She cocked her head, looking at him, waiting for an answer.

He cleared his throat. "Not since I reached puberty."

She grinned. "How old are you, John?"

He considered lying. He'd lied to young Grace. Why not Emma? "Sixteen," he said, knowing that Leslie would have told her how old he was. "How old are you?"

"Twenty," she said. His heart sank. Why couldn't she be nineteen, like Leslie. Nineteen he could cope with. "I've been twenty, emotionally and psychologically, ever since I was about twelve," she said. "I better take that bath, John."

"Sure." He led her to the bathroom, said, "This is the hot, this is the cold. And here's the soap and I guess these are your towels. The guest always gets the clean towels. If you want anything, just yell."

"Thanks, sweetie," she said. "I will, don't worry."

"Just yell," he repeated, heading for the stairs. Halfway down, he stopped and listened. He thought he heard her laughing. At him, no doubt. What did he care. Leslie had called it. She *was* outrageous. He liked having new people around, in the house. It was exhilarating. *She* was exhilarating. Wait'll he told Keith.

Dinner was very festive. His father was laid back under the influence of Leslie's presence, also Emma, also two martinis. Emma sat across from him at the table, shimmering in the candlelight, eating her lamb with mint sauce and roast potatoes and carrots. He caught her pushing most of the carrots off to one side, hiding them under some bits of lamb, and that endeared her to him further.

His mother sipped her wine and watched his father showing off for the girls from behind her thick black eyelashes, smiling faintly. She wore a lavender dress he'd never seen before.

"You look nice, Ma," he told her.

His father leaned toward him. "Your mother always looks nice, John. Always. This lamb is perfectly cooked, Ceil, perfectly." He said everything twice to make sure he'd been understood. Les and Emma told a story involving a red Volvo and an ardent suitor of one of them, which caused a lot of laughter and didn't make any sense to him at all. His mother tucked her hair behind her ears and put her chin in her hand, smiling, enjoying herself. He got up and cleared away the plates, anxious to get at the blueberry pie he knew was for dessert. While he scraped the plates, the telephone rang.

"Get that, please, John, and tell whoever it is to call back." His father had a thing about telephone calls at dinner time.

He held his nose and picked up the receiver.

"Yeth?" he said.

"Is John there?" a girl's voice said.

"Who ith thith?"

"Grace Smith from Seattle." In his mind he hyphenated her name. Grace-Smith-from-Seattle.

"He ithn't home. He'th out. Gone to the picthure show." He hung up and loaded the plates into the dishwasher. The phone rang again. When he picked it up, a voice said, "Ith John there? If he ithn't, tell him hith wallet ith over at Lerners'. Ith empty, but thath where it ith." Bang. She had slammed down the receiver so hard it made his ear drums sing. Reluctantly, he decided maybe she did have a sense of humor after all. He hadn't even missed his wallet. It must've fallen out during the orgy.

"Who was that?" his mother asked when he went back to the dining room.

"Grace Lerner's niece. I left my wallet there. She called to tell me." Absentmindedly, he fingered his hickey.

"God, John, you'd think you invented that thing," Leslie said. "Grace Lerner's niece must think you're pretty cute." She and Emma went off into gales of laughter, which he ignored. His father, zeroing in on the liquor closet, squinted over his shoulder to see what he was missing.

"What are you doing, Henry?" his mother inquired. She knew darn good and well what he was doing.

"Just getting out the calvados, my love."

"Not tonight, Henry." She always said, "Not tonight, Henry" when his father headed for the calvados, and his father always proceeded on course.

"This is an occasion, Ceil. We're going to celebrate with some fine old calvados."

"But tomorrow's a work day, Henry."

"It's Leslie's first night home, and we have a charming visitor. That's cause for celebration." And his father poured some calvados into each of the glasses with a practiced hand.

"None for me, thanks," he said facetiously, watching them drink. He had never been as sick as when he and Jimmy Howard had nipped some of that stuff back in the fourth grade.

"I didn't think you wanted any, John," his father said. "You'll have to wait a few more years." He and Leslie exchanged glances. She had never told, even though he'd barfed on her when he thought there was no barf left in him. And she'd held his head and said, over and over in unconscious imitation of their mother, "Just let it come up, John. Let it come up." And he had.

"I love calvados," Emma said, sniffing at her glass. "It smells so earthy. I had some when we went to Normandy and it hooked me for life." She smiled around at them. In this light, her eyes looked green, although this afternoon he could've sworn they were gray.

His father beamed. "See, Ceil, this is a girl after my own heart." His mother smiled thinly. Spots of color rode high and bright in her face, a sure sign of danger.

"It's very hard to find good calvados in Oklahoma City," Emma said.

"Emma." His father leaned toward her. "Everything is hard to find in Oklahoma City, I understand."

"This is good, Daddy," Leslie said. "The best we've ever had."

His father took a big sip of his calvados and rolled it around in his mouth, making a show, imitating a wine taster.

Emma giggled. "Now you have to spit it out and eat a cracker to dry your palate."

"Ceil, have we any dry crackers?" His father poured out more calvados into his own glass. Theeothers still had some.

Bunching her napkin beside her plate, his mother rose, lips pursed, and laid a firm and significant hand on his father's arm and said, "Come on, Henry. Let's go to bed."

"It's too early," his father protested. "We have guests, Ceil. We have guests." But he went, complaining all the way.

"Way to go, Dad," he said under his breath.

"Your father is adorable, Les," he heard Emma say as he carried out the remains of the roast. "Just adorable." He was so struck by her comment that he stood for a moment, platter in hand, trying to see his father as adorable, and failing.

"Your mother is very protective of your father, isn't she?" Emma then said. He turned, thinking her behind him, that she'd been speaking to him. But she was in the dining room still, talking to Leslie.

"Yes," he heard Les say. "I guess she is. My mother is very protective of us all. When I'm a mother, when and if, I'm not going to be as protective of my children as she is of us. I'm going to train mine to be independent when they're young so they'll know how to operate on their own. "Well," she gave a little laugh, "that's what I say now. You never know what you're going to do with your kids until you have them. But I'm going to try. I think you do kids a favor when you teach them early on to be independent."

When he returned to the dining room, Emma sat, one elbow resting on the table, watching the remains of her brandy she was swirling around in its glass.

"Yes," she said, agreeing with Leslie, "in the end, the only person you have to rely on is yourself. So you better make damn good and sure you don't lean on, count on, anyone else."

"That's sort of cold-blooded," Leslie said. "I didn't mean that exactly. You can be independent and still count on other people. Usually, I think, if you can count on someone, you can love him, too."

"You sound just like Ollie," Emma said.

Who was Ollie? Her steady?

"Who's Ollie?" he said.

"He's my stepfather. My most recent stepfather. And the nicest one, so far. And," Emma picked up a spoon and leveled it at him as if it were a gun, "the richest. By far the richest."

"How many stepfathers have you had?" He may have sounded like a twit, but he had to know.

"Four. Each one cuter than the last." She was teasing him now. He knew she was teasing him.

Thinking of Keith, he said, "Sometimes parents have to count on their kids, too, even though that's not the way it's supposed to be, not the way it's planned."

"What I meant was," Leslie's eyes looked very dark in the candlelight, "it's easier to love someone if you can count on him than if you can't."

"Oh well, love." Emma tossed the word across the table as if it were weightless and not worthy of her concern. "I wasn't talking about love. Love makes people vulnerable. If you train yourself to be totally self-sufficient, you're better off. In the long run, you're better off if you count only on yourself. Love doesn't enter into it."

Later, lying on his sofa bed, trying to concentrate on the dumb poem he was supposed to have memorized for English tomorrow, he thought about what Emma had said. What does she know? She's only twenty. Twenty isn't so old. Only four years older than he was. I suppose she thinks she's never going to fall in love. I'm only four years younger than she is. That's nothing. Older women went bonkers over younger men and, in fact, were doing it more and more these days. Four years is nothing. He felt very sophisticated at the moment, very worldly. Very horny. It's a good thing Emma wasn't around right now. Boy, watch out. Just watch out. A man's in his prime at sixteen. When he'd read that, he'd thought, man, is that true. Is that ever true. The only trouble with being in your prime at sixteen was that the rest of the way is a downhill trip. By the time you're twenty-five, you're over the hill. Sexually speaking, that is.

There wasn't a moment to lose.

If she thinks Dad's adorable, what does she think about me?

13

He overslept. Last night he'd got into *Catcher in the Rye* for about the fifteenth time. Once in, he couldn't get out. That old Holden Caulfield was a smartass, but you couldn't help liking the guy. If only Salinger would pull himself together and move out of his hermit's hideaway and write a sequel to *Catcher*, he might find out what had happened to old Holden, find out how he'd turned out. Christ, he must be about forty-four by now. Almost as old as his father. He tried to imagine Holden as a middle-aged man. Would he be duded up in a three-piece suit, talk about the stock market and where the Dow had closed for the day? Play golf, sit behind a shiny desk, go to his club for lunch. Or would he still be hacking around New York City, getting drunk, calling up prostitutes in the middle of the night, sneaking into old Phoebe's room, snuffling around until she woke up, stuff like that.

He lay with his arms behind his head and looked at his feet. They didn't look all that erogenous to him. The sun rested a tentative finger on his big toe. His mother yelled, "Get a move on!" and banged on his door. He snatched his foot out from under the sun's warm touch.

"Thanks a lot, Ma!" he yelled back.

He got out of bed and trudged down the hall. The doors were all closed. Suppose Emma emerged from her room and they collided. He had a feeling she slept in the nude. Either that or in a see-through nightgown with her initials over the nips. The thought revved up his groin. He took a hot shower, changing to cold. Plenty of guys he knew told him the shower was the best place for fantasizing in.

Oh, sorry. Emma stepped daintily into the tub. I didn't know anyone was here. Do you mind if I share?

That's okay. Sure, plenty of room. Here, have my soap.

I'm done with it. Temperature all right for you? He tried not to
stare. Good manners were important, never more so than in the
shower. Emma began to wash her hair. Maybe she'd want him
to hang around to soap her back. He stood under the cold
shower, daydreaming, exchanging witticisms with her, until
goose pimples started creeping up on him.

Stay as long as you like, he said as he exited. No rush.
Wrapping a towel around himself, he peeked behind the shower
curtain. She was singing with her eyes closed against the spray,
neat and trim, her skin taut and rosy. He checked the nips.
They were in place, just where they were supposed to be. He
was relieved. She was perfect. An older woman, nevertheless
perfect.

He'd have to ask Les about her. Find out what she was
like, what she was interested in, what kind of guys she went
out with. Slept with. He had a feeling she wasn't a virgin. He
was pretty sharp about things like that. But she wasn't promis-
cuous. Choosy was the word for Emma.

She was enchanting. He was enchanted. Not only that,
but he was also a prince of a fellow. An enchanted prince and
she was the princess who felt the pea lousing up her mattress.
There was something about Emma that put mattresses in his
mind. And to think they'd only met yesterday. How would it
be when he'd known her a week? How long was she staying?
He'd never thought to ask.

For the first time in his life he chose what he would wear
with care. Clean everything: underwear, socks, chinos, button-
down shirt, tie. He went for broke and even parted his hair.
His hickey glowed discreetly, somewhat diminished in luster.

Usually, he played at being seedy. Mostly to aggravate his
father, who never even appeared in shirt sleeves. When he was
dressed, his father stayed dressed. He had his hair trimmed
every other week, his shoes polished to a high gloss; his garters
were kept busy holding up his socks. If they knew what was
good for them.

He, John Hollander, however, in order to offset the ridiculous, to him, anachronism of shirt and tie demanded by his school, went as far as he could to the other extreme. He affected white socks stiff with dirt, so stiff no garters were necessary. A soiled white T-shirt worn in lieu of an undershirt. And, when his father complained about the long hair, he'd hack at it with dull kitchen scissors so that, if another complaint arose, as it surely would, he could truthfully say his hair had just been cut.

Last year, during the February vacation, he'd met a girl on the towline at Butternut. She was a pretty nice girl, a much better skier than he was. They'd gone to the lodge to get warm and high on cocoa and, when he'd pulled off his ski hat, she'd let out a little shriek.

"My gosh!" she'd cried. "What happened to your hair? You look like you have a case of the mange." So he'd made up a story about how he had to take medication that made his hair fall out and then she'd been embarrassed, thinking he had some terrible disease. They'd finished the cocoa while she told him a long, involved story about her dog, who had the mange, only the vet hadn't diagnosed it until the poor animal was practically bald. He was about to tell her a funny tale about his dog spraining his knee jumping off the newly upholstered couch when a bunch of people the girl knew showed up and they all went to ski the top of the mountain. They told him in supercilious tones that the top of the mountain was the only trail worth talking about at Butternut. They hadn't asked him to come along, which was probably just as well. And he'd been left there, staring into the fire, mange and all.

Emma probably had a line of guys reaching around the block, he figured, waiting to take her out. There was a look about her, a look he'd never run into before, that he found disturbing. The look was trying to tell him something. The way her body moved, her eyes, her shoulders, all of her, spoke to him in a foreign language, one he didn't speak or understand, but one he knew without question he would very much like to become fluent in.

Big hangover, eh, Dad? he thought as he watched his father pick at his half grapefruit, his gray face matching his gray suit. You never learn, do you? I coulda told you to steer clear of that calvados, Dad. That stuff's bad news. If you'd asked me, which you didn't, I coulda told you.

"Girls not up yet?" His father rattled his newspaper and settled in behind it as if it were the Declaration of Independence and he was John Hancock checking it for errors before he signed on the dotted line.

"You know how they are. They'll probably surface in time for lunch," his mother said. The telephone rang. His father's hand jerked, sending coffee flying. He was surprised. His father almost never made an awkward motion, never spilled things. Boy, he must really be hurting.

He elbowed his mother out of the way, saying, "I'll get it." His father put down his paper and listened as he said, "Hello."

"Trouble here," Keith said. "Big trouble."

His father stood, clutching his paper to his chest. "Who is it, John?" he asked.

"It's Keith." His father sat back down and again hid behind the paper.

"She's in the hospital," Keith said.

"How come?" He was becoming an expert at monosyllabic answers and questions.

"I was baby-sitting next door at the Irvings, and she called and said 'Come and get me.'" Keith's voice faded as if he were holding the receiver at arm's length. "From next door she called and said 'Come and get me,' so I knew it was bad. I left the oldest kid in charge and skinned home. Told the kid I'd give him a quarter if he kept the others apart, kept 'em from killing each other. Man, you oughta see those kids go for each other. It's like the battle of Little Bighorn. The kid said he wouldn't do it for less than fifty cents. I couldn't believe it. Anyway," Keith took a long breath, "when I got here, she was zonked out on the couch. There was an empty pill bottle and an almost empty booze bottle on the floor. So I knew. I called the cops, they came and took her to the emergency room in a squad car. They got her in time." Keith stopped and he heard the sound of heavy breathing, an obscene caller. "They pumped her out in time," Keith said.

Whatever he said now counted.

"You did good, kid." Noncommital, words Keith needed to hear, words that meant nothing to his mother and father, who were listening, he knew. "How about today?"

"I have to sleep. She's still there. I don't know for how long. I don't know what the doc's going to say. I'll set the alarm for noon." Keith sounded exhausted. "They got her in time. I don't believe the whole thing. The intern told me five more minutes and it would've been curtains."

"Don't worry about a thing. I'll tell Gleason," he said and hung up.

"Keith's mother's in the hospital." If she asked, he'd say the doctor didn't know what was wrong. She didn't ask. "He didn't get much sleep last night. He wants me to tell Gleason he'll be in after noon some time."

"I'm sorry to hear that," his mother said. "Poor kid, he has a rough time of it, doesn't he?"

Little did she know.

"Why don't you ask him for dinner? I'm taking Mrs. Hobbs to the doctor this morning, but I'll have plenty of time to go to market, maybe bake a cake or something festive. Les would probably like it if I made cheesecake. Whatever we have, it'll be better than Keith going home to an empty place, eating alone."

"Thanks, Ma." It was the first time she'd ever suggested he invite Keith for dinner. Usually he had to ask. "Thanks, I will." On his way out, he checked the windows of Emma's room. He wouldn't have been too surprised to find her leaning out, grinning at him, maybe even waving good-bye. The windows were blank, blinds down. He thought of throwing a couple of small boulders up against the glass to get her attention. Nah. With his luck, he'd break the window and his father'd have him up in small claims court for damages.

"So long!" he hollered to a nonexistent person across the street, hoping he'd wake her and she'd stagger to the window to see what all the ruckus was about. He waited, nothing happened. All right, so she was a heavy sleeper. He skimmed the fence like a decathlon runner and almost wiped out when he hit some ice. Never mind. She would be there, in his house, when he got home. The thought cheered him all day. Even after he'd seen Keith.

"She really did a job." The shadows under Keith's eyes were like bruises. He'd made it to school in time for lunch, which he ate ravenously, without criticism, not having eaten in some time.

"She must've taken the whole bottle. Washed 'em down with Scotch. She's done it before. I told you, didn't I?" Keith's eyes were puffy and bloodshot. "I don't know what to do, where to go from here. Sooner or later she's going to pull it off. That's what the doctor told me. If they really want to die, they'll manage."

"Why don't you call your father?" He spoke before he thought. "Maybe he could help." Keith's face turned dark. He didn't answer. He plunged on, as if this day were like any other. "My mother wants you to come for dinner. Les is home and she brought a friend. She's really something."

"Your sister isn't all that great," Keith said, not looking at him.

"I meant the friend, not Les." He wouldn't allow himself to get sore at Keith now. Keith was like a grizzly woken early from its nap. He had good reason. "She's from Oklahoma. She has these fantastic boots made of red snakeskin. They're custom-made."

"So?" Keith said.

"What's 'erogenous zone' mean?" he asked, knowing that would get Keith if nothing else would.

"Why do you want to know?" Keith smiled a strange smile.

"Because she said feet were an erogenous zone and I figured it meant something sexy."

"Why?"

"The way she said it."

"How'd she say it?"

"I don't know. Everything she says is sexy." He wanted to go on and on about Emma, but, for once, discretion prevailed. He decided against overkill. Keith would find out about Emma. All in good time.

"I have to go to the hospital after school. I said I would."

"You want me to come with you?"

"That's okay. I'll go alone, thanks anyway. But thanks for offering. And tell your mother thanks, I'd like to come for dinner. I've gotta split now."

"But what's it mean? Do you know?" If it was sexy, Keith would know.

"Hey, man." Keith smiled. "It's every zone in your bod. It's your teeth, your toenails, your knees. You're loaded with them. You probably have more erogenous zones than most people. Hang on to 'em, kid. Hang on. I have a shitty date with Simons. See you." Keith took off.

"Do you spell it with one *R* or two?" he shouted, but Keith by then was too far away to hear. On his way home he stopped at the library. The dictionaries were kept in a room off the main room where harried college students on vacation pored over reference books; haggard, earnest, procrastinators all. Procrastination is the thief of time. He'd had to write that one hundred times last year for one of his teachers. Boy, that was depressing. One hundred times when he could've been doing something constructive. The room was loaded now with hunched figures, writing feverishly. In a couple of years, that might be him. Would be him. He lifted one side of his mouth in a thin, Woody-type smile. Suppose he skipped college, took a year off to find himself. Suppose, when he found himself, he felt like puking. Entirely possible. He winced, thinking of the roars his father would let loose if he suggested finding himself.

Maybe he should run away. He could travel across country, notebook in hand, gaining experience from living. Sort of a Jack Kerouac type, only more lovable. Or he might opt for art school, learn the mechanics of drawing. That way, if he turned out to be a writer manqué, he'd have something to fall back on. Life was full of possibilities.

His hickey. He clapped a hand to his neck, causing heads to snap up. People were looking at him. No one had mentioned his hickey. He'd forgotten it himself. His encounter with young Grace had been for naught. He could've sworn that hickey was a winner. A standout. But here it was, afternoon half gone and the hickey was fading, drooping on the vine. Too much else was going on.

He found the dictionary, thumbed to the *E*'s. There was Eros, Greek god of love. Yeah. Right on. One *R* or two? He found it. Erogenous. Sexually sensitive or gratifying. All right.

He stared down at his feet with new respect. If feet had something to do with sex, then everything did. Sex was everywhere.

14

Woody put it another way. "My brain is my second favorite organ," he'd said in some movie. *Sleeper?* He wasn't sure.

Was the brain an erogenous zone?

It bore some thinking about.

"Keith says thanks, Ma, he'd like to come for dinner. He'll come over after he gets back from the hospital, all right?"

"Fine. Get me the milk, would you, please, John?"

"What're we having?"

"Shepherd's pie and cheesecake."

"What's in shepherd's pie?" He sniffed. It sure didn't smell like steak.

"Leftover lamb. You love it," she told him firmly, "it's one of your favorites."

"It is?" She had a way of telling him things were his favorites when he couldn't remember them ever having been such. "Where are Les and . . . her friend?" He wouldn't call her by name. It might make him seem too interested. Where's what's her name? I'll never forget what's her name.

"Shopping."

"How long is she staying?"

"Why, I guess the usual time. Ten days. Isn't that how long she stayed on her spring break last year?" She was talking about Leslie, he about Emma.

"How's Mrs. Hobbs?" he remembered to ask. "She still forging ahead in business?" Mrs. Hobbs was one of the little old ladies his mother chauffeured around town as part of her volunteer work. Mrs. Hobbs was a gas. A few years back he'd been in the back seat, the old lady in front, talking nonstop about her dear departed husband.

"Why, I lived with that man for more than fifty years, don't you know," Mrs. Hobbs had said, turning to look at him, to make sure he was listening. "And I don't believe I ever did anything right, to hear him tell it. I washed his shirts, shined his shoes, made him bran muffins for his digestion, and he never said so much as thank you' once. He liked his shirts done soft, don't you know, but I put starch in 'em and you could hear him all the way down to the corner." Mrs. Hobbs had smiled then and taken off her small black hat to punch up her wispy white curls.

He'd seen a little pink spot on top of her head, which he'd realized with a start was Mrs. Hobbs coming through her hair. He'd opened the car window a crack and let his fingers hang out and had thought seriously of resting one cold finger on Mrs. Hobbs's bald spot. Just to see what she'd do. But she'd put her hat back on, turning again to look at him with her little watery eyes, as if she read his mind. The moment for touching Mrs. Hobbs's bare skin had, regrettably and finally, passed. He hadn't seen her since.

"Oh, she got her dates mixed," his mother said, sniffing at the milk to see if it had gone sour. "She called right after you left this morning and said her appointment was tomorrow, not today. She's fine. Getting a little fuzzy, but aren't we all."

The telephone rang and she said, "Get that, will you, John. If it's the young man for Emma, tell him she isn't home yet. He's a pest, must've called four times today."

"Emma there yet?" a silky male voice inquired.

"Nein," he said, tracing a little Hitler mustache on his upper lip with a handy ball-point. His mother called this dude young? He sounded pretty old. You could tell a person's age over the telephone pretty well, if you'd made a study of voices. This one was at least thirty.

"You vant leave message?" He clicked his heels, not easy while wearing sneakers, and saluted with his free hand. You turkey, how do you get off calling her four times in one day?

"Just tell her Ralph called. Tell her I'll wait to hear from her about tomorrow night, okay?"

Say please, you turd. Ralph? What kind of a name was that?

"She have your number?"

"She should have, but she's a little flaky." Ralph gave a somewhat snide laugh. "Some days she has trouble remembering her own name. I better give it to you."

Listen, turkey boy, don't hand me that crap. Don't give
me that familiarity crap, like you know her so well. I'm not
standing still for that kind of garbage, turkey boy.

"Wait a second while I get a piece of paper." He left the
receiver dangling, went into the hall, took his father's old hat
out of the closet, turned down the brim all around, and practiced looking sinister in the mirror for a couple of minutes.
Then he studied his gums to see if they were receding. Receding gums were all the rage these days. Were the gums an erogenous zone? He considered going up to floss his teeth.

"Okay." Reluctantly, he returned to the phone. "I'm set.
Shoot."

"I thought you fell in," Ralph said in a clenched voice.

"You want to give me the number? I'm in sort of a hurry."

Ralph gave him the number. "Would you mind repeating
that?" he said, not once, but twice. Pushing Ralph to the brink.

"You oughta get your ears cleaned out, sonny," Ralph
snarled.

"Emma know your last name?" he asked cheerfully,
pleased with his interrogation technique. "In case this is a bar
and grill she's calling you at."

"Whose monster kid brother are you, anyway?" Ralph was
on the verge of an explosion.

"Heil Hitler," he said, and hung up fast.

"What was that all about?" His mother backed out of the
refrigerator, both hands loaded with fur-bearing leftovers. "Was
that Emma's young man?"

"Making soup, eh, Ma?" he asked, not answering her question. The less said about Ralph the better.

"Things get so crowded. I should've cleaned it out before
Les got home, but I forgot." She had the grace to look sheepish.
"You know how I feel about throwing perfectly good food
away, John. With people starving all over the world. What do
you think of Emma?" She was changing the subject. You could
practically hear her shifting. She was sensitive on the subject of
her leftovers. "She's . . . different, isn't she?"

"Well, she's not Grace Lerner's niece, Ma, if that's what you mean. She's okay." He was slippery as an eel when it came to committing himself about people. Girls, especially. He didn't want to be quoted. "I've never known anyone from Oklahoma before." As if Oklahoma were Afghanistan. Mercifully, a car pulled up in the driveway just then and he heard them talking and laughing. He went out to greet them, glad to get away from what he thought of as the inquisition.

"Johnny!" Leslie embraced him as if she hadn't seen him in months, He stood there thinking Emma might get the idea and do the same, but no luck. He helped them carry in their packages.

"This is for you." Emma handed his mother a package wrapped in shiny dark-brown paper, tied with a huge, classy white bow. He was pleased that his mother didn't say, "Oh, you shouldn't have," the way phonies did when you gave them a present. He couldn't stand it when people did stuff like that. Instead, his mother said, "Thank you so much, Emma," and picked carefully at the bow, no doubt having some future plans for it. She also collected string.

Inside was a mohair throw the color of ripe apricots. Even he could tell it was expensive.

"Why," his mother's face flushed, "it's perfect. It's lovely. Thank you, Emma." He wished he could have bought his mother a present as grand. She held it up against her cheek.

"I've never had such a beautiful thing; well, anyway, not in years," his mother said. "I can't thank you enough."

Emma ducked her head in mock shyness. "I'm glad you like it. All right if I use the shower? I promise I'll make it fast. My hair's filthy."

She excused herself. He felt the tips of his ears get hot at the mention of "shower." Did she know?

Les put the kettle on for tea. His mother placed the pink cyclamen in the center of the kitchen table. He got out the jar of cinnamon and sugar to sprinkle on the toast. While they waited for the kettle to sing, Les tried on her new running shoes; pale blue and guaranteed to make her run faster than anybody. "They were on sale," she said. "I would've bought two pair but I ran out of money. Emma wanted to buy me another pair, but I wouldn't let her. She's very generous. She has scads of bills crumpled up in every pocket. It's the most amazing thing." Leslie shook her head. "I've never known anyone as rich as Emma. She's always lending people money. Half the time I don't even think they pay her back."

The kettle began to keen. Les made the tea and he put the bread in the toaster. Cinnamon toast was his responsibility. Leslie got down the most fragile teacups.

"Sit, Mother," she directed. "Let the slaveys do the work."

"You've become very bossy," his mother said. "Hasn't she, John?"

"Higher education done it to her," he said. The smell of burning filled the room. Both he and Les leaped for the toaster. "God, Mother, you've simply got to buy a new toaster," Leslie said. "This thing is the pits."

When they'd got everything settled down, Les did the honors, balancing a strainer carefully as she poured tea into each cup. They ate and drank and a feeling of well-being overcame them all.

"How about some for Emma?" his mother said.

"Oh, she won't be out for hours," Leslie said. "When she washes her hair, she also does her nails and her exercises and about a hundred other things."

Exercises? What kind of exercises? He saw her doing sit-ups in the bathroom, the mirror fogged over with steam. Or push-ups. Or maybe chin-ups on the shower rod. He shook his head to clear it.

"Anybody call?" Leslie asked.

"Ralph," he said.

"Ralph who?"

"Ralph for Emma. How long's she staying, Les?" He had broken the ice by saying her name.

"She might go to North Carolina for a few days. Mother, I have a lunch date in town tomorrow. Thought I might go in with Dad on the train in the morning. That all right with you?"

"How about Emma?" he said. "She going with you?" There, he'd said it twice.

"Oh," Leslie waved her hand vaguely, "she wants to stick around for a phone call. You don't have to worry about her. She's good at amusing herself."

North Carolina? What does she want to go there for?

"If you want," he said, "I can get home early, in case she needs anything. Or anything like that."

"Good boy, Johnny. You're a real sport, sport. Do anything for a pretty girl, wouldn't you?" Leslie leaned and kissed his ear, then blew into it.

He jerked away. "Quit it," he said, not really sore. "How come she's not going into New York with you?"

"I told you. She's expecting an important phone call. She wants to stick by the phone all day."

"You don't mean Ralph?"

"No, not Ralph."

"The plot thickens," his mother said. "I'm going up to write some letters and read. Clear up here, will you? Thanks for the lovely tea."

After she'd gone, he said, "Then she's in love." Gloom settled over him like a shroud. Leslie's eyebrows shot up. "But of course, dahling. Who isn't? I am."

"You always are," he said. "Who's she in love with?"

"No one you know. This time it's a married guy, somebody she met on her last flight from Oklahoma back to college."

It sunk in. "She's in love with a married guy?"

"Don't worry." Leslie patted him on the knee. "It won't last. She's flighty, is our Emma. She never stays in love for long. It's part of her charm, Johnny." Les took the cups and saucers over to the sink, began rinsing them and stacking them in the dishwasher.

"Keith's coming for dinner," he told her, not wanting to talk about Emma anymore. He had to digest what he'd heard. "His mother's in the hospital."

"Keith as crazy about himself as ever?" She had never liked Keith. And Keith didn't like Leslie. He wasn't sure why.

"Listen," he turned on her, "give the guy a break. His mother tried to kill herself. That's why she's in the hospital. He's having a rough time. She drinks, takes pills. His father's no help." Leslie's face was instantly sad. He noticed how her high cheekbones caught the light, looked glossy, as if they'd been oiled.

"I didn't know," she said. "No wonder the poor guy's so loused up."

He told her about Keith's father getting the cold toe and chickening out of his wedding. "How'd you like it if Ma tried to knock herself off?" he said, wanting to make her feel something for Keith. "How'd you like it if when you came home she was laid out on the couch drunk as a skunk?"

"I'm sorry—"

"You'd be loused up, too."

The doorbell rang. He went to answer and met Emma in the hall. She was done up in a gray miniskirt over red tights and a black turtleneck sweater that looked a little too small for her. She wore yellow clogs, which made her very tall, and her freshly washed hair was braided around her head like a coronet.

"I told you I'd make it quick, didn't I?" Emma said. "I can when I want to."

She smiled at him and he just stood there while Leslie let Keith in.

"Hi, Keith," he heard her say. "Come in. Nice to see you. Emma, this is Keith Madigan. Emma's a friend of mine from college, Keith." As they shook hands, he watched to see how Keith would react to Emma. Nothing happened. Keith didn't twitch a muscle. He didn't know what he'd expected, but something. He still hadn't said much to Keith about Emma, hadn't had a chance. Just as well. Let her speak for herself. Keith couldn't help but be impressed. Emma was impressive, even to someone as jaded as Keith.

His mother came downstairs, hand out in welcome. "How's your mother, Keith?" she said. "We were so sorry to learn she wasn't well." She'd always been sort of standoffish around Keith, but tonight she was warm and cordial, shaking his hand, concerned about his mother, and he was grateful.

"Pretty good, thanks, Mrs. Hollander. The doc says she can come home in a couple of days." For all the concern Keith showed, his mother might have had an attack of gastritis. Les and Emma went to the kitchen to get some drinks. He knew Les would fill Emma in on Keith's situation, most likely. He put on some records. Music might get things going. It had been pretty stiff, up to now. Keith sat uneasily on the edge of his chair, his big hands dangling down over his knees. Leslie brought him a glass of ginger ale. It struck him that Keith wasn't used to family gatherings.

"Do you do touch dancing here?" Emma came over to Keith and sat on the floor at his feet. A pang shot through him and he thought, why didn't she sit on the floor beside me? Her miniskirt, he noticed, was minier sitting than it had been standing. It was either luck or careful planning that she had on tights. She had terrific thighs. He couldn't take his eyes away from her thighs. Her knees weren't bad, either. He decided he was a thigh man.

Next thing he knew, Emma had Keith by the hand and was pulling him to his feet, teaching him how to touch dance. He could've sworn Keith already knew how. "That's right, put your hand around my waist, like so," Emma directed. Smiling faintly, Keith did as he was told. Leslie grabbed his hand and said, "Johnny, let's show them how the big kids do it." She grasped him in her strong arms and they were off, Leslie leading. Leslie always led. She wouldn't dance with him unless he let her lead. That was all right with him. He just wondered if she insisted on leading the other people she danced with. It was okay if you happened to be her brother, but if you were just a date, you might not take kindly to being propelled masterfully around the dance floor by the girl you were dancing with. People might stare.

"Hey, you're good!" Emma said, leaning back to look into Keith's face. "You can't tell me you never touch danced before. You're putting me on."

He watched Keith pull Emma close and silently gnashed his teeth. What's going on here? he wondered.

"I had some lessons when I was in Palm Beach," Keith said. "My father's a regular Fred Astaire and thinks I should be one, too."

He slipped out of Leslie's firm embrace. "Let's change partners." He touched Keith on the shoulder. "May I cut in?"

"No," Keith said, dancing away from him. Taking Emma with him.

"Hey, Johnny." Hands on hips, Leslie watched. "You can't leave me in the lurch like that. It ain't gentlemanly."

He felt his face grow hot, felt the blood travel down to the tips of his ears.

"Be cool, Johnny," Les whispered. "Hang loose."

"I'm going to see if I can help Ma," he muttered, and went out to the kitchen. Who did Keith think he was, hogging Emma? Emma was *his* guest, staying at *his* house.

"It's all ready, John," his mother said when he offered help. "If you'll just carry in the shepherd's pie for me, please. We'll go ahead without Dad," she said. "He's going to be late. Just sit anywhere you like. John, will you see who wants milk." Milk. Boy, it was a good thing his father wasn't around. He wouldn't sit still for milk, especially when it was practically a party.

Emma went ape over his mother's shepherd pie. "It's the best I've ever had, Mrs. Hollander. Absolutely terrific. I've had it lots of times in England and it's practically their national dish, but never as good as yours."

No good cook could resist such blandishments. His mother warmed perceptibly. He'd known that first night that Emma wasn't his mother's cup of tea—she had a way of letting such things be known right away—but give Emma another couple of days and his mother would be eating out of her hand. Figuratively speaking.

"When I was seven or eight," Keith said suddenly, "my father took me to the Tower of London. I can still remember the size of those jewels and the size of those hats the Tower guards wear. Those hats scared me. I thought at first they were alive."

"Oh, I love the Tower!" Emma said. "I love London, all of it. We stayed at the Connaught and I thought someone had stolen my shoes because my mother put them out in the hall at night, and someone came and took them away to polish them and I got all excited because I thought they'd been stolen and they were brand new." She laughed at her own foolishness and they all joined in.

"That's where we stayed," Keith said. "The Connaught. My father keeps a running tab there. It's a pretty classy joint."

"Classy is the word," Emma agreed. He saw her regarding Keith with new interest, thought briefly of telling his story about making his own bed at the hotel in Montreal, and decided against it.

A rare shot of intuition told him it wouldn't fit.

By the time the cheesecake was cut, Emma and Keith were buddies. He tried to get a word in edgewise, then gave up. Leslie caught his eye and winked. He had never seen Keith so animated, so obviously having a good time. Good thing they'd invited him for dinner. Too bad he'd hit it off so well with Emma. Don't be shitty, he cautioned himself. Can Keith help it if all the girls were wild about him?

After dessert, Keith checked his watch and said he better go. "I told her I'd call her tonight, see how things were," he said. "Thanks, Mrs. Hollander, for a delicious dinner. Nice to meet you, Emma. Leslie, good to see you again." There were no flies on Keith when it came to saying adios.

"I'm going to walk Keith to the corner, Ma," he said, going out with Keith and closing the door behind them. "Be right back."

They went a way in silence. "That was really nice," Keith said. "Thanks for asking me. It was great."

"Well, what'd you think? Isn't she something?"

Keith laughed. "I better keep her away from my father."

"Your father?"

"Yeah. He'd really go for her. She's his type."

He swallowed once or twice. "She's only twenty," he said.

Keith looked at him in the dark. "That's right. But she *is* his type. I told you my father was an old goat. Listen, I better go. See you tomorrow. Thanks for dinner," and Keith jogged off into the night.

Keith's father? She wouldn't give him the time of day. What kind of a thing was that to say about a girl? He stuffed his hands deep into his pockets and headed back, stood for several minutes staring up at the lighted windows in Emma's room.

I better keep her away from my father.

15

"Of course, Mr. Hollander," and the doctor's eyelid twitched rhythmically, "you must feel free to consult another doctor. Get another opinion. Or several, if you like. We believe that second and third opinions, in a case like yours, are a good idea."

The air in the room was suffocating. "In a case of this sort," the doctor's voice seemed to deepen, gain momentum, "it's best to explore all possibilities, all options. There should be no doubt whatever in your mind as to what the proper procedure should be. As to the proper steps to be taken, that is. I want your complete confidence. It's important to have that between patient and doctor."

There was a ringing in his ears. He swallowed hard and shook his head to clear it.

"The X-rays show a mass in the abdomen, Mr. Hollander, as I said. It's hard to know what we'll find until we go inside and have a look around."

He wanted to shout, "You're talking about my insides, goddam it! You're not talking about spelunking. What are you, a real estate agent!" He heard Ed say, "They said they'd know more after they take a look inside." It *was* like a real estate agent. Go ahead. Feel free to look around, see what's what. This is your gallbladder, this your pancreas. Nice location. If there's something you don't like, why, we'll just eliminate it, cut to fit. We aim to please.

"As far as the liver goes," the doctor's voice was inexorable, "the tests show some damage. We'll do a biopsy. That's the usual procedure. But perhaps you have another doctor you'd like to consult. Before we proceed." The doctor fixed him with a stern glance, waiting for some feedback.

"If the liver is cancerous," he said. "If my liver is cancerous," he corrected himself, showing the doctor he was facing reality, "if it's cancerous, then that's it. Nothing can be done. Is that correct?"

The doctor's gaze shifted to a point just over his shoulder. "Usually this is the case, yes, Mr. Hollander."

"I mean, if the liver is cancerous," he knew he was saying it again but he couldn't seem to stop, "there is no hope. Is that about it?" Perspiration slid from his armpits down his sides, where his belt made it captive.

The doctor lowered his head, thinking this over. "That is true," he said, without inflection. "But we don't know for sure, we're not absolutely positive that this is so. The biopsy will tell us more."

"I understand they do lots of things these days with diet," he said.

"Diet?"

"I read a magazine piece not long ago telling of wonderful cures for cancer brought about by diet, a change in diet. By eating certain foods in quantity and eliminating others. Some man who had been told he had only a short time to live cured himself by changing his diet drastically. Did it on his own, too. No medical advice was involved." He liked saying that. "And now," he sat up very straight and put his hands on the edge of the doctor's desk, "now that man is hale and hearty. Did it on his own, too, the whole way."

"Well," the doctor smiled. "There are lots of quacks around. If you are going to consult another physician, Mr. Hollander, I would suggest a need for haste. Time is important. The sooner we get to the bottom of this, the better."

"Another?" the bartender asked, swabbing down the bar unnecessarily.

"No," he said. "No thanks. I shouldn't. I've had enough." He laughed. "I sound like my wife." He got down from the stool, patted his pockets to see if he had everything. The bartender smiled tentatively, waiting for him to leave before scooping up his tip.

"I'm a dying man," he said. "You may not think it to look at me, but I'm a very dying man. Don't feel bad." He lifted a hand in admonition. "Don't say a word. It's all right. I don't blame you. I don't blame anyone. It's no one's fault. Good night."

He went out into a stinging downpour. His body felt weightless, his head enormous, almost touching the stars. His feet seemed huge, black platters skimming the ground. How could there be stars when it was raining? Stranger things have happened. Alcohol had made him strong and brave; at least he felt, momentarily, very strong, very brave. But he knew he was a coward, too.

"No!" His voice rang out, a high, hoarse croak. "No! No! I am not!" He lifted his fist and shook it at the sky. In a dark house on the corner, lights went on, and someone came to a window. A terrible sound was wrenched from deep in his throat, a sound like an animal in a trap.

He was still there a few minutes later when the police caught up with him. The headlights of the squad car picked him out, and the driver said to his partner, "Jeez, he's in bad shape."

"I reserve the right to remain silent," Henry said as he climbed in, giving them his name and address. They drove him home and escorted him to his front door, the cop checking the house number to make sure it was the right place. Lights were on downstairs, the cop noted, and the drunk's key fitted the lock. The door swung open.

"See!" Henry crowed. "I told you this was my house."

Over his shoulder the cop saw a woman standing in the shadows. Poor guy, the cop thought. He's in for it.

"Thank you," the woman said.

"Good evening, Ceil." Henry turned and said to the cop, "If you leave your card, I'll send the money around in the morning." The cop touched his fingers to his cap and left quickly.

Henry climbed the stairs slowly, stumbling over each one. Ceil walked behind him, thinking she might have to catch him if he fell, wondering if she could manage that. Please God, don't let him fall. This was bad enough. Leslie and John and Emma were still in front of the TV set; she could hear canned laughter as she closed the bedroom door.

Henry took off his shoes, lifting each one in order to inspect it carefully before he let it drop. Then came his tie, his shirt. She helped him out of his suit, shocked at his color, his sunken eyes. He crawled into bed, closed his eyes, and began to snore. She sat on a chair, heart pounding, listening to his rattly snores, smelling his whiskey breath. If it hadn't been for the strong odor of Scotch, she might've thought he'd had some sort of a stroke. Rage constricted her throat. Where had he been? With whom? And why had he come home in this condition? She would have gone into the guest room, but Emma was there. After a long time she got into bed and slept fitfully, her arms rigid at her sides, careful not to touch him.

In the morning, when she woke, she could hear him in the shower. She lay there, waiting. He emerged, fully dressed, and went directly to the closet to get his overnight bag. Turning, he saw she was awake. He came toward her with a gesture of conciliation.

She was carved of stone.

"I have to go to Dallas today," he said, going to his bureau, rooting through the drawers.

"Today!" Anger propelled her from the bed. "Where were you last night to get so drunk? How could you do that to me?"

"I didn't do it to you," he said. "I did it to myself. I'm sorry, Ceil."

"Sorry!" Her voice became uncharacteristically shrill. "Sorry isn't enough. I'm embarrassed for you, Henry. And ashamed. In front of Leslie and her friend. And John. You set a fine example to your children. And humiliated me in the bargain. You could hardly walk."

"I'm sorry," he said again.

"Don't keep saying that," she said, teeth clenched. "I want an explanation. A man doesn't get falling-down drunk and come home in a police car and say 'I'm sorry' and that's it."

"Then I have no excuse," he said, his back to her. He stuffed in socks and a tie. He'd buy some handkerchiefs in town. There were no clean, ironed ones in the drawer. He wouldn't ask her if she knew where his handkerchiefs were, which he often did. They were usually in a pile in her ironing basket. It as a standing joke between them.

Had he taken off his clothes and paraded naked in front of them all, lined up so tidily in front of the TV? He remembered seeing them when he staggered in. He remembered the rain, the bar, although if his life had depended upon it, he couldn't have found his way back to it. He remembered the nice cop.

"What the hell are you going to Dallas for?" She almost never swore, considering it beneath her dignity.

"Burrell wants me to go out to speak to some hotel people about a rather advanced design they want, wants me to talk them out of it, if possible. Offer them several alternatives." He was amazed at his own glibness.

"Oh, then I suppose you'll see Ann and Ben while you're there. Play some golf, have a nice little visit, is that it?" Her voice was so thick with sarcasm it didn't sound like hers.

"I'll be back tomorrow or the next day." Tell her the truth, a voice within him said. Tell her now.

No, that's a terrible idea. Not yet. Not until I know for sure. I won't put her through that unless I have to.

The idea had come to him in a dream he'd had just before he woke, the time they say most dreams occur. It had been a strange dream in the way it had surged and receded time and again, like the tide. The idea formed so perfectly in his head, despite the amount of alcohol he'd consumed, that he wondered why he hadn't thought of it immediately, it was so right, so perfect. He would go to see Ben Nilson, his old friend, his doctor. Ben would give him the straight dope. He could believe Ben, trust him as he was unable to either believe or trust the new young doctor. Ben would fix him up, tell him the other man didn't know what he was talking about. Relief washed over him. When he turned himself over to Ben, his troubles would be over. He longed, at that moment, to hear the sound of Ben's voice; longed the way a lover longs for the sound of his beloved. He longed to feel Ben's agile hands, so steady, so soothing, so full of healing. All doctors should have healing hands: big, thick-knuckled, as Ben's were. This new doctor couldn't help being young. All he lacked was experience. You can't hang a man for that. Experience and compassion. Experience comes with time. Compassion does not necessarily. Either you have it or you don't.

Like sex appeal. Or cancer. Either you have it or you don't. There were no in-betweens.

"Maybe that's why you got so drunk," she suggested. "Because you have to fly to Dallas. You always get nervous when you have to fly, Henry. You know you do. Is that it? You want me to believe that?"

"Ceil, I've had a rough week. Please. Everything sort of piled up."

"Baloney," she snapped. "That's baloney, Henry, and you know it." A thought occurred to her. "Are you seeing another woman, Henry?"

He laughed. He couldn't help it. He broke into peals of laughter. She burst into tears, but he couldn't stop himself.

"All right, then!" she shouted. "You're leaving me, that's why you got out your suitcase. You've got some girl. I should've known!" She felt a sliver of pain in her heart muscle. She had trouble breathing. She had never expected anything like this of him.

Get hold of yourself, he told himself. And still couldn't stop. She went for him, raking her nails along his neck. He held her hands together tightly, still laughing, further infuriating her.

"Stop it!" she cried. "You're hurting me."

He let her go. "Oh Ceil, forgive me. It's nothing like that. I love you. I'll always love you. You know that." He tried to take her in his arms, but she would have none of him. She ran from him, stood near the door, hands cradling her face, staring at him. He saw smudges of mascara beneath her eyes and knew she'd gone to sleep without washing her face. Ceil, the most meticulous of women, had gone to bed without washing her face because of him.

"There could never be another woman for me, Ceil. Never. You are my heart. Without you, I am nothing."

Against her will, she was moved by the tenderness in his voice, and by the expression on his face.

"What is it, then, Henry? Your job?"

"No, Ceil, the job is fine. It's cumulative, I guess. Things build up, things bother me now that never used to. And I haven't been feeling well, as you know."

He felt himself stretched to the limits of his endurance and was fearful that if he didn't escape now, this minute, he might break down and tell her the truth.

He brushed her forehead with a kiss.

She reared back and demanded, "Why can't you give me a real kiss? Pretend we're courting. Pretend you're trying to get me into bed, that you can hardly wait."

She grasped his upper arms and shook him and was so inadequate to the task that he surprised himself and laughed at her.

"For Christ's sake, Henry!" she exploded. "Open up! Why can't you open up to me, to all of us? We're your best friends. Let us in, let us know what's bothering you. Maybe we could help." Ceil released him, exhausted by her outburst, and stood, quivering, waiting for him to speak.

In his usual quiet voice he said, "I have to go now, Ceil. I've got a cab coming at eight."

He made a gesture toward her.

"All right," she said coldly, "have it your way."

Upstairs, in the bathroom, he heard them and felt sort of sorry for his father. When his mother got up a head of steam, watch out. He heard the front door slam and took his time going downstairs.

"Where's Dad going?" he asked cautiously.

His mother drew a deep breath, composing herself.

"To Dallas," she managed in an almost ordinary voice. "On business."

"For how long?" He wiped his mouth on his sleeve, getting rid of some excess toothpaste, willing her to look at him. Her eyes skimmed over him, unseeing. She was in a state, he knew.

"I don't know, I'm sure," she said, as if his father were a casual acquaintance whose comings and goings she wouldn't dream of prying into.

He went into the kitchen and she followed. "I didn't have time to make any oatmeal this morning, John," she said. "You can have eggs or cornflakes."

He didn't want either, but he settled for cornflakes because it seemed easier.

"Don't forget, John. Today is my day for Mrs. Hobbs, and Les is going to town for lunch. If she isn't up in ten minutes, I'll wake her. She was planning to go in with Dad, but obviously that's out. I'll run up and get dressed and drive her to the station. And," she turned on her way out, "Emma's on her own."

"Yeah, Ma." The mere mention of her name provoked ennui. He yawned elaborately. "I might be able to get out of gym early so I could take her on a tour of local spots of historical interest." His mother must have changed her mind about leaving, because she came back, rolled up her sleeves, and began to scrub the skin off the kitchen sink.

"I scarcely think that's necessary," she said in a cold voice. "Emma strikes me as being a young woman who can take care of herself. You better get going. I'll be home by five-thirty, John, certainly no later than six."

He kissed her ear good-bye and trudged down the front

walk. She went to the window to watch him go, saw him look up at the bedroom windows, saw him break into a run as his bus came into view. He reminded her of a colt set free on a spring morning. Never let them get the upper hand, Henry liked to say. Being a parent, Ceil, is a power struggle. Once they get the upper hand, and they're in control, you've lost it. Lost the whole thing. One of the reasons Henry was so stiff with John, she knew, was his way of dealing with what he thought of as her softness with him, her efforts to keep her children protected from the woes of the world. Her desire to protect them, Henry had told her, was sometimes overwhelming. It was all right to see that they had their shots, to see that they went regularly to the dentist and that their shoes should fit properly. Anything further, he thought, was coddling and cosseting. In the final analysis, protection meant pampering, which he was against.

"I'm not running a popularity contest, Ceil," he'd said during a recent disagreement they'd had about his treatment of John. "I'm interested in developing his character, not in making myself the best-loved dad on the block. If you don't expect a great deal from your children, if all you expect is the barest minimum, then that's what you get. And I'm not willing to settle for the barest minimum."

She considered she'd been greatly overprotected by her mother and father, probably because she was the only child, and had long ago resolved not to make the same mistake with her children. But she found herself fighting a constant battle with herself not to repeat the errors of her parents. Wrap them in cotton batting, guard them against the germs and evil, against life. It didn't work.

Already she regretted her behavior of this morning. She knew she'd behaved badly and was sorry for losing her temper and accusing Henry of lying. Henry had never been a liar. Just as he had never been a philanderer, despite that silliness over Emma the other night.

He was a proud man, though. She couldn't imagine why he'd allowed himself to get into such a state, to be so drunk he could hardly navigate. To be brought home, like some recalcitrant child, by the police. Had he lost his job, or invested all their savings in some bum scheme, lost it all? It didn't sound like him.

She ached all over. Unwashed, uncombed, she felt like a slattern. She heard someone in the bathroom. Probably Leslie. Hastily she climbed the stairs and went to her room to try to repair the damage the past twelve hours had wreaked on her face as well as on her psyche.

A discarded Ace bandage buried in the general detritus in his desk triggered it. Just as his father's plan to go to Dallas had sprung, perfect, whole, exactly right, from the dream, so then did John's modus operandi take shape.

Skillfully, he wrapped the bandage around his knee. He'd had enough knee injuries to know how to fake one convincingly. He limped to the gym, wincing theatrically. The soccer coach saw him coming out of the corner of his eye and thought, what the hell is this, Hollander was okay yesterday. Looking woebegone, he told the coach that the doctor had advised staying off the leg as much as possible. It might be nothing, but to avoid complications—surgery, even, he hinted—stay off it. The coach heard "surgery" and his skin tightened on his face. People liked to sue. Steer clear, Gleason had said, of problems resulting in surgery, due to inadequate care on the coach's part, the school's part; he got Gleason's drift. On the slightest provocation, they used the shit out of you. Gleason had told him to be especially careful with the boys. This careful stuff, the coach privately thought, was keeping him from winning his matches.

"Okay." The coach turned his back and blew his whistle to show he had other things on his mind. What a crock. The coach let him know by the way he hunched his shoulders and shouted orders at the other players that he thought his story was a crock.

He sped home, heart pounding, unimpeded by the Ace bandage. He let himself into the house. It was empty. He knew an empty house the minute he stepped inside. Emma's Saab was in the drive, though. He hollered, "Anybody home?" to be sure. No answer. He prowled around some, pretending he was a cat burglar. He checked the pad by the telephone.

In a cramped, felonious-looking hand, someone had written "Back soon. Hang loose." He smiled, delighted. No big, round Palmer-method stuff from this cookie.

I break my buns so she won't get lonely, he told himself, and she's off and running anyway, probably with the milkman, though they hadn't had a milkman in years. He swung on the refrigerator door, looking for sustenance. All right for you, Emma, he told himself. See if I cut soccer practice again for you. He loosened his tie, turned on the stereo to cheer himself up, and started to dance. Then, thinking he heard someone, he turned off the music, not wanting her to catch him in action. He strained for the sound of approaching footsteps, heard nothing. He went to his room, undressing along the way. By the time he got there, he had the bandage off his knee and was down to his skivvies. He lined up the crease in his gray flannels and hung up his jacket, making his mother proud. He saw his camouflage suit nestling on the closet floor and put it on gratefully. Army surplus, with the voluminous crotch known and loved by all GIs, it was guaranteed in the magazine to be the real thing. A suit made for real men, real danger, real combat. Odd that he thought of this garment as his leisure suit. When he put it on, he thought of himself as invisible. He had never worn it anyplace but here, in his secret room. He had thought of buying one for Keith, who needed camouflage more than most people. Keith could crawl inside and he, too, would be invisible. Keith's mother and father could shout and argue and OD and chicken out all they felt like and Keith would be out of their reach. Safe. But the price of the suit had gone up, according to the latest ad, and he couldn't scrape together enough bread. In the summer he planned to mow lawns, clip hedges, guard lives of importunate, exhausted swimmers, counsel campers, teach them how to make first-class lanyards so they'd have something upon which to hang their front door keys. Now, in the dead of winter, his hands were tied.

He settled back, fished under his sofa bed, and came up with *Dandelion Wine*. He loved Ray Bradbury, loved the idea of the Happiness machine. Had tried, years ago when he was young, to make one in the garage. Another time he'd tried to make dandelion wine—stuff so bitter he could hardly open his jaws to retch.

This time he was sure he heard someone moving around downstairs, or was he? He sat up in order to hear better. If it was a burglar, ripping off his mother's silver and the stereo, the two most valuable things in the house, then let him. Or her. He wasn't messing with any armed robber. Even in this camouflage suit.

Once more he fell back and took up his book.

"So this is where you get your jollies, is it?" It was Emma, standing on the threshold, her eyes glinting through the murk. To his dismay, a hoarse cry escaped from him. He leaped to his feet, impeded by his suit's low-hanging crotch.

"Hi," he said, super casual. "Come on in." She already was. Slowly, she approached, her roving eyes taking everything in. With a wide swath, he cleared the bed of its flotsam, shoving everything underneath with his foot. From the way the load resisted the burial, he knew it was getting fairly crowded under there.

"I got home early," he said lamely.

She smiled, and dimples—which he hadn't remembered— jumped in her cheeks. Too much, he thought, despairingly. Too much.

"I thought you would," she said, sitting on the edge of the bed.

"Where were you? Your car was here but you weren't. I thought you had a date or something." He tried not to sound plaintive.

"I do," she said. "With you." This left him speechless.
"What're you reading?" She picked up his book and turned a
few pages, pretending to read, and he wondered what came
next.

"I thought you were a burglar," he said into the stretched
silence.

"And if I had been?" Calmly she lay down, fitting the bed
as if it, too, had been custom-made for her. She crossed her
ankles, put her arms behind her head. "This is cozy," she said,
her eyes at half-mast. "I can see why you like it here. This is
where you hide to get away from things. People. How come
you came home so early?"

"I told Les I would," he said, knowing he sounded like a
sanctimonious twit. "She asked me if I'd see that you didn't get
bored." That was a white lie, one that did no harm. And was
therefore justified. And justifiable. He thought of asking if her
expected phone call had come and decided not to.

"Oh, I'm almost never bored." She smiled sleepily, kicked
off the yellow clogs, and lay back again, wiggling her toes. He
stood at the side of the bed and wondered if he should put the
moves on her. She liked him, he could tell she did. She was
perfectly relaxed, she even closed her eyes. What would he do
if she fell asleep, if his mother came home and found her sleeping in his bed? And eating his porridge?

"I like your suit." She opened her eyes and looked at him.
"It's adorable. I wouldn't mind having one like it."

"It's army surplus. Maybe a size small would fit you. I'll
check and see if they have a size small."

"That would be nice," she said, dreamily.

"They run sorta big," he said. She laughed and said, "So I
see." Then they both laughed. She patted the mattress and
said, "Sit down, why don't you?" He sat. Her fingers ran up
and down his back absentmindedly, as if she were practicing
scales on a piano. They touched the skin at the back of his neck
and he jumped, but only a little. Then he shivered. If only he

had some experience. He didn't want her to think he was a loser, a nudnik. Which he was. What would Woody do?

With each stroke of her fingers, he sank lower until, finally, he was lying beside her. Emma lifted herself on one elbow and kissed him on the mouth. Like a child kissing another child, her kiss was ingenuous. Prim at first, then authoritative. Dazed, he suspected she might mean business. Otherwise, why had she begun to kiss him with her lips opened, why was she slipping in her tongue. There was no doubt about it, this kiss was distinctly French.

She gave him a series of little nipping kisses on his face and neck. He felt woozy. Spots formed in front of his eyes and he wondered how they got there, two of them on the bed, so fast. He was dazzled by the speed with which he had moved. His head was as light and empty as a gourd. His body felt weird, like a jug into which some strange, combustible liquid had been poured, making everything inside tingle. His nerve ends were all hanging out. His insides were a mass of sensation. It was as if he were a puppet and Emma the puppeteer. The master puppeteer. No matter what he'd read and imagined and heard, none of it bore any resemblance to what was going on now.

She began to unbutton him. Slowly, slowly, she made her way. She had all the time in the world. Her fingers skimmed over his stomach, under his skivvies. All the while she was working on him, she made little chirping noises, like birds on a summer morning before the sky filled with light. Her body settled over him, very slender, very hard.

As hard as his; harder, even. Except for her little pointed breasts that came to rest against him from time to time, only to pull away, tantalizing him beyond belief. She smelled delicious. His breath was short, erratic. His chest was heavy, his eyelids leaden. Desire lodged in his throat like a piece of improperly chewed meat. Desire, newly felt, wasn't always easy to recognize. Desire wasn't lust, he thought, it was on a much higher plane than lust. A plane he had always wanted to reach. He watched as Emma shed her jeans and T-shirt. Underneath, she was all skin. Rosy, shattering, pink-and-white skin. She nibbled at his earlobe, which tickled. He tried to sit up and she pushed him back down. Her tongue fiddled around with his ear and entered it. Her hands were as light as a moth as she stroked and caressed him. It was the most exquisite agony he had ever known. She kissed her way from his collarbone to his navel, worked her way around it clockwise, then counterclockwise. Her moist little mouth sucked on his thigh, his kneecap. He felt her moving toward his feet and scrunched up his toes in an effort to make them smaller, smell sweeter.

She hummed as she worked, a queen bee. Her body moved rhythmically, light and drifting, like fog. He entered her. Unbelievably, he entered her.

He opened his mouth to tell her something, then closed it, unable to remember what it was he wanted to say. Words hung on the end of his tongue like shreds of tobacco. He shuddered in ecstasy, willing this to last forever. She continued to caress him, her mouth delicate, sure.

"Yes," he heard her sigh. "Oh, yes."

A cataclysm seized him, wrenching, tugging, pulling, sucking at his insides. In a throaty voice she said, "Don't stop now, damn it."

The sensation was indescribable. Ineffable. That's what it was: ineffable.

She held him in a vise. "Keep it going, John," her voice was husky, her eyes closed. "Don't leave me behind. It's not fair. That's not nice, John. Don't leave me." He tried to go on, tried to hang on, but a sensation of falling took over; falling, falling into a deep place.

"Oh, Johnny, yes, that's nice, yes, that's lovely. Keep going, John. Keep going!"

He collapsed, like a balloon with the air let out, lay there flat on his back, smiling foolishly at her. "I'll give you five min-

utes, kid," she said briskly. "This time it's my turn." She rolled
off him, got up, stretched, smiling at him over her shoulder.
    "Want to try again?"
    He nodded, awash in a sea of satiation.
    "I have to go to the loo," she said. "Be right back."
    He closed his eyes. He had dreamed it all. God knew he'd
had plenty of practice, dreaming dreams like that.
    "Here I am, love." Was the five minutes up already?
Emma stood by the side of the bed. He tried to look surprised,
as if he'd forgotten she was coming back. She burst out
laughing.
    "You're so cute." She reached under the sheet and again
her warm little hands went to work.
    "Johnny." She cocked her head and stood with her hands
on her hips, smiling, shaking her head. "Take it easy, Johnny.
Easy does it. Make it last. Move over." She snuggled in. "Let's
see how it goes this time."
    Fearless, well-armed, dauntless in love, he plunged in. He
lunged and parried and thrust, a true swordsman. Time passed,
time stood still. Emma rose to meet him, his willing partner
found at last. And he hadn't even been looking. He felt as if he
could go on forever. His pecker was okay, after all. No need for
him to write Ann Landers.
    "Oh, yes, please, yes, yes, now!" Emma cried out. He
didn't have to be hit over the head. He knew what she meant.
It was okay to let go. A good thing. He'd been trembling on the
brink for a long time. It was a question of balance, among other
things.
    The cataclysm came again, this time more prolonged, more
cataclysmic. In all the room, nothing moved. He felt as if he'd
had a near-death experience, like the guy who almost drowned.
Maybe he had died and this was heaven.
    "I could do this all night," Emma said, eyes still closed.
    Elated, he made quick plans for a raid on the kitchen, a
quick trip to the head, then lock the door. . . .

From a great distance, he heard a telephone ringing. Emma heard it, too, and bounced off him, her stomach pulling away from his with a slight plop.

Stay! he cried silently. Don't leave me! Let the bastard ring. But she was gone, as lightly, as unexpectedly as she had arrived. He could hear her talking, laughing.

Laughing! He sat up, clutching his camouflage suit to his chest, a virgin surprised by a unicorn. Presently he heard her returning and lay back in readiness. Through the slits of his eyes he could see her come in, bend to retrieve her clothes. He reached out. Her lips barely touched his forehead, like his mother checking him for fever. He grabbed out at her. His hands came up with air.

She'd be back. Probably she was taking another shower, getting set for him all over again. He smiled to himself. She didn't need to bother. He liked her as she was. But why was she taking so long? Hadn't she said she could make it quick if she wanted? It wasn't nice of her to tease him. Maybe this is what girls did; they gave you a taste of honey and then they closed down the hive until they felt like putting out again.

A fuzzy outline of a gag—a hive pulsing with sex-crazed bees engaged in an orgy—passed fleetingly through his befuddled brain before he was overcome by a paralyzing lassitude. Weakly, he raised his head from the pillow. Did he hear her coming? Was she sneaking up on him, ready to assault him one more time? He certainly hoped so. There were lots of things he wanted to ask her. His head swam with myriad questions that had occurred to him.

He dozed. He didn't want to, but he couldn't help it. When he woke, the room was almost dark. He was very thirsty and he had to go to the bathroom. He studied his face in the mirror and, even to his eye, it was not the face of a great lover. His hair stood in peaks, the ends looked wet, like a dog's coat when it comes in from the rain. He was as pale as an oyster. He stuck out his tongue to see if it had turned black. Once, years ago, a kid told him you can tell when someone's done it because their tongue turns black. Like so many bits of miscellaneous information he'd stored in the dim recesses of his brain, this one turned out to be fake.

He went to his mother's room to look out. Emma was tripping down the front path, hanging onto a mountainous oaf with a thick neck, sixteen and a half, easy. They were talking animatedly and she reached up to pat the oaf's cheek. Was that Ralph? Or was it the married man? He was helping her into his red Toyota.

He got dressed and went to the telephone to call Keith. "Hello?"

"Guess what?" He could hear music playing. "I just got laid." A baby wailed in time to the music.

At the other end, there was a pause. A man's gruff voice said, "Wish I could say the same."

He hung up. His head fell into his hands like a ripe coconut. He tottered back to his room and stood looking down at the bed.

He had been had.

16

He'd forgotten that Burrell, his boss, would be in Minneapolis for the rest of the week. Explanations wouldn't be necessary, after all. On the train coming in, he'd prepared an elaborate story, too elaborate, like most lies, outlining the reasons for his sudden trip. The truth would have been so much easier, if only the truth weren't so impossible right now.

"Book me on the first available flight this afternoon for Dallas, would you, Jane?" he said to his secretary. "I'll probably be gone two days. If anything comes up, Allan can handle it."

When he got to the airport and discovered the plane was a DC-10, he almost changed his flight. Then, ashamed of himself, he went on board.

He braced himself as the plane took off into a cloudless sky.. If you made it through takeoff, you were almost safe. Home free. Landing was the next big hurdle. Everything in between was a piece of cake. He felt light-headed, lighthearted. Making it through takeoff was like making it through a doctor's examination. You were safe until the lab reports came back. Lab reports were his landing. If he could get through the next couple of days, the rest would be gravy.

"Can I get you something to drink?" The stewardess was at his side with her drinks cart. It was eleven-fifteen in the morning. He'd checked in early for a one o'clock flight, and they'd talked him into going early on this plane, which was only half full. That in itself, he felt, was tempting fate. Better to stick with your original flight, he always said. A bit early for drinking.

"I'd like a Bloody Mary, please." Tomato juice was high in protein. Or was it potassium? Ceil, if she'd been with him, would have drawn an audible breath and tugged at his arm. But she wasn't. He was on his own. The stewardess was not young. Heavy makeup accentuated lines around her nose and mouth. Wash her face and she'd drop four, five years just like that.

In the old days, stewardesses had looked like runners-up in a beauty contest. Now they could pass for checkers in a supermarket. Where are all the pretty girls? he wondered. Gone, all gone. No more good-looking nurses, no more smashing stewardi. Maybe he was turning into a dirty old man. High time.

"You going to Dallas on business?" A woman had sat

down in the seat next to him without his noticing. She over-flowed the seat, her tiny feet scarcely touching the floor. Her fingernails were a work of art. Set into each talon was what looked like a tiny diamond. Her long-sleeved white blouse bil-lowed out at him provocatively.

What business was it of hers what he was going to Dallas for?

"I'm visiting a doctor, an old friend," he said pleasantly. "And you?"

She, it turned out, worked for the airline. Every week she flew to Dallas to check on her ailing mother. Left her kids in care of her husband, who ran their jewelry store in New Jersey. Something about the way she curved her lips as she spoke of her weekly trips tipped him off. He saw the ailing mother, shaving for the second time that day, lavishing pungent after-shave with a liberal hand, checking the drape of a new suede jacket.

Her flights, the woman informed him, cost her virtually nothing. She and her family had also traveled to Russia last year and were scheduled to go to Hong Kong in a few weeks' time. Working for an airline had its drawbacks, she said, but the free air travel made up for them. The woman drank orange juice, dark eyes glinting at him over the rim of her plastic glass.

Lunch was baked chicken or soup-and-sandwich.

"Take the chicken," the woman whispered. "I happen to know the soup's left over from yesterday, and it wasn't so hot even then." She laughed merrily, exposing perfect teeth. He had trouble with nicotine stains and admired people with per-fect teeth. He thought of complimenting her on her teeth, and decided against it.

Presently, when the NO SMOKING and FASTEN SEAT BELTS signs went off, the woman unstrapped herself and went down the aisle on her stiletto heels, greeting the attendants by name. He watched her go, watched her fulsome rear. It was very enticing and doubtless would have commanded respect in

certain parts of South America, where well-developed behinds
were held in high esteem, he'd read someplace. He liked watching women walk. No matter in what country.

They had both decided on the chicken. The stewardess
delivering their trays said, "Gorgeous!" eyeing the fingernails.
"How on earth do you get them that way?"

"Oh, they're not real." The plump woman laughed.
"They're phonies. I take them off at night."

Did she mean the fingernails or the jewels?

They ate their chicken and limp broccoli. "You got children?" she asked, emptying the little packet of sugar into her
coffee.

"Two," he said. "And you?"

"Same. A boy and a girl. The girl's giving me heat about
getting her driver's license. My husband says let her. I say not
until she shapes up. Although, God knows, she's shaping up
sooner'n I'd like." She made a face and he pictured the daughter, flat stomach, tilting breasts, the works.

"That kid of mine thinks she knows it all," the woman
said.

"That seems to be symptomatic of that age. My son's sixteen, too." It was a bond between them.

"He on anything?" The woman stirred her coffee vigorously.

"On anything?"

"You know. Like marijuana or coke." She lifted her cup to
her mouth, little finger extended. She was very dainty in her
habits, he could see.

"Not that I know of," he said. "John's all right; a little
flaky, but he's basically sound, doesn't give us much trouble.
Doesn't seem to know what he's going to do with himself,
where he's going. My daughter's nineteen, a sophomore in college."

"She living with anyone?"

"She's got a roommate in college."

"Male or female?" Her teeth weren't as perfect as he'd thought. Perhaps she took them out at night, too.

He laughed. "Leslie's been in and out of love so often I figure when it's for real, it'll be a relief."

"Well," the woman shrugged, "sounds like you got it made. My boy's fourteen, already been picked up for B and E. Possession of illegal drugs, too. My husband says throw him out, he doesn't toe the line. Give him a curfew, he breaks it, out he goes. I say no. He's my boy. I love him. I lay awake at night and figure out ways to keep him safe. Then I tell myself there's no way to keep him safe. No way." He looked into her swimming eyes and put his hand into his pocket in search of his handkerchief. She dove into her handbag and came up with Kleenex. He was embarrassed, feeling responsible for these sudden tears.

The stewardess took away their trays. He closed his eyes and settled back in his seat. Better not to talk to strangers.

The pilot's voice came over the loudspeaker. "This is Captain Schultz. Passengers please fasten their seat belts. Flight attendants be seated, please. We're headed into a little turbulence."

"Oh, boy," the woman said.

Once, years ago, he'd been in a terrible electric storm, lightning and thunder bouncing off the plane, having their way with it. Terrified, he'd prepared himself for death. He hated electric storms, on land or in the air. He was ashamed of this unmasculine weakness and had never told anyone about it, not even Ceil.

The plane dropped. He put his hand over his mouth to keep himself from crying out. He was sure they'd been hit by lightning. He waited for the smell of burning plastic to fill the plane's cabin. Behind him, a baby cried.

They were flying at about 32,000 feet. One time he'd figured how long it would take a plane to hit the ground at that altitude, but now, when it mattered, he couldn't remember.

The first few moments would be the worst. Those moments when you realized you were going down, that nothing could stop you. Airline inspectors, doing their job after a crash, were frequently quoted as saying, "Those on board never knew what hit them." How did they know what passengers knew? That seemed presumptuous to him.

Look at the bright side. No long illness, no hospital bed, no evil smells. Disagreeable odors were always mentioned in stories of terminal illness. He hated the thought of being surrounded by his own stench. A plane crash, at least, would be quick. Clean. And Ceil could collect from the airline for loss of his services.

Relax. His hands gripped the arms of his seat. If he had a deck of cards, he would ask his seatmate to play gin. His father had always played gin on planes. His father knew no fear, had told him with relish of flying over the Alleghenies in a single-engine plane, dodging mountains, caught in downdrafts. On a flight to California, he and his father had orbited San Francisco for hours, waiting for clearance, playing cards, his father chuckling and declaring "Gin!" in the same resounding voice he used when he was safe in front of the fire.

Last month he'd read of a particularly bad plane crash in which more than 200 people had died. Newspaper stories of the aftermath of a crash always seemed distressingly graphic to him, and this one certainly was. Two arms, buried in the wreckage, the hands clasped, were found by rescue workers. The hands and the arms of a man and a woman. No bodies, only arms. He found it impossible to get the image of those two arms out of his head. Now, out of the corner of his eye, he stole a glance at the woman beside him in her billowy blouse. She looked calm. The storm's intensity grew until it seemed unbearable, yet the crying baby had fallen quiet. He imagined the plane suddenly swooping toward earth, a gigantic, flaming bird. Would he and the woman hold hands, gaining comfort and strength from each other as they plunged toward the ground? Would they, perhaps, make some pledge of endearment, as that other pair might have done? Had those arms belonged to husband and wife, sister and brother? Lovers? Or total strangers? It was something to contemplate in the night's small hours.

Apprehension kept its grip on him as the plane careened through the atmosphere. Soon. This must end soon.

"If we had some cards," the plump woman's mouth was almost touching his ear, "we could play Hearts." She was a sweetheart, after all, reading his thoughts as if they'd shared years together. Unable to speak, he nodded, and leaned back in his seat, exhausted by the effort of staying alive. His stomach felt sour. He should never have had that drink. He swallowed a couple of times, forcing the bile back to where it belonged.

The woman was still speaking.

"My mother was past forty when she had me," she said. "She thought I was a tumor."

Something was required of him.

"Is that so?" he said, absently.

"So you see." The woman's hand touched his with tenderness. He started, almost pulled away, controlled himself.

"I'm all she has." The woman's face lengthened, grew dolorous. "I'm an only child."

"Yes," he said. "Well, I'm sure you're doing a good job."

"My mother's seventy-seven." Her voice would not cease. "She has diabetes and the doctor said they might have to amputate her feet." For some reason, she smiled as she said this.

"Well, seventy-seven isn't old these days," he babbled. "I'd never have known you were that old."

The smile slid off her face. She sat up very straight, holding up her head so her chins melted into her collar.

"I have a very young face," the woman said, staring straight ahead.

The loudspeaker crackled. He held his breath, waiting for bad news. The voice of Captain Schultz told them the worst was over and they were making their approach and should be landing at Dallas–Fort Worth in approximately twenty minutes. Until the plane came to a stop, all passengers would please observe the no smoking signs and keep their seat belts fastened. Thank you for flying with us.

He roused himself, studying the other passengers. Their faces looked untroubled as they arranged their clothing, tucked their magazines into the little seat pockets. He was proud of them, of himself. Only the baby had lost its cool. If the plane's brakes failed now, if a tire blew or a vital pin fell off the plane's undercarriage, he would have no strength left to fight. What will be will be. He found it easy to be philosophical with the ground so close. He felt the change of altitude in his ears. The plane touched down delicately, taxied bumpily, came to a stop.

"Nice talking to you," he said, turning to his little fat companion. She, however, wanted no part of him, was up and away, moving down the aisle like a broken field runner.

She thought I was a tumor. He wished Ceil had been with him to share that. She thought I was a tumor. The skin at the corner of his eyes felt tight. His whole face felt as if its skin had shrunk and was now too small to fit over his bones.

He shouldered his bag and walked toward the gate, trying to keep the woman in his sights, hoping to catch a glimpse of whoever was meeting her. But by the time he reached the main terminal, she'd disappeared, a figment of his imagination.

"Henry!" he heard someone call. "Over here!"

He wasn't expecting to be met; he had told Ben he'd take a cab. A large blonde woman wearing an orange T-shirt and blue leather running shoes, one hand clutching her denim wraparound skirt, came toward him, out of breath. It was Ann Nilson, Ben's wife. When last he'd seen her, she'd been a brunette.

"Hello, Ann," he said, glad to see she hadn't succumbed to Dallas chic.

"Ben asked me to meet you and I got caught in the most

awful traffic jam. I was afraid you'd get away without my finding you. He'd never forgive me." She hugged his arm. "Henry,
how nice to see you. Have you got everything? Your baggage,
everything?"

He held up his small bag. "This is it," he said.

She led him out into the glaring sunlight to where her car
was parked. "Don't worry, once we get inside it's air-conditioned. Everything's air-conditioned out here." The car smelled
new, its dashboard a Byzantine complexity.

"Now you just sit tight." Ann was off, driving like someone out to win the Grand Prix. He averted his eyes from the
oncoming traffic. He wondered if he could outwit death twice
in one day. Ann had never been much of a talker, but now she
was chattering away like a nervous squirrel, pretending this was
a social visit, to see old friends in their new setting, to examine
their house, their swimming pool. To exclaim at how their children had grown.

He was tired, talked out. Ann was doing her best. He
started to tell her about the woman on the plane. About halfway through his tale, his voice gave out. The car's air-conditioning was too cold.

They were surrounded by glass skyscrapers in various
stages of construction. "This place must be an architect's
heaven," he said, clearing his throat.

"Isn't it extraordinary." Ann drove more sedately now, in
deference, perhaps, to his pale face and agitated hands.

"A friend of mine, a native of Dallas," Ann went on, "told
me she couldn't imagine what they were thinking of, putting up
all these glass buildings. She said, 'What will we do when a
tornado comes through?'"

They stopped at a red light. Ann's skirt parted, revealing a
long white thigh bisected by a mauve vein as frail as a spider's
web.

"Would you mind turning down the air-conditioning?" he
said. "It's awfully cold."

"Of course." In silence they rode the rest of the way, turning at last into a flower-bordered drive that led to a gleaming bronze door set into an expanse of dark brown glass.

"The bluebird of happiness must lie on the other side," he said.

Ann smiled and checked her watch. "We're right on time," she said. "Ben will be waiting for you." He opened the car door, leaned back in to kiss her cheek. It tasted salty. Then, holding his bag in front of himself like a shield, he got out, slammed the door, and went into the hospital.

17

Ben was there, waiting for him.

"It's been a long time, Henry," he said. None of the usual amenities friends observe when they haven't seen one another for some time applied here. "Did you have a comfortable flight?" Ben led him through the waiting room, which was empty. A nurse seated behind the desk rose, smiling welcome.

"This is Henry Hollander, Nancy. An old friend from Connecticut," Ben said by way of introduction. "Henry, this is my right-hand man, Nancy Adams." They shook hands. "If it's possible, Nancy, we'd like a few minutes alone. See if you can arrange that, would you?"

"I appreciate your fitting me in, Ben," he said as they went into Ben's office. "I know you have a very busy schedule."

"Never too busy for you, Henry." Ben waited, his eyes listening for what Henry would tell him.

"As I said over the phone, I wanted another opinion." He found that if he crushed the fingers of his left hand by squeezing them hard with his right, it helped him to maintain his composure. "The doctor, Dr. Hall, the one who took over your practice, said it would be a good idea. I don't know why I didn't think of it myself, but I'm getting somewhat addled in my declining years." He tried for a smile and didn't make it.

"He said I shouldn't waste any time. Time is of the essence, I believe. So, of course, I thought of you. I shouldn't have wasted any time with him in the first place, should have come straight out here to see you. But, you see, it all came as a shock. I was only feeling tired, you see. Not quite myself, but nothing really serious, nothing really wrong, I thought. I thought it might be my gallbladder. My brother, Ed, had just had his taken out and I thought . . . well, anyway, I had a complete physical last year. Remember? Everything was okay then. Clean bill of health, for what that's worth. Now it seems I have some sort of mass in my stomach. The X-rays showed it. And he seems to feel my liver is damaged. That hepatitis thing, I suppose, although that was a long time ago. Ten years, maybe more." He stopped, exhausted.

"I'm glad you came, Henry. We'll do the best we can for you. Put you through the standard tests, blood sample, everything. Then we'll do a biopsy."

"How long will that take?" He leaned forward. "The biopsy, I mean."

"We'll rush it through. A couple of hours, maybe." A buzzer sounded. Ben answered. "Yes. All right. I'll be right down."

Ben got up. "I have to leave you now, Henry. Mrs. Adams will look after you. If you need anything, ask her. I'll be back as soon as I can."

"Ben. Just one thing. I want you to promise me you'll give me the straight goods. I don't want any half truths. What I mean is, I trust you, Ben. I'll believe whatever you tell me. Just don't hold anything back."

"Have I ever?" Ben said.

Alone, he prowled Ben's office, checking the pictures of the children and Ann, lined up in a tidy row on the desk. They were a good-looking bunch. That was what he wanted, wasn't it. The truth.

"Can I get you anything, Mr. Hollander?" Mrs. Adams's seemingly disembodied head peered around the doorjamb. He started to say no, thanks, then reconsidered. "If you wouldn't mind, a couple of aspirin would be a help. And do you have anything to settle the stomach? I had lunch on the plane." They exchanged a smile of mutual understanding about airline food. She brought him two aspirin tablets in a paper cup and some pink, syrupy liquid for his stomach. She handed him a spoon and said, "One tablespoon should do it." He went into the small lavatory off Ben's office and took the medicine, washed it down with some water. When he came out, she was waiting, her eyes a brittle blue in her lightly suntanned face. Mrs. Adams was what his father called "a fine figger of a woman." Built of firm flesh, roundly contoured, her face, under its pouf of white hair, was young-looking. Pushing fifty, he thought. Older than I am. He had never thought of age as much as in the last few weeks. It irritated him that he'd fallen into the habit. Mrs. Adams was the best-looking nurse he'd seen recently.

"How nice you and Dr. Nilson are old friends," she said, smoothing her crisp uniform over her rather formidable front. "He works so hard, it's nice for him to see folks from home. We feel very lucky to have him here with us. He does a fine job." She tilted her head, obviously expecting some rejoinder from him.

"He's the best there is," he said. "I'd say that even if we weren't friends." He stole a look at his watch. How much longer would Ben be?

"My family is originally from Ohio," Mrs. Adams said, as if he'd asked where she was from. "In Dallas, almost everyone is from someplace else," she explained. He nodded, looking out the window. He already felt better, glad he'd made the trip. It was a tonic just to be here, in Ben's office. Mrs. Adams excused herself and he began to pace, stirring up the orange carpet. Obviously new, it covered his shoes lightly with orange fuzz. He bent to wipe them clean with his handkerchief. Then he went to the window. The skyline of the city stood out as sharply as if it had been cut out of black construction paper and pasted against the brilliant sky.

I've had a good life, he thought, bending over again to get a spot of orange he'd missed. Vertigo, the result, no doubt, of last night's excess, overcame him, and he straightened, still dizzy. I'm middle-aged. There you go again. Age, age. But you are. There's no escaping that. My father is old. My father will go on forever. He's indestructible. There are lots of things I haven't done, places I haven't been. I've never been in a war. Or a battle of any kind, except with myself. I've never seen the Piazzo San Marco. Or China. Or the rain forests of Brazil.

He was cold. It must be that damned air-conditioning. In February. He sat down and cradled an issue of *Science Today* against his stomach, thinking he would read it in a minute. It comforted him to know he had something to do to fill the time.

At last Ben returned, saying he'd made arrangements for some X-rays. They would also do a biopsy, and if he'd follow Mrs. Adams, she'd show him where to go.

"We'll do our best, Henry." Ben laid a large warm hand on him. "I'm assuming Ceil knows you're here."

"No," he said. "I haven't told her anything."

Ben's face suddenly developed the wrinkles it hadn't had before. "Oh, Henry, that's not right," he said sadly, sounding, somehow, exactly like his father. It was what his father might have said. "Ceil's a strong woman," Ben said. "Very strong. She can help you through this. It's not fair to leave her in the dark. Why didn't you think you could tell her?"

He managed a shrug. "I don't know. I didn't want to worry her. Ceil's against ailments, infirmities." It was the wrong thing to say to a doctor. He realized that the minute he'd said it. "She never gives in to aches and pains and doesn't think others should. I thought it would be easier, all the way around, better if she didn't know. At least until there was something concrete I could tell her. Why worry her until I'm certain of what it is?"

"She's your wife, Henry. I think it would have been easier for you, if not for her, if she knew what you've been going through."

"I'll tell her the minute I get home," he said. "Bad news or good, I'll tell her."

The technician this time was a Mexican with gold showing in one front tooth. The man, whose English wasn't very good, said little and understood everything. His hands were small and wide, very quick and deft in spite of their stubbiness. There was no occasion for conversation, though once or twice he patted Henry on the shoulder, as if to reassure him. When he'd finished taking the X-rays, Henry thanked the man, who said, "You bet, boss. Have a good day." Then he went out and Henry was alone again, feeling that there is no aloneness quite like that of being in a hospital examining room, waiting for the word.

He studied the palms of his hands. His lifeline stood out clearly. He wondered what the next step on the agenda would be.

"Dr. Nilson will see you now," a beautiful black nurse said briskly. What had happened to Mrs. Adams, he wondered. "Follow me, please," the nurse said, and he did as he was told. Her hips were very trim and she moved like a dancer, he thought, following her down the hall. She would have been a knockout if there'd been any warmth in her eyes.

He got on the elevator with the nurse and saw the old man in the wheelchair a split second too late. The man, tiny, seeming to be made of bleached papier-mâché, made indistinct squawking noises at Henry, telling him something. The male nurse pushing the chair said, "Smile and nod your head. He knows what he's saying, even if no one else does. He likes it when people respond." So Henry did as he was told.

God, don't let that happen to me, he thought, don't let my family ever see me like that. That's the way they'd remember me. Making noises like a parrot.

Before she got off at five, the nurse told him to ride the elevator to six and Dr. Nilson would be waiting. "I'll push the button for you," she said.

Slightly addled by this time, he rode the elevator all the way up, then down to the lobby, where he got off, bought a roll and Life Savers in the coffee shop, then strolled around as if he were in a resort hotel waiting for his wife to come down so they could go off together to see the sights. Then he boarded another elevator and rode it up to Ben's floor.

18

"Hey, John Boy." Leslie slouched in the doorway. "You alone?" She only called him John Boy when she was feeling frisky. She knew he hated it.

"No, there are eight or ten guys here with me, turkey." He pushed aside the mounds of books and magazines to make room for her.

"I always haf time for one so beautiful as you, Mother Walton," he said. Les sprawled, flinging one of her long legs over him, pinning him in place. "You are my captive," she said. Les had big feet, made bigger by old-fashioned high-top basketball sneakers, a holdover from her high school days. She always wore them when she was home. They were very ugly, but they had class, she'd once told him. "Are you aware, Johnny, that there are things in life that combine ugliness and classiness? One of life's imponderables." He loved it when she said stuff like that. Half the time he didn't believe her, but the other half he did.

"Emma said I should kiss you good-bye for her." Les leaned over and planted a juicy kiss on his cheek.

"Quit it." He scrubbed at the wet spot with his hand. Last night he'd gone to his room, put on his camouflage suit, and waited, reading the same page in *Madame Bovary* over and over without remembering a single word. He'd only read *Madame Bovary* after reading Woody's short story about her and the guy in the leisure suit. Woody had it all over M. Flaubert, as far as he was concerned. Emma hadn't showed. Emma, his Emma, not Flaubert's and Woody's Emma. It had struck him as a coincidence of the most enormous magnitude that Madame Bovary's first name was also Emma. It had endeared the fictional Emma to him, although she wasn't an endearing character.

When his Emma hadn't come back to visit him again, he'd had a serious discussion with himself and decided he was going to quit horsing around with girls for a while, settle down, and lead a celibate life. Anyway, anyone else after Emma would be a letdown. That he was sure of. Idly, he wondered what stories of rape and lust on the eastern seaboard Grace Lerner's niece had carried back with her to Seattle. She probably made him out to her chums as a regular Jack the Ripper. What did he care. Next time he had a sexual experience, he figured he'd aim for someone without any experience at all. And looking for same. He might even put an ad to that effect in the *Village Voice.* "Young, experienced male, looking for young, inexperienced female, willing to learn." That ought to bring down a barrage of replies on his head. He'd probably have to rent a post office box to handle them all.

"That Emma is something else," he said nonchalantly, feel-

ing the blood run out to the tips of his ears, an embarrassing
habit his blood had that he couldn't seem to control.

Leslie gave him a bear hug.

"You're having hot flashes. Don't feel bad. She has that
effect on lots of men older than you, if that makes you feel any
better. She's a siren." He smelled Leslie's peppermint breath.
In the old days, before college, or B.C., as she called it, Leslie's
nickname had been Peppermint Patty. P.P. Les brought up her
other leg and arranged it tidily over his, pinning him to the
mat.

"She put the moves on you, John?" she asked cosily.

"Take your big fat feet offa me!"

"Did she? Come on, did she?" He was sorely tempted to
level with Les, but he didn't. The time wasn't right. Maybe in
five years, ten years, when they were both grown up and un-
shockable, he'd tell her. Not now.

After a brief tussle, Les let him go. He sprang up and
away from her, scuffling through the pile of papers on the floor.
He needed space, needed time to regain his composure, after
his first foray into the world of real live sex. He felt bruised and
used and also exultant at having achieved the loss of what was
euphemistically called his maidenhead. What did they call it
when a woman seduces a man? Plain old seduction, that's what.
Forget maidenhead. How could he lose what he never had.

"She ever call that Ralph character back? Was he the guy
in the red Toyota? Or was that the married geek? Poor guy,
calling her four times in one day and she doesn't even call him
back. She doesn't care how she treats people, does she?" He
smiled, thinking of poor old Ralph and how shamefully she'd
treated him.

"What's she doing in North Carolina anyway?" he asked.

"Riding to the hounds," Les said. "Listen, John, I want to
ask your advice on something very important." This was what
she'd come for. She was suddenly tense, watching him.

"I charge two hundred a day plus expenses," he said, borrowing a line from Rockford. Looking at her he realized that she wasn't in the mood for any more horsing around. "Shoot," he said, overwhelmed. Leslie didn't ask him for advice very often. This was the first time, as a matter of fact. Les usually had all the answers.

"I've been seeing a lot of Michael Varney." She lingered over the name. "You remember Michael?" He shook his head no. "You do so! You met him last fall when you and Mother and Daddy were in New York. We went to the theater. You remember."

"Oh, yeah, okay," he said, not really wanting her to go on in this intense way about a total stranger. Well, almost total. "You mean the long drink of water. Is that the dude?"

"He's tall and dark and fit, not a long drink of water." Her voice tripped lovingly over the adjectives that best described Michael. "He lives in Boston. He's an engineer. And he's got this terrific job offer to go to Saudi Arabia to work for a couple of years. The pay is fantastic."

"Yeah," he said sourly, "and there's a good reason for that. Saudi Arabia is the pits. The climate, everything. They have to pay people big bucks to lure them there. That's what I hear."

Leslie tugged at her sweat shirt, frowning. "It's not *that* bad," she said.

"I'll tell you one thing, women are definitely second-class citizens there." He was angry without knowing why. "I saw a TV documentary about Saudi Arabia, and it didn't make me want to rush over there, even for the big bucks they dish out, that's for sure." Why were they talking about Saudi Arabia, for Pete's sake? "Yeah, so, anyway, go on. I'm listening."

"I want to go with him," Leslie said softly. "He wants me to go with him. It's only for two years. That's what his contract's for. It'd be a terrific experience."

"Two years can be an awful long time," he prophesized gloomily. Then the full import of what she was planning hit him and he turned to face her. "You telling me you want to leave school and go to that place with this guy I don't even know? A place where they put women down like you wouldn't believe. Is that what you're saying?"

"You sound just like Daddy." Leslie's mouth pursed disapprovingly. "That's exactly what I expect him to say. Don't be judgmental, John. You're too young to be judgmental."

"I'm not being judgmental!" he shouted. "I'm telling you I can't believe you're saying what I hear you saying. What about graduating? Getting a job? If you go for two years, you might stay five. Then where'd you be?" A thought occurred to him. "You in love with this guy?"

"I think so. I'm almost sure I am." Her eyes were like drowned violets, her hair drooped in a lank curtain around her troubled face.

"It'd kill them, Les. You know it would. You can't do that to them. They pin all their hopes on you to make it big. You know that. You're the star of the family. You gotta shine, kid. It's up to you." It was what he'd thought all along but up to now had never put into words. Never had to. She was the great white hope of the Hollander family and now she was talking about letting them down.

"Oh, no! You're not getting away with that, John Hollander!" Leslie leaped up and gathered him to her in a crushing embrace. "You're not pushing off that responsibility totally on me. You're the one, the heir, the son and heir of the family. Someday you'll control the purse strings, John Boy. Oh, please, please, kind sir, give me a fiver for a cup of coffee. Only a fiver to buy milk for my baby. Alms, kind sir, alms for the love of Allah!" She grabbed him and made him dance with her. Round and round they went. Leslie liked to dance more than anything. She danced when she was happy and when she was sad and always had.

"For God's sake, John, quit looking at your feet!" she hollered. "Look at me. Give in to the music."

"There isn't any."

"Abandon yourself!" she cried. "Let your feet take wing!" And for a minute, they forgot what they'd been riled about. Eventually, Leslie pulled them both down and they lay on the floor, in a heap, chests heaving, laughing until their stomachs hurt.

"I'm old enough to know my own mind," Leslie said quietly, after a while, crossing her ankles, watching one of her big feet in its ugly sneaker moving up and down, as if there'd been no interruption in their argument. "It's my life. I'm a responsible person."

He sat up. "Not if you do that to them."

"It'd save Daddy a lot of money." Leslie sat up, too. "He's always worried about money. My tuition goes up every time you turn around. And there's you coming along. Just think of the money it'd save if I dropped out of college for a while."

"Don't give me that crap." He stood and brushed himself off. "That's a cheap shot and you know it. Trying to make yourself look noble by leaving college so your kid brother can get in his licks. That's crap and you know it." He turned to stare out the window and when he looked around, she was gone.

God, he thought dismally, wait'll she lays that one on them. They'll freak out. And she knows it. She was trying it on me to see how it went. An enormous disappointment welled inside him. He'd thought Leslie was perfect. He no longer did. Not if she was going ahead with the plans for Saudi Arabia. She'd said she wanted advice, but she didn't want advice, she wanted his approval. Well, he hadn't given it. He didn't think that would stop her. She'd probably hit them with it tonight. He got all tight inside, thinking of their reaction. He didn't want to be around for that blowup, that was for sure.

Instead of going into the office, he took the limo from the airport to Norwalk, then caught a cab for home. He needed time to think. To plan. The house would be mercifully empty. John at school, Ceil off at the hospital or the library or one of the many places she frequented during the day. The girls, he knew, wouldn't be sitting at home twiddling their thumbs, not on a vacation day. The driver went down the Post Road, and he thought how much the place had changed. Apartment buildings going up, condos, office buildings, even hotels. It was getting to look like Dallas.

He paid the driver, walked up the path, thinking how much he liked his house. Thinking, too, how the flowers would be up before much longer, sprouting buds. Everything would be budding in a little while. He fitted his key in the lock, feeling as if he'd been gone for a long time. As the door swung open, he smelled something delicious, something baking in the oven. Ceil was home, after all. His first instinct was to turn and run. He wasn't ready. Ceil came out to see who it was, wearing her old blue jeans—her cooking jeans, she called them—and an old shirt of his, almost buttonless, tied in a knot at her stomach, an equally disreputable sweater underneath.

"Henry!" Her face showed pleasure at his homecoming and she almost ran to him. Then she remembered how they'd parted and held herself back. "I didn't expect you so soon," she said in a distant voice. "How was Dallas? As swinging as they say?"

"Ceil." He set down his bag and took a step toward her. "I have bad news."

She struck her chest with her fist. "The children," she said. "John?"

"No," he said. "It's me."

"You," she said. "What is it? What's wrong?" Her hands met in front of her and clung together for comfort.

"I went to see Ben." His throat was suddenly so dry he had difficulty talking. "Could I have a glass of water, please?" She ran to the kitchen. He stayed where he was, trying to find the right words to tell her. She brought him the water, and although he drank it all, it didn't seem to help.

"It seems I have cancer," he said, not knowing how else to put it. There was no other way, no way to say it without making it real. Her hand went over her mouth. She didn't make a sound.

"I went to see Ben because the doctor I saw here told me the tests had shown a mass in the stomach and the biopsy indicated a malignancy. So, of course, I thought of Ben. I knew I could trust him. I didn't trust, not completely, anyway, the other man. He was too young, too . . . impersonal, I guess. Ben confirmed the diagnosis."

He stood there in the hall, coat still on, hat in hand, wondering what to do now. He had told her the worst. Had got the words out, and now what did they do? Everything led up to the terrible moment of telling, and then they leave you, balancing on the edge of the abyss. How does one fill in the time left?

To spare her asking the question, he said, "Ben said I have maybe three months, maybe four or five. Not more than six, at the most."

"No," she said in the thick silence. "No, I won't have it. It simply won't do, Henry." She went to him and took his face in her hands. "This can't happen. There must be some mistake. It can't be happening to you. To us."

She smelled of chocolate.

"What are you making?" he said. "It smells good."

"I told Les I'd make her favorite cake. Henry, we'll find another doctor, one who will know what to do. I'm always hearing of people who beat it. Only the other day Mrs. Hobbs told me about—"

"Ceil," he said, "don't." His skin was ashen. She was afraid he might faint.

"Go up and get into bed, Henry," she said, almost briskly. "I'll fix you some tea and toast. How would that be?" Without waiting for an answer, she scurried into the kitchen, glad of something she could do for him. He went up the stairs, lifting each foot as if it wore an iron boot. He turned down the spread,

got out of his clothes, and, still in his underwear, crawled under the covers. He shut his eyes and listened to her moving
around downstairs. Even then, his hands moved over his stomach, exploring, trying to locate the thing that they said was
there. He felt nothing. Maybe even Ben had been wrong. No,
impossible. Ben had told him the truth, the truth he'd asked for
and, it turned out, didn't want to know.

"Henry." She put the tray down on the top of her bureau.
She came and sat on the edge of the bed. "I won't let it happen
to you," she said, as if anything she did or could think of to do
would be of any use.

"I don't think I want any tea now, Ceil. I'm sorry, when
you went to the trouble. I don't think I could get it down."

She didn't argue with him, but instead, took off the old
shirt, the sweater under it, slipped out of her jeans and her bra
and pants, and got under the covers beside him.

"I'm sorry I called you a liar, Henry. I was so angry. I'm
ashamed of myself for saying such a thing." Her breath lifted
the hair on his chest, her voice caressed him, her arms went
around him, as warm as they had ever been.

"I want to make love to you," she said.

He laughed. "It's been a long time since we've made love
in the afternoon."

"Pretend it's the first time. Pretend we're in that apartment
on Third Avenue. Can you remember how it looked, how it
smelled? Can you remember Mrs. . . . oh, what was her name,
the nosy little woman who lived across the hall and was always
borrowing things she never even made the pretense of paying
back?"

"Mrs. Romero." He had a good memory for names.

"Yes, that's it. Remember when we thought we were the
only ones who ever felt the way we felt then? Remember, we
thought we'd discovered sex. It was lovely, discovering sex.
Henry. Pretend we can't keep our hands off each other," and
she stroked him with long, delicate movements. "Henry, my

love. Remember when we were so new to each other's bodies
we could hardly bear going to parties and on Sundays sometimes we didn't get out of bed until it was dark." Her mouth
moved over him in a way he'd forgotten, a way she'd told him
years ago she'd read about in one of her sex manuals.

"I don't think I'm up to it, Ceil," he said in a cracked, old
man's voice.

"Yes, you are," she said fiercely. She put her length
against his. "Yes, you are." She touched him and touched him
and touched him until he groaned and heaved himself up and
over to her. "Oh, my dear God," he said, moving very slowly
at first, then faster until she cried out and threw her legs around
his waist, crushing him to her.

She aroused him, as she had always done. He had thought
himself incapable of being aroused, but she had soothed him
into it, had aroused him once more, in the old way. They were
young again, their lives before them.

"Henry." She lay at his side, smelling of whatever perfume
it was she used. "My darling, don't despair. We'll think of
something. We'll go to the best cancer specialist in the country.
You'll see." She put one leg lightly over him.

"Once it hits the liver, Ceil," his voice was patient and
very tired, "there's nothing that they can do, no recourse to
take. They both said that. Ben and the other doctor, they both
said the liver was damaged and the cancer had reached it.
Nothing except a miracle will stop it now."

She raised herself on an elbow and looked down into his
face through her tears. "Then we'll work a miracle. If that's
what it takes, that's what we'll do."

He looked at her and knew she believed what she was saying.

"I have to tell the children," he said.

"No!" she cried. "Not yet. Not just yet. Give yourself
time." Give me time.

Under the blanket, his hands explored his stomach once

more. "I'll put the lettuce in tomorrow," he said. "Lettuce is hardy. Even if we get another frost, the lettuce will survive."

Downstairs, John let himself in and headed for the kitchen. In the hall he stumbled over his father's bag. The sink was filled with bowls and spoons and the electric mixer, coated with cake batter, rested on its side. A cake was in the oven. He checked, hoping his intrusion wouldn't make the cake fall. His mother must be home, too. He went quietly up the stairs, stopping halfway. Sure enough, the door to their room was closed. He went back down and made himself a peanut butter on rye.

They're making up. He was absurdly pleased by the thought. How do you like that.

19

"She's coming home day after tomorrow," Keith said. "The doctor says he doesn't think it'll work, having her home, I mean. But she said if she has to go back into the bin, she'll kill herself. So I guess the doctor decided that home is the lesser of two evils."

Keith's face seemed to have developed new hollows. "I have to clean up the joint before she shows up. If she came in here right now, she might be so grossed out she'd jump out the window to escape. Lucky we're only on the second floor, huh?" He kept his face entirely without expression.

"You want me to help you?" he said. "With the cleanup, I mean. I'm pretty good at swabbing down floors, changing sheets. I even do windows."

"That would be great," Keith said. "I feel kind of over-whelmed by the whole thing." Keith's smile was precarious, his mouth tilted slightly downward, threatening the smile with ex-tinction.

"I don't blame you." He was on the verge of asking Keith if his father had been informed of his mother's hospital stay and shoved the words back just in time. He'd learned his lesson. Keith didn't like him asking questions.

"I've been thinking." Keith's voice was matter-of-fact. "If this doesn't work, if she can't handle it, we might work out something. The two of us."

Did Keith mean himself and his mother, or did he mean the two of them?

"It might be a first." Keith's tone was falsely jovial, his eyes bleak. "A mother-son suicide pact. I never heard of one. Husband-wife, sure. Old hat. Plenty of those hanging around. Boyfriend-girl friend, loads of those. But mother-son? Never. What do you think?"

There was no answer he could give that could conceal the horror he felt at Keith's remark. So he remained silent.

"I said, what do you think?" Keith hadn't laid a hand on him, yet he felt as if he'd been assaulted.

"I think it's not worth talking about," he said. "Anything I say now would only mean you and me ending up fighting. I'm not up for talking about shitty stuff like what you just said. I can't handle it, Keith."

To his surprise, Keith laughed and said, "You're right. I was only putting you on, anyway. Tomorrow we do a number on what I think of as home sweet home, right? I've got plenty of soap and stuff to swab down the floors with. I appreciate your help, John. I really do. You're a good friend."

Just when he was ready to blow his cork, Keith had a way of saying something that got to him.

"That's okay," he said.

"Why don't you bring Emma along? We can let her scrub

the tub. Then after, we could all sit down and play strip poker. I've got a special deck I use for strip poker with female provocateurs." Keith also had a way of giving with one hand, then taking away with the other.

"She's gone," was all he said.

"She coming back?"

He shrugged. "I doubt it. Les didn't say anything about her coming back. She's in North Carolina riding to the hounds."

"Hey, I knew my father would like her. He's very big on riding to the hounds, stuff like that."

"I've gotta go. I'll wait for you tomorrow outside study hall. I'll be the one with the mop and the broom. See you."

The house was empty when he got home. He prepared a gargantuan sandwich, using five slices of bread and all the leftovers he could find in the refrigerator, and carried it up to his room. On his way, he let his imagination soar, settled Emma cosily on his sofa bed, waiting eagerly for him. They had a tryst. Tryst was a word he was fond of and had little opportunity to use. He set the sandwich down and divested himself of his straight clothes to get into his camouflage suit. That suit was definitely an aphrodisiac, he figured. It sure had turned Emma on. He'd promised he'd see if he could get one for her. Size small. Right at the minute, he didn't feel much like following through. Maybe later. He'd see how he felt. Maybe she could buy a custom-made camouflage suit. He'd read someplace that General MacArthur had worn one. Maybe the general's tailor could whip one up for Emma. It was a cheering thought.

Emma was a tryst type. No doubt about that. He ate his sandwich, belching loudly to show his Chinese friends how much he'd enjoyed it, and wondered what he should do next. He didn't feel like reading. Instead, he slitted his eyes so he could barely see out of them, and contemplated his sofa bed. Even through those eyes, he could tell Emma wasn't there, would not be there. Emma was lost, perhaps forever, to him.

She had been his brief encounter with romance. Sex. Do sex and romance go together?

"Tryst," he said aloud, and went to look out the wobbly paned window, checking to see if the willows showed any yellow. They were brown. It was barely March, three weeks until the first official day of spring. Under the waters of the pond, circled now by a ribbon of mist as wide as a watchband, he imagined the slugs stirring hopefully, getting geared up for the coming season. One small boy, fishing pole over his shoulder, hurtled down the hill to the pond, looking furtively over his shoulder, checking for the fish and game warden who was famous for handing out stiff fines to people who dared to drop a hook before he blew the whistle saying it was okay.

The kid tucked himself onto a rock and assumed the position of a thinker. Chin in hand, he stared down at the water, probably sending up a few prayers for a big one. He thought of knocking hard on the window to scare the kid, then thought better of it. At that age, nine or ten, hope sprang eternal. It was only when encroaching age got a good grip on you that you knew the fish were as elusive as most everything else in life. Prayers didn't help much, once you hit your teens. Let the kid find out for himself.

He thought idly of dropping Emma a line. "If you're ever in the vicinity, drop in. My mother would love to see you." Signing it "Faithfully Yrs.," he sighed deeply. He would never be a letter writer. They'd never get him for breach of promise. Never put anything on paper, he always said. That way you were safe from designing females.

He heard someone moving around downstairs. Maybe the burglar he'd been expecting for so long had finally arrived. His heart beat faster as he crept toward the stairs. If ever a camouflage suit came in handy, now was the time. He had always wondered if he would rise to the occasion if confronted by a burglar in a stocking mask and carrying a gun. Would he tackle the intruder, put him in a chicken-wing or a half-nelson, then, bringing the old Boy Scout knots into play once more, secure the bandit's arms and legs and call the police, telling them to hurry on over, he had a live one for them.

Whoever it was was in the dining room. He could hear the faint clink of glass against glass. Probably toasting each other before they filled their sacks. What if there were two of them? Caution was indicated. Maybe he better call the police before he tied up the buggers. Suppose they were armed?

He leaned over the stair rail and looked into the dining room. A man was standing at the sideboard with his back turned, pouring out a drink.

"Dad? Is that you?"

He bounded down the last few steps, somewhat relieved he hadn't had to be a hero, after all. "How come you're home so early? I thought you were stealing the silver."

His father took out his pocket handkerchief and carefully wiped his mouth. "I thought you were at soccer practice," he said. "I thought the house was empty. What's that you're wearing?" His father's eyebrows went up.

"It's my army surplus camouflage suit. I wear it when I don't want anyone to see me."

His father tossed back his drink and laughed. "Get one for me, will you?"

Amazing. He'd expected a monologue concerning the weird and wasteful dress habits of the young. That was one of the most amazing things he'd ever heard his father say.

"Sure, Dad. I'll see what I can do." He never knew what to get his father for his birthday. Now he did. All he had to do was figure out how to pay for it.

They stood looking at each other.

"John," his father said, as he'd said plenty of other times, "I'd like to talk to you." Only this time his voice was different.

Oh-oh. What now? He felt himself tense up. What had he done? He racked his brain. My God. The thought hit him. Maybe he found out about Emma. My God, what do I do now.

Maybe he thinks I took advantage of her. Had my way with her. In spite of himself, he smiled.

"Sure, Dad." His voice trembled ever so slightly. "What's up?"

His father stood looking at his glass.

"My mother lost a baby who was born when I was two and Ed four. It was a girl. My mother never got over losing that baby." Deep lines appeared at either side of his father's mouth as he spoke. "For a while, she want to a sanitarium, a rest home, they called it. She'd had a nervous breakdown, you see. We had a housekeeper, a woman named Mrs. Quirk. She was a terrible cook, but she was kind to Ed and me. My father didn't tell us much of what was going on. Ed and I thought our mother was never coming back. My father said she was resting, regaining her strength, but we were convinced she had gone forever. In those days, parents didn't tell their children everything, the way they seem to do these days. They thought children should be protected from painful things so they kept the children in the dark, thinking they were doing them a kindness."

Where was all this leading to? What was his father trying to tell him?

"Nowadays," his father continued, "it's very much the fashion to let children in on all family events, to spare them nothing." His father frowned at him and he smiled back.

"I'm not sure that's a good idea, John. What do you think?" His father put down his glass abruptly and waited for his answer.

"Maybe somewhere in between would be good," he said. "I think kids should be let in on things if they can do anything about them. If they can help, I mean."

"You may be right, John." His father looked at his watch. "I've got work to do, John, and I don't want to be disturbed." Then, instead of going into the study, his father went up and shut the door of the bedroom quietly behind him.

Some days you eat the bear, some days the bear eats you. Ain't it the truth.

By the time he made another sandwich to tide him over until dinner time, and trudged back up to his room to eat it, peering out the window, checking the pond again, the little kid with the fishing pole had disappeared.

20

There was something going on. He heard them, late at night, when they had every reason to think he was asleep. Furtive footsteps passed his door, going down the stairs. The sounds of crying; terrible, ragged sounds that brought him out of his warm bed to listen at the door, trying to figure out what was wrong.

Maybe Les had sprung her Saudi Arabia scene on them after all, although she told him she hadn't. She'd gone back to college early, to finish a paper, she said. He thought she'd left because of the oppressive atmosphere in the house these days, the fact that he didn't approve of her defection, the way his mother and father were acting; as if something heavy was happening.

They'd asked her to stay, wanting more time to talk to her, they said. But she insisted she had to get back. He was glad she'd held off telling them, glad of the part he might have played in her decision. But even Leslie's announcing she wanted to quit school wouldn't be reason enough for those awful, tearing sounds that came from their bedroom. In the daytime, his mother maintained her composure, avoiding his eye, moving about the house, almost the same, but with a nightmarish, sleepwalking way about her that was new. His father said very little, spent long days at his office, cleaning up a lot of things, as he put it, coming home to eat his dinner, and excuse himself early, saying he'd had a hard day and was whipped. He *looked* whipped, that was for sure.

A night came when the sounds of crying woke him and he crept to his door, opened it a crack, and heard his father say in a harsh, almost unrecognizable voice, "He should be told. He's old enough to know." And then his mother's voice bit off the word "No!", leaving no room for doubt.

It hit him with the force of a stone. They were getting a divorce. Just like everybody else. Like Keith's father and mother. Like the parents of lots of kids he knew. He'd been proud of his parents because they were still married to each other after all those years, putting them in the minority. They had staying power, a virtue his father was always plugging. He'd had them pegged for a lifetime trip. They were going to make it, go hand in hand into the sunset, a couple of white-haired stalwarts.

Not that he wasn't aware of plenty of tension between them—filling the house, at times. Sometimes he caught a look on his mother's face that told him plenty about her, stuff she probably didn't want him to know. But you can't live in a family and not get clued in to things that would be better kept secret.

His father had had a monkey on his back for some time, he figured. It could be any one of a number of things: his job, the fact he hadn't forged ahead the way he'd planned, would've liked; or, more likely, money problems: tuition bills for him and Les, mortgage payments. That everyday shit that tried men's souls. Lots of times his father was testy and irascible for no reason. It's me, he decided. He takes one look at me and Wham! he gets sore. What was this strange power he wielded, he wondered, wishing he could change things.

They thought he didn't notice the battle of wills his
mother and father often waged. Once, when they'd had a fight,
his mother had left the house before his father got home and
hadn't returned until late. He'd heard her come in. The light
was already out in their room. She slept in the guest room. The
next morning he'd asked her where she'd been. He'd been
younger then, more forthright, less cautious.

"To the movies," she'd said, giving him the brush-off. She
never went to the movies, hated them, as a matter of fact.

"What'd you see?" He was like a detective in a two-bit
mystery, checking his witness's alibi.

"I don't remember." She hadn't even bothered to make up
a story. "My mind was elsewhere." For days after, his mother
and father had prowled the house, not speaking, feeling their
way back to the norm. He and Les discussed their parents endlessly, trying to figure out what made them tick.

During one of those discussions, he'd hit upon a likely explanation. "I figure," he'd said solemnly, "the bloom is off the
rose. I read in the paper today that romantic love only lasts
three years. Did you know that?" Leslie hadn't known that.
"That means theirs flew out the window long ago. You know
what?" He snapped his fingers, inspiration at hand. "I think Ma
has the hots for Mr. Wilson." Well, that had thrown them into
such spasms of merriment they'd almost hurt themselves
bouncing around the room, thinking of their mother and Mr.
Wilson locked in carnal embrace.

Mr. Wilson was the principal of their elementary school.
He had an intricate network of dark warts on his face and neck,
and a breath that would bring a dragon to its knees.

After they'd calmed down, Leslie said, "They still hold
hands. And last week I caught them with her sitting on his
lap." Les then studied the ceiling and he the veins in his wrists,
trying to figure that one out. Lap-sitting, for parents, that is,
was pretty heavy stuff, they both knew. "And Daddy thinks
she's the most beautiful woman he's ever seen," Les tossed in
for good measure. "He told me so."

He was always reading statistics about the numbers of married men and women who had affairs. It interested him that this was no longer called "committing adultery." As far as he could figure, adultery was obsolete. An anachronism. He wondered if the *Reader's Digest* condensed version of the Bible said "extra marital affair" instead of "adultery," although three words as against one technically broke the *Digest's* code. He made a mental note to check on this. Thou shalt not commit an extra marital affair didn't sound too hot, when you thought about it.

The statistics were high, at any rate. And climbing fast. He wondered if his father was making it with some liberated woman, maybe some divorcée who couldn't do without a man, or, more likely, someone in his office. Not his secretary. He'd seen his father's secretary and it definitely wasn't her. Office romances, however, continued to flourish, if he could believe what he read in the papers. He'd read about a woman who went after her boss with a revolver because he'd rejected her for someone a lot younger. It turned out the woman was a lousy shot, however, so the guy wound up with only a little nick on the side of his head. But he suspected that the experience of being shot might make the guy think twice about fooling around with anyone else. It wasn't worth it, never knowing when that old bullet might come winging toward your head.

And, even though he fantasized about his mother going to a male strip joint when she was supposed to be out doing good works, he could never work up a really good fantasy about her having an extra marital affair.

A while back Keith had said, "My father keeps telling me how much we have in common. About the only thing I can see that we have in common is we both like girls." That set him to thinking. Did *his* father like girls? As opposed to women, that is? He knew a kid whose parents were divorced, and when the kid spent the weekend with his father, the father tried to be a pal by telling the kid about the latest girl he'd slept with. And the funny part was that the father wanted the kid to tell about some girl that he, the son, had slept with. So the kid freaked out because he hadn't slept with anyone yet. It was bizarre. He figured sleeping with girls didn't necessarily bring father and son closer together. He didn't know what did, but that wasn't one of the ways.

He was pretty sure they loved him. Well, he was certain his mother did, anyway. She hollered plenty at him, and sometimes clouted him on his rear end when he did something bad. Every time she punished him or Leslie she used to say, as her hand came down on the old backside or a treat was withheld, "If I didn't love you, I wouldn't be doing this." He could never see the logic in this, but he could tell from her face that she was telling the truth.

She baked muffins and cakes and pies, made casseroles concocted of strange and wondrous things: chicken wings and blue cheese, Chinese dumplings. Once, even, incredibly, brains. She believed in experimenting with food. In eating everything. He had friends, as did Leslie, who, when invited to their house for dinner, demanded to know what was on the menu before they'd agree to come.

His mother had a way of placing the food on the table and standing back to watch their faces carefully, watching as the fork and spoon carried the food to the mouth, watching as it was chewed. It could be unnerving. He remembered a friend he'd had in second grade who became his mother's favorite. The kid, whose name was Benny, had eaten everything his mother put in front of him, rolling his eyes, smacking his lips, exclaiming, "You're a wonderful cook, Mrs. Hollander," after every meal. His mother loved Benny.

"Very tasty, Ceil," his father always said, but in such an absentminded way you knew he wasn't really aware of what he was eating. When his father bit into food, if it didn't bite back, it was very tasty, by his lights. And, when he and Leslie were sick, his mother made them Junket and custards with a pool of maple syrup hidden in the bottom.

"Cooking is an act of love," she told them. Especially if it was liver. She also made soup of chicken feet, which the butcher magnanimously handed over for nothing, wanting to be rid of them. Chicken feet, she said, gave soup an extra flavor. Once she stashed a bag full of chicken feet in the freezer, and he'd come upon them while foraging for ice cream, showing off for someone he'd brought home from school. The bag of chicken feet had popped unexpectedly out onto the floor. The friend, who had a notoriously weak stomach, had almost lost his lunch then and there. "It's only chicken feet," John had said, feeling very worldly, making his friend look at them. They resembled little hands, the nails curved and yellow, looking as if they belonged on a tiny mandarin. . . .

Inevitably, the time came when he was again wakened by the familiar sounds of crying coming from their room. He had made up his mind that the next time it happened he would confront them, ask them what was going on. He had a right to know. He was old enough. He was sick of being treated like a child. He was not a child. He got out of bed and stamped his way down the hall, knocked on the door, softly at first, then, when no one called out to him, and the sound of weeping continued, he pounded with his fists.

"It's me, John," he called out. "I want to come in." A heavy silence followed. Then his father's voice said, "Come in, John." He opened the door boldly, knowing he had a right to be here. His mother, wearing an old sweater over her nightgown, was sitting up in bed, tears falling down her cheeks. When she saw him, she sank low, pulling up the covers, until all he could see of her was her head and her fingers gripping the edge of the blanket.

His father stood in a corner, smoking a cigarette.

"I thought you gave those things up," he said. His father went on taking big drags, letting out the smoke so the room looked cloudy, as if a fog were rolling in.

Nobody said anything.

"What's going on?" he said in a wavery voice. "I want to know. Every night I hear you and it's driving me nuts. If you're getting a divorce, I can handle it."

He crossed his arms on his chest, a habit he'd developed in nursery school when he'd wanted to feel brave. His feet were cold.

His father put out his cigarette, taking a long time about it. "You're right, John," he said at last. "You should know. Your mother and I should have told you before this. We might have known you'd hear us in here." His father's face was pinched and waxy looking. He looked like a man who'd been shut up for a long time, a prisoner of war.

He waited, his hands gripping his upper arms in an effort to keep his cool. So what if they were splitting up? There were worse things. Lots worse.

"I have cancer." His father was speaking to him, his pale, bloodless lips forming the words that made no sense. "I haven't long to live. The doctors say maybe three or four months. Six at the most."

He heard his mother draw a deep breath and didn't dare, didn't have the heart, to look at her. He wasn't sure he'd heard right. He'd got himself ready, psyched up to hear they were getting a divorce. He didn't want to hear about a death, an imminent death. He wasn't prepared to accept this news. He shook his head. There must be some mistake.

He watched his father go over to the bed, sit down, and put his arm around his mother. All right, he told himself. You wanted to know. Now you know. What good does that do. What can you do to help, asshole. Standing there looking at them, asshole, doing nothing . . . they don't need you. Look at them. They don't even know you're here. Get lost, get back to your beddy-bye, asshole.

He went, shutting the door quietly, not wanting to disturb them. They wouldn't miss him. They had each other.

His room was very cold. He shut the window and put on

the socks he'd discarded on the floor. He lay rigid under the covers, arms at his sides, staring up at the ceiling. When he closed his eyes, terrible pictures floated there, pictures of people dying. So he couldn't close his eyes. He'd have to keep them open all night.

I should do something, he thought. Something must be done. We mustn't take this lying down. I'm sorry I know. I wish I didn't know. I wish they hadn't told me. If I didn't know, everything would be all right. I don't know what to do. I want to help but I'm helpless.

Up until now, he'd never really known what helpless meant.

You're such a big shot, storming in there, demanding to be let in on the secret. Now that you know, big shot, what next?

He felt as if someone had a hand over his face, shutting off his supply of oxygen. He felt as if a big, hairy hand had clamped his throat, as if someone hugely fat were sitting on his stomach. He sat up, turned on the light. He was alone. There were no more noises coming from their room. Then he thought he heard someone pass his door and stop. He thought he saw the doorknob turn. Quickly, he turned off the light and flattened himself in bed. Closed his eyes and pulled the covers up over his head. Minutes passed. No one had tried to come in. There had been no person, no presence, no hand laid on his shoulder, no voice had said, "John." Nothing. After a long time, he came out from under the blankets.

The docs might be wrong, he thought. Plenty of times he'd read or heard about doctors making mistakes. That was why they had to fork out such big bucks for malpractice suits, wasn't it. Why they had such heavy insurance policies against malpractice suits, wasn't it. Docs were only people. They made plenty of mistakes. How many times had he read about people who'd been told they had cancer and it turned out they didn't. That happened all the time. He needed someone to talk to. He'd call Leslie, except it was the middle of the night by now.

Anyway, all that would accomplish would be to upset her and probably make her hop on the next bus or train and come home. Anyway, maybe they'd already told her. No. They wouldn't tell one of them and not the other. He could call Keith. Keith would have to listen, for once.

He opened his mouth to try out the words. "My father . . ." he said out loud, and could go no further. If he said the words out loud, all of them, then the enormity of it would sink in; it would prove to be true. If he refused to say them out loud, then what his father had told him wouldn't be true, would never happen.

Now he did hear someone coming. He flipped over on his stomach, facing toward the wall. The door opened. He stayed stiff as a board. He was a coward. Someone was there, waiting. He screwed his eyes and began to count, as if he were playing hide and seek and he was giving them all time to hide before he opened his eyes and began to look for them. The door closed.

So it was a dream. That was it. In the morning, when he woke, he'd realize it had all been a dream.

I will never sleep. Never again will I sleep without having terrible dreams.

And, when he slept at last, he dreamed not of death and dying, nor of his father's face. He dreamed of Emma.

21

They had become a family of pale people, stepping softly through pale rooms, eating pale food from pale plates. Even their voices were pale. Everyone spoke in whispers. His mother had given up her volunteer work, pleading fatigue. Then Mrs. Hobbs called to say she had to have some corns cut off and needed a ride to her foot doctor.

"Oh, Mrs. Hobbs," his mother's voice rose despairingly, "I don't think I can." Then she did anyway. Afterward, she told him: "I'll have to find someone to fill in for me, John. I lost my patience with Mrs. Hobbs twice and snapped at her. Poor thing. It isn't fair to her."

The telephone seldom rang. When it did, it sounded pale, too, as if it were hidden under bales of old clothes waiting to be collected by the Salvation Army.

He felt like a good fight. He felt like screaming.

His father continued to go to his office, to straighten out his affairs, tie up loose ends, his mother explained. At the office, did they know?

His mother haunted the library, collecting books on cancer, its causes, its effects, its cures. She took notes frantically, as if she were overdue with a term paper. He found her when he came in from school, filling pages of yellow-lined paper with her small, precise handwriting, telling her everything she needed to know about cancer.

Les called. She spoke to him last and said, "What's with them, John? Mother sounds clutched, and Daddy sounds like a zombie. Do you have any idea what's going on?"

"Oh," he answered blithely, "it's the weather. It snowed for two days straight. School was called off and I made thirty bucks shoveling driveways. I'm buying Dad a camouflage suit for his birthday with the dough."

He played soccer like a madman. The coach took him aside, said he was getting downright vicious. "You got something against your fellow man, John?" the coach said, attempting to lay an arm around him. He ducked, dodged, wanting no man to touch him.

"What about Les?" he said to his mother that evening. "When are you going to tell her?"

"When he's ready he'll tell her, John."

"How about Grandy?"

"Soon," she said vaguely. "Soon."

He caught himself staring at his father. Then, when his father turned toward him, he averted his eyes, not wanting him to see what was in them. Which was: Now I'll never get a chance to know my dad. Never find out what he's really like. What he's thinking. Find out why he never loved me. That was the crux of the matter. Why had his father never loved him. Had he done something? Did he, perhaps, look like someone who had, in his father's youth, caused him pain? Maybe his father had never wanted children. Maybe he only wanted girl children. But didn't most men want a son? He knew he'd never figure it out.

His dreams became mixed with real life. For instance: He dreamed that he and Woody and his father were in Elaine's, sitting at a table usually reserved for Warren Beatty. His father ordered champagne. The waiter, bowing and scraping, called his father "sir." Woody was attired in a tattered nightshirt and sported a flashy cravat tied with a Windsor knot that fought with his Adam's apple. Autograph seekers, brandishing pencils and paper, besieged their table, asking him, John Hollander, for his autograph. His father kept saying "Woody who?", which sent Woody into a snit. His nostrils flared and his cheeks quivered with indignation. No one knew who he was. Woody drew an old fedora from a secret pocket in his nightshirt and placed it low on his brow so his face was partially obscured.

"I want no limelight, no publicity, no paparazzi," Woody said. A beautiful, slender brunette, not unlike Emma, wearing a one-shouldered, flame-colored culotte, perched herself on Woody's lap.

"Please." Wearily, Woody held up one hand. "No pictures. I am a very private person. I want nothing but my fireside, my slippers. Maybe to make a movie or two. Write a play now and then, a short story, perhaps. I do not seek fame. It seeks me. Everything must be kept secret. I do not divulge my plots. I want no bright lights," he said, blinking into the strobes for which Elaine's was famous. "No parties." His voice could scarcely be heard over the din. "I want only to travel the world incognito. I want only to be free to do my own thing."

"And what *is* your own thing?" his father asked.

The brunette, waving a wand she had concealed in her flame-colored culotte, had the answer.

"As you wish, sire," she said in a New Jersey accent. "From henceforth, you are the man in the street." The wand grazed Woody's shoulder and he flinched. "The average John Doe, pulling down two hundred big ones weekly as a carpenter's apprentice." It appeared that the brunette, now that she had center stage, was reluctant to leave it.

Woody leaped to his feet, sending her spiraling into the air. Fortunately for her, she was as agile as a fox and landed on her feet twenty feet away, scuffling her running shoes in the sawdust that was indigenous to the boîte in which she found herself.

The crowd applauded her wildly, putting Woody into an even bigger snit. "Carpenter's apprentice!" he howled. "Every time I hear the word 'carpenter' I think of Jesus Christ. Was he not a carpenter, the noblest of them all? If I grew a beard and assumed a different expression, more soulful-like, I might be mistaken for the Messiah. It is entirely possible that this will be the theme of my next flick, although of course it is too early to tell and, at any rate, must be kept a secret. I may even star in this flick, which would sure beat fighting off fans in some grubby gin mill."

Hands clasped in a prayerful attitude, Woody studied them from under his hat brim.

"Of course," he mused, "Christ did not wear glasses. A small matter, taken care of by contacts. I plan to renounce the Hamptons, the fleshpots, the constant surveillance which my fans subject me to. I may even renounce my yellow Rolls." A great sigh went up. Woody drew his nightshirt close about himself and scuttled off into the night. Alone. That was the worst of it. He was alone.

His father said, "Who *was* that man?" and John woke up laughing. It was the first laugh he'd had in days.

Grandy was coming.

"I didn't want to tell him so soon, John, but your mother insisted. She said he had to know. I know she's right, but I feel he's too old to be dragged in. What can he do? He shouldn't have to deal with this."

It was the first time his father had spoken to him of his illness. He was dumbfounded. Tongue-tied.

"He's your father, isn't he?" he said, without thinking. "He has to know. Wouldn't you want to know if—" He'd been on the verge of saying "if I was sick." And said only, lamely, "If it was me?"

His father looked stunned. "Of course," he agreed, looking, for the moment, almost cheerful. "You're right, John. That's very wise of you."

It was his turn to be stunned. He rolled the word around in his head for a long time. Wise. His father had said he was wise. A first. Was it possible he'd gained wisdom overnight, and would it be wisdom that would enable him to cope with this horrendous thing that had happened, was happening, to them all?

He and his mother drove to the airport to pick up Grandy. He was arriving on a flight due in shortly after noon. The thin March sunshine picked out bits of detritus strewn alongside the thruway, caught in the greasy snow remnants from the last storm. It was Wednesday. His father had gone in to the office. His mother, after saying she would go alone to Kennedy, had changed her mind and asked him to come with her. She'd even called Gleason to tell him she was keeping him out of school today on a family matter.

When they were near the airport terminal, he said, "Are you going to tell them at school? About Dad?"

"I will if you want me to."

"I wish Dad would let me talk to him about it," he said. "The only thing he's said to me is that you made him call Grandy."

She only shook her head. They parked the car and walked toward the terminal.

"What did Grandy say?" he asked her.

"Only that he would come. Your father didn't want him to, but there was no stopping him." She stepped off the curb into the path of a taxi. The driver blew his horn, leaned out of his window, and shouted at her. "Watch it, Ma," he said, putting his hand on his mother's arm. He had to learn to be her protector. Up until now, he had never been anyone's protector. Without acknowledging his touch, she hurried across the street. "Your father told me this morning if he can get through this, seeing Grandy, I mean, handling that part of it, he can get through anything. Poor man. He dreads it so."

The automatic doors opened and they went inside. Why does he dread seeing his own father so much? he wondered. Grandy might be old, but he was also tough. He wouldn't break down. Grandy would know what to say to his son. John was certain Grandy would know the right words. He counted on Grandy, was glad he was coming. How did people act in situations of this kind? How did they handle a notice of impending death? Either their own or that of someone deeply loved. Maybe Grandy would know what to say because he was old and—until now, anyway—closer to death than any of them.

They got to the gate just in time. Grandy was walking briskly toward them, a middle-sized man, his silver hair cut just so, dressed in a pin-striped suit. He was carrying an overcoat, his Homburg, and a briefcase.

They waved and Grandy came over to them, kissed his mother, and shook his hand. He liked that, was glad Grandy hadn't kissed him, as if he were a child. "Helen sent her best," Grandy said. "She wanted very much to come, but I told her no. I thought it was better if I came alone. How is he, Ceil?"

"As you might expect, he's perfectly contained and very brave," his mother said evenly. "He's handling everything methodically, wrapping up all sorts of loose ends in a very businesslike way."

Grandy peered down at her, his brown eyes sad. "And you," he said, "you are also brave." It wasn't a question, it was a statement of fact. She braced her lips against smiling, but a little laugh, tremulous but not without pleasure, came from her. "I'm so glad you're here." She hugged his arm. "It was good of you."

"As you can see, I came prepared." Grandy indicated his overcoat. "I almost forgot a coat, Ceil. I'm getting used to the California weather. I forgot it was March, that it'd probably be cold here. But Helen reminded me." They walked toward the luggage pickup. "She also insisted I bring two bags." Grandy smiled slightly. "If it had been up to me, I would've managed with one. Helen has me under her thumb, as you can see. She even packed for me. I had to unpack when she wasn't looking and do it over my way." He grimaced and they all laughed. "I'm set in my ways. Can't help that, at my age, can I. But Lord knows, if I can't pack my own suitcase at my age, I'm in bad shape."

They waited at the carousel for the bags to come down the chute.

"It's hard on you, John." Grandy regarded him intently. "Terribly hard. And on Leslie. I know you'll both bear up, for your mother's sake, as well as your father's." Grandy cleared his throat and brought out an immaculate handkerchief to blow his nose, not expecting any answer from him, for which he gave thanks. "I'm prepared to stay as long as you want me, Ceil. As long as I'm of some use. Thought I'd play it by ear, as Helen is fond of saying, although what that means I'm not precisely sure. Now." He turned as the bags began their trip around the carousel. "Let's get this over with. Hope they haven't lost mine. All of my friends in California have stories of luggage winding up in the Azores or some such fool place."

They saw Grandy's bags almost immediately. "Helen read somewhere that bags should be marked conspicuously with their owner's initials, so she cut out some huge white letters and taped them on mine. I feel rather like a schoolboy going off to summer camp. Only thing she didn't do was sew name tapes in my socks and underwear. Helen is a born executive."

He grabbed the big bag, his mother dealt with the smaller of the two. Grandy hailed a porter, who loaded the bags onto his cart. They followed the man out to the street.

"You stay here and I'll bring the car around," his mother said.

"Nonsense. John and I can manage," Grandy told her. "I'll take the little one, John can have the big one. Why do we have strong teenagers around if not to wrestle with the luggage, eh, John?"

"I can take them both," he said masterfully. "Stand aside," he ordered, and they did as they were told, giving him a feeling of immense power and satisfaction. For a minute, he forgot why they were here, at the airport, loading Grandy's bags into the car. For a minute, he knew a moment of pure happiness. Then it came back to him with almost physical force that Grandy was here on a terrible mission, and guilt at his little instant happiness took hold of him. He put down the bags and took a deep breath. When he picked them up again he felt smaller, diminished, a child once more.

They had tea when they got home, and Grandy gave them a large bag of artichokes, a present from Helen, he said, who made a regular trip to the heart of artichoke country, which was near where her sisters lived. Nothing would do, Grandy said, but that Helen must send them a little part of California. "Henry told her how much he liked artichokes when he was out with us," Grandy said. "He made a big hit with her. And with les girls. Henry was wonderful with all of them, Ceil. They come on pretty strong on first meeting, but he handled them as if he'd been doing it all his life."

John put too much cinnamon on the toast, his hand shook so. His mother kissed Grandy and thanked him, although she knew as well as he that artichokes had always been well down on his father's list of favorites.

All his life. The simplest remark took on new meaning.

"Henry said he'd be home early," his mother said in a strained voice. "He's very busy at the office. He carries on as if nothing is wrong, and there's nothing I can do to stop him working. I suppose it's just as well. He comes home exhausted, but he says he has to keep going. While he still has the strength." Grandy laid his hand over hers and they sat there quietly for a moment. She put sugar into her cup and stirred so vigorously the tea slopped over into the saucer. "He sees the doctor every other day. There isn't any change. There will be no change for a while. Henry's very thin, but otherwise he looks the same. It will take a while, I imagine."

It was as if he wasn't in the room. It was Grandy and his mother talking to each other.

She walked aimlessly about the kitchen, nipping off dry leaves from the geranium on the windowsill, wiping imaginary spots off the stove with a sponge. Grandy drank his tea, letting her talk.

"What about Ed?" he said at last. "Did he let Ed know?"

She stopped moving. "He said he'd wait until you got here. I don't know why, but that's what he decided. I don't argue. He knows what's best for himself."

Then Grandy said in a soft voice, "How about Leslie?"

All three of them seemed to stop breathing. He heard a plane go over the house, heard the mail drop through the slot in the front door.

"Leslie," his mother said. "Well, we haven't told her yet. I was going to call her and he said to wait. She was just here, you see. On vacation. When he got back from Dallas, where he saw Ben Nilson—you remember Ben? Well, he's chief of staff in a new hospital out there, I guess they all love it, it's a whole new way of life, and Henry went to see Ben. They've been friends for years. And when he got back, Les had to leave sooner than she'd thought to write a paper of some sort, and he didn't want to upset her just then. He had to sort it out, had to get used to the idea." She raised a hand to rub her eyes. "You know what I mean. Of course, he will never get used to the idea but," her eyelids fluttered, "you know. You know Leslie, I mean. She will have to be told, of course. He wants to be the one to do it."

He took Grandy's bags up to the guest room, wanting out of the kitchen, which suddenly was stifling. He picked up the mail from where it had fallen. If they didn't tell Les soon, she might spring the Saudi Arabia plan on them. That would be the end. He knew she'd never forgive herself. He was tempted to call her in secret, tell her, but he knew it wasn't up to him. His father had to do it. He only hoped it would be soon.

It seemed an eon since he'd brought Emma and Emma's bags up here, but it had only been a little over a week. He thought he smelled Emma's scent in the room. He wondered if, in her distracted state, his mother had remembered to change the sheets on the guest-room bed. He put down the bags and pulled down the bedspread to sniff at the pillowcase. It smelled of the sun and air. He was glad about that. His mother would never, no matter how distressed she might be, forget to change the sheets. He peered into the hall bathroom and saw fresh towels hanging there. If he closed his eyes he could hear the shower running, imagine Emma was there, washing her hair. He was overcome by a wave of guilt at thinking about Emma's bare skin when he should be thinking about his father.

He went to his room, lay down on the sofa bed, and fished under it, coming up with *Moby Dick*. He'd made a rule that he had to read at least one chapter in any book his arm discovered.

It was a form of random self-discipline. He couldn't always read just what he wanted to read. He'd recently decided he couldn't go through life doing exactly as he pleased, either. He knew that tended to soften a person, and he wanted to be hard. Tough. When he was small, he'd gone to church and Sunday school and could never figure out why. He planned on canceling religion entirely when he got to college. It didn't mean anything to him, he'd announced somewhat belligerently, expecting an argument. His father had simply lowered his paper, peered over his glasses at him, and said he might regret that decision.

No one at school knew about his father. That's the way he wanted it. He knew his secret was safe. He hugged it to him like a lump in his chest. And began to check himself for signs of cancer. Oh, didn't he know them all. Hadn't he read, plenty of times, lists of the telltale signs. Nightly he checked himself for sores or cuts that didn't heal. Moles that changed color or shape. Change in bowel movements. He overlooked nothing.

What will we do without him? Who would chew him out, keep him in line? Crack the whip, tell him to shape up, grow up, take on responsibility? He decided he might have to quit school, go to work to support his mother and Leslie. Forget college. College cost a bundle. There'd be no money for college. He felt a pang, had sort of been looking forward to it. Remembering the music and laughter always behind Leslie when they talked on the telephone, he regretted having to give that up. Football games, house parties. Orgies. He'd heard there were plenty of orgies at house parties. One way or another, it looked as if he might never get to go to an orgy.

He was afraid; afraid for himself, what he would do without his father, what they would all do. Afraid for his father, because death was something to fear, he thought. Was it nothing, or was it grand and gentle, with a benevolent God waiting just over the line, hand out, welcoming smile on His face, ready to lead the newly dead to a paradise that could only be dreamed of. Or was death just the end of everything. Or a beginning. His head swam with the thoughts of death it entertained. Was his father afraid? And, if he was, would he speak of his fear to alleviate it?

Would his father be in pain? Would he take drugs to lessen the pain? Would he, if the pain grew too severe, contemplate suicide? No. That was one thing his father would not do. Follow through what you've started was his father's creed. You've got to follow through, John. That's the important thing. Finish what you start.

Unable to concentrate, he closed his eyes without relinquishing his book, although he'd never found *Moby Dick* so tedious. He thought about dying, what it meant to the person who dies, and the people who were left behind. He wondered how Grandy felt about his own son leaving him, an old man, behind. It was all backwards. Did Grandy feel any small triumph about hanging in there at seventy-three, or did he feel only the sorrow that he was going to have to see his child die soon?

Grandy had called his mother brave. How odd. He'd never thought of her that way. Probably Leslie was brave, too, or would be. The only coward in the bunch was him. He'd turn out to be a son that everyone would be ashamed of, when what he wanted most was for his father to be proud of him. He tried to think of the last time that had happened and drew a blank. Probably his father had never been proud of him. What if his father died without ever once having been proud of his only son?

There were worse things. Yet at the moment he couldn't think of any.

22

"John! John Hollander!" Mrs. Arthur's ratchety voice made the hairs inside his nose tremble. "Come back to us, John. Join the crowd." Appreciative laughter from one or two sycophants stirred her curls, brought a blush to her cheek. She tilted her head to one side, looking at him like a coquette. If you knew how you looked when you do that, he thought, you wouldn't.

"Sorry," he said, unsure of what he was sorry for.

"We're reading *Macbeth* and you are to take the part of Lady Macbeth, John." Inspired casting, that. "Please pull yourself together. One has the feeling your head is not on straight this morning, John."

Mrs. Arthur made the mistake he'd discovered many middle-aged people made. She believed that by using current idiom, keeping abreast of terms young people used these days, she appeared younger, more au courant. In his eyes it only made her appear silly.

He didn't feel up to being Lady Macbeth today. Or anybody else, for that matter. Not even himself. He wanted to hide, crawl inside some warm and secret place, take a long nap there and wake refreshed. A long, forgetting nap, which would cleanse him, make his father well.

"All right, boys. Places, please." Mrs. Arthur waved her arms in the manner of an orchestra conductor. "*Macbeth*!" she trilled. "Act one, scene seven, if you will, please."

Macbeth was Larry Dunne, who was possessed of a strangely nasal voice, even when he didn't have a cold, which he now did. "If we should fail . . ." Macbeth said through his stopped-up nose.

"Ready, Lady Macbeth, please." Mrs. Arthur sent him a piercing, yet winsome glance.

He found his place. "We fail! But screw your courage to the sticking place and we'll not fail!"

At the word "screw" there was an outburst of laughter.

"Boys! Please!" Mrs. Arthur clapped her hands together smartly. "Come to order!"

The more frantic she became, the more chaos reigned. He put down his book, went over to the door, and let himself out into the quiet hall. It would be some time before order prevailed and Mrs. Arthur missed him.

He leaned against the wall, wondering if he should just cut for home and let the demerits fall where they may. Maybe they thought he'd meant to be funny. He had the reputation of playing the clown, and playing it to the last row in the balcony. Maybe they thought that he had doctored Shakespeare's lines.

"Screw your courage to the sticking place," he said aloud.

"Hey, what's going on?" It was Keith, coming toward him.

John ran his hand across his face, finding that his eyes were moist. "Nothing much. It just got too much in there." He gestured toward Mrs. Arthur's room. "She made me Lady Macbeth for the day, and I wasn't up for it. That's all." Hardly a reason for crying, but it was the best he could do on such short notice.

"Well, let's split, then," Keith said. "Let's get on with the cleanup job. We can start a little early. You know, work-study program. We've got a lot to do."

So they left. They hitched to Keith's apartment, catching a ride in a Ford pickup on the first try. When the driver saw their ties and jackets, he tried to charge them for the gas. Keith turned out his pockets to prove they were broke, and the man's eyes turned small and hostile. He jammed on his brakes and said, "Out," having driven them a good part of the way. "Little bastards," they heard him muttering as he drove off.

Keith's kitchen had a stale smell. Several bulging plastic garbage bags leaned tiredly together, holding one another upright in one corner. Dirty dishes crowded the sink, and an open container of heavy cream stood congealing nicely on the counter.

"Don't look too closely at anything," Keith warned. "I've been leading a bachelor existence since she did a number on herself and, believe me, bachelorhood ain't what it's cracked up to be. Want something to drink? Water? Orange juice? Maybe even ginger ale, if I've got any."

"What do I drink it out of, my hands?" he said. They opened the refrigerator and peered in at its dismal contents. "What's this?" Gingerly, he poked at something that resembled a pygmy's head.

"Half a lemon?" Keith guessed. "How about some cottage cheese?" Keith opened the plastic container and sniffed. "Over the hill," he said, chucking it in the direction of the garbage bags. "I know. I just bought some frozen fish sticks and frozen french fries. They're dinner. You think it's too early for dinner?"

"That's okay," he said hastily. "Let's do the cleanup first. I came to work, I want to work. And baby, it looks like I came to the right place." The place looked as if it had been trashed by professionals. There were cigarette burns on the tables, one on the arm of the couch. Empty glasses lolled about, under the chairs, one under the TV set. A pair of dusty shoes with run-down heels sat on the thick-piled carpet, which bore several large stains. A layer of dust covered every surface, even the glass-topped coffee table and the copies of *Architectural Digest* and *Town and Country*, which, oddly enough, were neatly arranged, as if lined up in a doctor's office, titles showing.

"How about if we open some windows?" he suggested. It was far from balmy outside, but a little fresh air seemed indicated. "Then we can start with changing the sheets, maybe clean the bathroom." It had been his experience that fresh sheets and a clean bathroom perked up a place considerably.

"We have a cleaning lady," Keith said, looking around, but unable to find any sign of her touch. "I guess she hasn't been here for a while. Probably because my mother ran out of funds. We only have her come in when we're in the chips. I guess we

better start by getting out the rags and stuff." They foraged
under the kitchen sink and came up with some soap powder
and a scrub bucket. And a large bag of rags. "She collects rags,"
Keith said. "The vacuum's in her closet. I'll get it."

He followed Keith into Mrs. Madigan's room. He had
never been in it, and he was curious. If a stranger walked in
here, would he get any idea of the person who lived here? The
bed was enormous, stretching almost the width of the room.
There were masses of little pillows strewn on it, pillows that
seemed to serve no purpose. The spread and the headboard
were covered in matching fabric. The same fabric covered a
small chair that sat in front of the dressing table. Its glass top
was laden with bottles of perfume, bottles of moisturizer, bottles of what he called youthifiers. Keith opened his mother's
closet and a passel of dresses and coats seemed to leap out.

"It's in here somewhere." Keith went deep into the mass of
clothes. The floor of the closet was covered with the same
bright green carpet as the rest of the room. He thought that a
nice touch. Luxurious, kind of. Keith backed out, dragging the
vacuum.

They filled the bucket with hot water and soap powder.
"I'll do the bathroom," he said. "I'm an expert on bathrooms.
How about some rags?"

"Here," Keith said, handing him the whole bag. "Take
your pick."

"Hey," he said, rummaging through, trying to find one the
right size. A piece of towel was good. "This looks like a perfectly good blouse, shirt, whatever you call it." He held it up.
It was pink, with an alligator on its front. "Nothing wrong with
this. Maybe it got in here by mistake."

"That's hers," Keith said. "It might have a spot on it, or a
cigarette burn, maybe. She puts things away when she's on the
sauce, she doesn't know what she's doing. Check it out. If nothing's wrong with it, use another one."

He could find nothing except a small hole under one arm.

"Should I use it?" he asked. Keith shrugged. "Might as well. She's not much on the mending bit."

They heard a knock at the door. Keith went to answer it.

"Mrs. Madigan home?" asked a small, squint-eyed man in a brown suit.

"No," Keith said. "Can I help you?"

The man flashed his moist teeth in a joyless smile. "Not unless you got two months' rent stashed away, bud. Payable now."

"She's in the hospital," Keith said.

"Yeah?" The man's eyebrows expressed disbelief. "Sorry to hear that. But my problem is, the rent's due. Overdue, I should say. When's she coming home?"

"I'm not sure. How much do we owe?"

The man extended a folded piece of paper. "It's all down there. Two months, plus a third, so's we don't have to go through this again next month. My time's valuable, ya know. It takes a lot of time, collecting rents that shoulda been paid already. I don't enjoy it, believe you me." The man moved around inside his brown suit, which had been meant for a much larger person. "If she don't pay up in a week's time, then it's out." He jerked a stubby thumb over his shoulder, indicating where out was.

Keith took the paper, shut the door, and said, "Cripes."

From the bathroom, John called out, "One thing about this joint is, it's a real challenge. Have no fear. I'll have it looking like the Waldorf in jig time. This tub hasn't been scrubbed out in a month, I bet. The thing I hate about cleaning bathrooms is all the hair," he said.

Keith didn't answer. "I oughta be cutting down trees," John hollered. "Or splitting wood. What kind of job is this for a man. Or a woman, for that matter."

The telephone rang. As John scrubbed, he heard Keith say, "Oh, hi, Dad." Then silence. "Yeah, well, Mom's in the hospital. Maybe tomorrow. The doc says he's not putting her

away again. She won't go, anyway." Another silence. "No, I
don't think so. I can't leave her, thanks anyway. Yeah, okay.
Sure. Good-bye."

He ran water into the tub, watched it drain out, then laid
his head on the hard cold edge of the tub.

"You know what he wanted?" Keith stood at the bathroom
door.

He looked at Keith's feet and thought, I don't want to
know what he wanted. Screw him. Shakespeare, act 1, scene
23. Untitled drama. Just screw him.

"He's house-sitting in the Berkshires for the summer.
Some faggy friend pays him to skim the bugs out of the swimming pool and chop up the Beluga for the dogs. He wants me
to come spend the summer with him. You know what he said
when I told him about my mother?" John stayed where he was,
kneeling on Keith's bathroom floor, knowing that Keith was
going to tell him without being prompted.

"He said, why didn't she marry a nice Jewish psychiatrist
and save herself a bundle."

John jostled the bucket, sending soapy water over the
floor, over his nice clean bathtub. He raised his head to look at
Keith, who was about to recite more atrocities he didn't want to
hear.

"What's bugging you?" Keith said.

He shook his head, unable to speak.

"That bad, huh?" Keith flipped down the lid of the toilet
seat and sat on it.

"Shoot. Maybe I can be of assistance," Keith said jauntily.

"My father's dying," he said.

Keith blinked once or twice and said, softly, "Shit."

That was as good a word as any to sum it all up, he figured. He got up and said in an almost normal voice, "Get off
the can so I can clean it, will you?"

"Christ, John, I'm sorry." Keith looked as if he were about
to bust out crying. "I can't tell you how sorry I am. Here I am,

shooting off my mouth as usual, laying my troubles on you, and you've got the big trouble. What can I do?"

"Nothing." He poured more soap powder into his bucket and filled it at the sink. "You got a toilet brush? Something to wash it out with? I can't very well use my hands, can I. The place smells like a cat latrine, for God's sake."

Keith fumbled behind the toilet. "Is this all right?"

"It's sort of bald," he said, "but if it's all you've got, it'll have to do."

He washed out the toilet bowl, flushed the toilet, contemplated his work with a critical eye. "If you have any Windex, ammonia, anything like that, I can clean off the mirror, too, in case you want to look at yourself."

"How do you know all this stuff?" Keith said, producing an almost empty bottle of sudsy ammonia.

"My mother. She thinks boys should know how to clean the bathroom." He lifted his shoulders so they almost touched his earlobes. "She's some hot ticket, my mother."

Keith was looking at him. "Is it the big C?"

"Yeah," he said. "The docs figure six months is the max." Now that he'd told Keith, he found he could talk about it dispassionately.

"That's terrible, John. I'm sorry as hell," Keith said.

"Thanks. I'm doing the best I can, but it's hard. My father's not the easiest guy in the world to talk to. He clams up. He doesn't let me in on what he's thinking or feeling. It must be awful for him. I'd like to help him, but he won't let me."

"If that happened to my father," Keith said slowly, "I guess I'd feel bad. Even if I don't see him very often. I'd feel bad, sure, but it wouldn't be like you and your father. He's there when you need him. He's not selfish, like mine. My old man operates on the theory that he's the most important man in his life. He's in love with only one person, and that's himself. Your father loves you, all of you."

"Sometimes I wonder."

"You know he does. If ever I saw a father who loves his family, it's yours."

Poor Keith. "How do you know your father doesn't love you? In his own way?" he said.

"Maybe in his own way, he does." Keith's voice was sarcastic. "But his own way is pretty shitty."

Someone knocked at the door.

"If it's that little lizard coming for the rent again," Keith said savagely, sticking out his jaw pugnaciously, "I'll blow him away. He'll never know what hit him."

"That suit will stop him from going anywhere," he said.

"Hello, darling!" he heard Keith's mother cry. He went out to the living room. "Hello, John. How nice to see you." Mrs. Madigan put down her small bag and turned to Keith. "Can you pay the taxi driver, darling? I haven't a sou to my name."

"Neither do I," Keith said evenly. "I thought you weren't coming home until tomorrow."

"I wasn't. But it was such a beautiful day and I felt so good, I packed my things, called a cab, and here I am." She clasped her hands in front of her and said, "Aren't you glad to see me?"

A horn bleated below, sounding like an angry sheep.

"Ask him to wait, will you, darling? Call down, tell him the money is on its way." She went into her bedroom and returned waving a twenty-dollar bill triumphantly. "I just remembered I put this in my jewel box. Isn't that fortuitous! Will you pay the driver, darling, and tell him to keep the change."

When the door had closed on Keith, John said, "We were cleaning up the joint so you wouldn't be grossed out when you got home."

"Oh, you are darlings!" she exclaimed, taking off her shoes and running her fingers through her hair. "It's marvelous to be out of there. You have no idea, John."

He smiled foolishly. "Well, I better split. Sure glad you're home, Mrs. Madigan. Keith's been worried about you." He wanted her to know Keith worried about her. She followed him out to the kitchen as he put his cleaning stuff back under the sink. "Stay for dinner, John, why don't you? I'll whip up something exotic."

"No, thanks. I really have to go. Thanks anyway."

She laid her hands on his shoulders and said, "I feel so much better about Keith knowing you're his friend. He really loves you, John." Her eyes glittered ominously and he backed off so her hands fell away from him. If she started getting emotional, things wouldn't be good.

"Right. So long," and he fled.

Outside, he met Keith coming toward him, counting a handful of bills.

"I tipped the guy fifty cents," Keith told him, pocketing the money. "He gave me some flak, but I told him I needed it more than he did. 'Keep the change,' she says." Keith snorted in disgust.

"Listen," John said, "if you feel like talking, I'm your man." Keith put out his hand and they shook on it.

He jogged all the way home. By the time he got to his own street, he had a painful stitch in his side. I'm out of shape, he thought. Sixteen years old and already I'm out of shape. What's this country coming to. He could picture the headline in tomorrow's papers: TEENAGER COLLAPSES, DIES, WHILE JOGGING. Up ahead, he could make out lights in his house.

They were home, waiting.

23

Everywhere he went, the news was not good. Friends, neighbors, children, the young as well as the susceptible old were being pulled into the vortex of terminal illness.

His body had betrayed him. His genes had let him down. His luck had run out. Somehow, he'd never thought this would happen to him. Others, yes. But not him. Or any member of his family. Spare them, Lord, keep them safe. I'll make a deal with you. Anything you want, anything. Only keep them safe.

Maybe this was the deal: his life for their safety. If he could hang on to that thought, it might make things easier.

He still couldn't believe it. Even after listening to Ben's carefully worded sentences, seeing the pain in Ben's face at having to impart the news, it didn't seem real. There must be some mistake.

The nights were the worst. He had taken to waking on the stroke of three, as if an alarm had gone off inside his head. At first, he was fool enough to think he might tug on the ragged edges of sleep, pull them around himself once more. Then he came to grips with the knowledge that sleep had flown. Music soothed him. He went downstairs and turned on the stereo, very low so that no one would be disturbed. After several such nights, John said, "You can use my headphones, Dad, if you want." He had always made fun of John and those idiotic headphones.

"Thank you," he managed to say with difficulty, "that might be a good idea." John must have heard him, late at night, listening to his golden oldies. What a good, tactful boy he was.

All things considered, his life had been rewarding. A beautiful, loving wife, good children, a good marriage. A job he liked, one that made him feel he was contributing something. Enough money. Not a plenitude, but enough. The respect of those he respected. Friends.

But he needed more time. He had thought he was good for another twenty, maybe even twenty-five years. Actuarial tables had practically promised him that much time. A minimum of that much time. It had just showed you couldn't count on anything.

Once or twice the thought had sneaked into his consciousness that Ceil might die before he did. He did not think he could bear up under that. Now he wouldn't have to. Ceil would prevail over her grief, would probably marry again. He had the financial thing worked out pretty well. There was enough for the children's education. Ceil might want to sell the house, buy something smaller. John would help with the lawn, the garden. The thought of his garden calmed him. The minute the frost was out of the ground, he would start digging. No matter what.

But there must be some mistake.

Leslie came back, pulled by Grandy's visit.

"Why didn't you come last week when I was here?" she cried, embracing her grandfather.

"You're grown up, Les," Grandy said, holding her at arm's length. "When I wasn't looking, you turned from a little girl into a big one."

"Not girl, Grandy," she said. "Woman."

She went to her room to settle in. John was home. He made the mistake of following her. He should've known better.

"If there's one thing I can't stand, it's being treated like a child," she said, turning on him. It could've been him talking. "What is it, John?" She brought her nose up to his.

"Will you tell me what's going on?"

He backed off and said, "What's with lover-boy Varney?"

"Is it Mother or Daddy?" she pursued. "Is something wrong with them?"

"I have to go now," he said. She grabbed him and hung on. He always forgot how strong she was.

"Tell me," she commanded. He broke away. He was strong, too. Pretty soon she would no longer be able to deck him and sit on his stomach, bouncing up and down while she farted and sang "The Star-Spangled Banner," a trick she had perfected in the ninth grade.

He attempted to escape, but Les tripped him and sent him sprawling. It was as if they were children again and he had taken one of her prized possessions and was making off with it.

"I've a right to know, John." She stood over him. "It's my family as much as it is yours."

He lay where he was, looking up at her. "It's Dad," he said. "He wants to tell you, Les, but he's scared."

She ran. He could hear her footsteps pounding down the stairs.

He put on his parka and went outside. The sky was pale lemon and apricot. A few sparse clouds scuttled to make it behind the horizon before the dark closed in. He went down to the pond to investigate any changes since the last time. There was still a skin of ice on the water. With his heel he pushed at it to break the coating. Water welled up, covering his boot. He thought again of the three little brothers who fell through the ice in New Hampshire. So long ago that seemed, yet it had happened only last month. So much had happened. He wondered if it would be safe to go back inside. It will never be safe again.

His mother was at the stove, tasting something on the end of a long-handled wooden spoon. She liked to taste, to season, taste again. She said it was part of the fun of cooking.

He shut the door noisily and she looked up, startled.

"Did he tell her yet, Ma?"

She looked at him and he thought she might be on one of those tranquilizers American women were supposedly addicted to. In fact, he had heard his mother talk disapprovingly of women who took pills in order to cope. But that was before she had all this to cope with.

"Your father is talking with Leslie now," she said. "Would you get down the green salad plates, please, John? Our strength is as the strength of ten because our hearts are pure. We don't have much time left. We've got to use every minute wisely."

She must have a book up in her room entitled *How to Deal With Death*.

"Don't forget the salt and pepper, John," she said, and went out to set the table.

"The doctor says it's cancer, Les." One down, plenty more to go.

"Oh, Daddy." She took him in her arms, almost as if she were the parent and he the child. "Oh, darling Daddy. Cancer doesn't mean you have to die. Not anymore it doesn't. A girl I know at school told me her father had cancer of the mouth and was given a ten percent chance of recovery if he took chemotherapy instead of having an operation, which would've meant he couldn't talk anymore, and he took the chemo and he's cured. Cured, Daddy." Leslie's eyes glistened as she told him of this miracle. "So you see. It will be all right." She kissed him and he almost believed her. He had passed the worst hurdle. He needn't have dreaded telling her. He had left some vital parts out, but the initial hurdle had been passed.

Oh, yes, the nights were very bad. And this night, when he'd told Leslie at last, outdid all the others. Leslie, the eternal optimist. She was so sure, so positive in her beliefs, she could almost lure him into thinking she might have something.

He would continue to grapple with life. He had made up his mind. He had read of miracles and knew in his heart there would be no miracle for him. But he had weeks, days, left to live. And he had his family gathered together now. The house throbbed with their breathing, their life. All the people he held most dear were there, under his roof. He protected them still.

Death doesn't end anything, he told himself. Not believing

it. Not an original thought, either. He had read it somewhere. Dying is a beginning of a kind. I am not interested in death. I reject the whole idea.

I want to see another spring.

Beside him, Ceil stirred. "No," she said. "No, no, no." He pulled at the corner of her pillow to make her stop. Then he put his own pillow over his head, not wanting to hear what more she might say in her sleep. And to smother the sounds he felt rising in his throat and wasn't sure he could contain.

Death is a beginning.

But I haven't reached the end yet. I'm not ready for a beginning until I've reached the end.

I'm hanging on for dear life.

Dear life. That's just what it is.

24

He woke with a start, hearing voices. There was light in the room. It must be close to dawn. Then he saw that the light was reflected from the kitchen windows, shining into his room. He got out of bed and put on the camouflage suit over his underwear. He'd taken lately to sleeping in his underwear for no good reason except he had a feeling he should be prepared. For what he didn't know. He was anxious about everything now, things he'd never given a thought to before.

He stood at the top of the stairs holding his breath. He didn't want them to know he was here.

He held himself still, wondering if he should play it cool

and sort of saunter down, into their midst, or if he should come
in rubbing his eyes, pretending he was still half asleep.

Maybe it would be better if he minded his own business
and made a fast retreat to bed.

He heard his father's voice, then Grandy's. He heard
Grandy say "gin." Were they drinking, then, in the middle of
the night?

By the time he'd decided to tough it out and was standing
in the hall barefoot and shivering, they'd moved to the study.
He looked in. They were playing cards at the desk. Grandy
wore his old gray bathrobe, and his silvery hair was neatly
combed. He wouldn't have been surprised to see his grandfather dressed in his pin-striped suit and wearing his Homburg,
even at three-thirty in the morning. His father was uncharacteristically untidy, dressed in his red and blue plaid shirt and
khakis that he usually saved for his gardening days.

They both looked up as he came in.

"I heard you talking," he said lamely. "I saw a light in the
kitchen and I thought it was time to get up, that I'd overslept."

"Well, now that you're here," his father said, "sit down
and you can referee the game. Grandy's beating the pants off
me. He's already schneidered me once."

"Helen and I play gin nearly every night," Grandy said
apologetically. "I've had lots of practice lately. Henry, do you
remember the time we flew to the coast and had to circle the
airport for hours and we played gin the entire time?"

"Do I remember!" Henry dealt the hands. "Dad, I thought
about that trip last time I was in a plane. I hadn't thought of it
in years, but we went through some turbulence and it got
pretty bad and I was scared silly. I was scared silly the time
you're talking about, too, which is why I remembered. But you
were so calm, so fearless, I had to pretend I was, too."

Grandy laughed. "I'm glad I pulled that off, Henry. I was
frightened out of my wits. I thought we'd had it for sure.
Here." He gave back one card. "You dealt me an extra one."

"Is that true, Dad? Were you really afraid?"

"Of course." Grandy arranged his cards with professional speed. "I'm not very brave when it comes to airplanes, Henry. I thought you knew that. Your mother was fearless, so I had to pretend a lot." Grandy smiled at his cards fondly. He must have a good hand. "I put on a good act."

"That's the secret, I guess," Henry said. "Putting on a good act."

"You want me to make some coffee?" John said. It was cozy in the study. There they were, three male Hollanders, playing cards and carousing in the wee hours. He liked to think they were carousing, he and his father and his grandfather. It was probably as close as they'd ever get. To carousing.

"That would be fine, John." His father sounded quite cheerful and seemed more relaxed than he had in some time. John whistled his way out to the kitchen, stopping at the hall closet to borrow a pair of Leslie's fleece-lined boots. His feet were blocks of ice by now and the boots didn't help much, but he didn't feel like going up for his slippers. Besides, if his mother heard him she'd make him go back to bed.

With John out of earshot, Grandy smiled and said, "It's amazing how his hands and feet get in his way, just as yours did at that age, Henry. Have you noticed?"

Henry shuffled the cards without answering. Then, in a voice that trembled slightly, he said, "Do you remember how you used to compare my coordination with Ed's, Dad? Ed had superb coordination, you used to say. You'd never seen such hand-to-eye coordination as Ed had. You told me that quite a few times, Dad. I used to go out to the field in back and practice my hand-to-eye coordination but it never seemed to get any better. Never close to Ed's."

Grandy cleared his throat. "I don't remember saying that, Henry. If I did, I'm sorry. That was exceedingly tactless of me."

Henry continued to shuffle the cards.

"What ever happened to Mona Abrams, Dad?" he asked.

Grandy pulled at his cheek. "Why, I don't know, Henry. I haven't heard of her in years."

"I don't know if I ever told you, Dad." Henry's hands were still, his eyes on his father. "Shortly before Mother died, the time I visited you out at the lake, she and I took a long walk and she told me that you and Mona Abrams had been lovers. For some time, she said. I was stunned. But, as we both know, Mother didn't lie. Or imagine things. I knew she was telling me the truth. I just couldn't figure out why she'd told me, after all that time."

Grandy's skin looked taut and grainy, his eyes almost black. He shook his head once or twice, but said nothing.

"What a strange choice for you to make, Dad. Mona Abrams. She wasn't even good-looking."

A heavy silence, like old draperies thick with dust, settled over them, held them in a stifling embrace.

The clatter of china, the sound of John's feet as he whistled his way down the hall, made them sit very straight in their chairs and rearrange their faces into a semblance of cheer, like two store-window dummies.

John set down the tray with a thump. "I let it perk ten minutes, the way Ma said." He backed off, squinting at his handiwork. "I didn't forget anything. I even remembered spoons."

"Good for you," his father said.

Grandy took a clean handkerchief out of his bathrobe pocket and wiped his face. "Perfect," he said faintly. "Just the thing."

"You okay, Grandy?" John said, dismayed at Grandy's pallor.

"Fine. It's getting a bit late for me but I want to try your coffee, John. I had no idea you could do such a good job in the kitchen."

"You should taste my french fries," John said proudly. He poured out the coffee and passed the cups. Watched as they tasted.

"That's first-rate, John," Grandy said. "Absolutely first-rate."

"Very good, John," his father said.

John looked from one to the other, trying to figure out what was different. They both looked wiped out. He probably shouldn't have made coffee, after all.

"Well, I better pack it in," he said. "Big day tomorrow. See you," and he went, taking the stairs three at a time. He almost fell over his mother on the top step. Her head was against the wall and her hands were dangling between her knees. She was asleep.

"You better hit the sack, Ma," he said, touching her lightly on the shoulder to wake her. She opened her eyes and sat up.

"I heard them talking," she said, "and I wanted to make sure he was all right. I'm glad I didn't go down. It would've spoiled it." She kneaded her cheeks with her fingers, trying to wake up. "Did you have a nice time, just the three of you?" She sounded wistful.

"It was okay. They played gin and I watched. I made us some coffee."

"I smelled it."

"I hear them coming," he whispered. "Better take off, Ma. You don't want 'em to catch you here." He watched her hurry into her room and close the door soundlessly. It wasn't often he called the shots with his mother.

He had overslept. Lucky for him he still wore his underwear. That was a real time-saver. When he stumbled down, his father was reading the paper, drinking coffee. Duded up in his city clothes. Otherwise he might've thought his father hadn't slept at all.

"Grandy and Ma still in the sack, huh?"

His father nodded, continuing to read the paper.

"You going to work today?"

"Of course. You better get going, John. You'll miss your bus."

"I already have. I can hitch."

Cars whizzed by, sending road crap onto his pristine clothes. He walked backwards, thumb out, trying to look like a harmless teenaged vagrant worthy of a ride in a well-heated BMW that also had some good tapes going.

Finally, an old codger, about forty, driving a '76 Chevy with a scabrous ruff of rust around its body panels, pulled up.

"Thanks." He hopped in. The codger was suited up in a Harris tweed balmacaan and smelled like a musk ox in heat.

"Where you bound for?" the driver asked, accelerating until the Chevy wheezed in protest.

"Oh, you can let me off a mile or two up the road," he said, leaning on his door. "I'm headed for school."

The man kept turning to smile at him. "Smoke?" He fished a silver case out of his voluminous tweed pocket. "It's good stuff. No weeds, no stems, no nothing. Pure gold. The best."

"Thanks," he said, taking the joint. "I'll save it for later. Last time I smoked when I was in a car, I tossed my best buddy out and he was doing eighty at the time." He managed an ingenuous look and the man's smile disappeared. The Chevy leaped forward, laying a strip of rubber on the road.

"Thanks," he said again as the codger let him out, presumably without regret. "See you around."

The man's glance said, not if I see you first. Probably the guy would've liked to ask for the joint back but didn't quite dare.

"You are some smartass," he told himself, starting to walk. "Some terrible smartass." But it came in handy at times.

25

Halfway through one of Simons's oft-repeated monologues on the glories of Appomattox, he allowed his mind to wander. Recently, he'd read about a well-known writer who'd gotten his start at age fifteen, writing a sports column for his hometown paper. This happened during World War II, of course, when manpower was scarce. But why couldn't he try writing a humorous column and sell it to the local weekly, which, as far as he was concerned, could use some humor. It would give him experience, which was what he sorely needed, if he was going to write for the likes of Woody. And the writer who'd gotten the early start was now so famous his name was a household word.

He smiled at the idea of his name becoming anyone's household word. And bent over his notebook, jotting down a few random thoughts.

"Mr. Hollander." It was Simons, breathing down his neck. "I hate to interrupt your train of thought. May we see what causes you so much amusement?" And Simons snatched up the notebook and read aloud in his high, penetrating voice, "Pulitzer for Humorist Hollander. Hollander Inks Six-Figure Contract."

The class, appreciating any diversion, guffawed.

"Get off his back." Keith's voice came, low and furious. "Let him alone."

A hush fell. Simons's angry face ripened into rage.

"This is a history class, Mr. Madigan, not one in creative writing. I will ask you please to butt out of what is not your concern. Mr. Hollander, your marks indicate your lack of attention has caught up with you at last. I will be forced to take up this matter with your father."

His throat tightened. He felt Keith looking at him but he

was too weary, too depressed to return the look. After the bell sounded, Keith said, "Why don't you tell him what's bugging you? He'd feel like a heel."

"Yeah, I tell the guy and he starts oozing guilt and gives me an A-plus for effort. To hell with it. But thanks, anyway, for standing up for me."

"You want to throw the Frisbee around?" Keith suggested. "Or we could try some lacrosse. I know a guy who has a couple of sticks he'd let us use."

"No, thanks. I think I'll head for home. I'm a real drag these days."

"You have a right."

"Thanks again, Keith. I'll see you." He began walking. The bus passed and slowed and Gus sounded the horn, but he raised his arm and waggled his hand to show he wanted to walk. He jammed his hands into his pockets and discovered the joint. No stems, no seeds, no nothing, the man had said. He found a moth-eaten pack of matches in another pocket and lit up.

The few times he'd smoked pot, it had loosened his tongue and words had spouted effortlessly from him. His own eloquence had astonished him. His friend at Duke, on the other hand, had told him he'd cut out smoking marijuana entirely because he thought it was destroying his brain cells. But that guy had started getting stoned when he was in the seventh grade. What did he expect.

This joint tasted okay. Not pure gold, but okay. He'd make it last—put it out halfway down so he'd have the other half to look forward to.

A car pulled alongside him and stopped.

"Hello, John," his father said.

Talk about being caught with a smoking gun. He considered tossing the half-smoked joint into the bushes and decided he'd tough it out.

"Hi, Dad. What're you doing here?"

"I took an early train." His father leaned over and opened the door. "Hop in. I assume you're headed for home."

He wasn't stoned, just light-headed and loose-tongued. His father seemed not to notice the joint, made no mention of it. He didn't think his father even recognized the smell of marijuana.

They drove in silence. If his father asked him what he was smoking, he'd tell him. What the hell. But his father didn't ask, and in an odd way, he was disappointed.

He leaned back in the seat, suddenly tired.

"Are you afraid, Dad?" The words slipped out. He was appalled at himself. But it was a question he'd wanted to ask for some time.

His father slowed for a red light.

"It's not so much fear," he said slowly, "as it is sorrow at leaving you all. I had so many plans. I worry about what will happen to you." They sat waiting for the light to change and his father looked directly at him.

"When I was a kid, a man lived on our street who was dying of some debilitating disease. He would walk up and down very slowly, waiting for someone to speak to him. I can see him now. No one spoke to him, they avoided him the way people avoid the dying. I'd hide behind the curtains and peer out at him and every time he'd turn in my direction, I'd duck down so he couldn't see me. I think of that man now, years later, and know how lonely he must have been and how he wished for someone to care, someone to talk to him, maybe even ask the question you've just asked me."

The car behind them honked impatiently. The light was green. He inhaled and held out the joint to his father.

"Want to try it, Dad? I got it this morning from a guy who gave me a ride to school."

"No thanks, John. I'd watch that stuff if I were you. I hear it's habit-forming."

"Not any more than alcohol is," he said. "Probably less."

In the old days, that would've started a fight. Now his father only shrugged.

"To answer your question, John. No, I'm not afraid to die. But if I am going to die, I'd like to do a good job of it. I'd like to be brave, not to whimper. I'd like people to remember I didn't whimper."

He looked out the window, too moved to speak.

"Dad." He swallowed hard. "I would lay down my life for you. If it would do any good."

His father pulled into the driveway and turned off the ignition.

"I know you would, John," he said. "I can't tell you how much it means to me to know that."

The joint had burned down dangerously low. He could feel the heat from it against his hand. Carefully, he opened the car door and got out, stubbing the butt against the garage floor. Then he put it in his pocket and he and his father went into the house.

26

"Henry." Grandy patted his son's shoulder, thinking, such fragile bones. He really is down to nothing. "I have loved you all the days of my life. I loved you even before you were born."

Grandy was going home. The visit had actually aged him. His beautifully cut suit, which had looked so natty on his arrival, hung on him now. Grandy took Henry into arms that trembled, arms that had once been the strongest in the world and he knew, with a terrible certainty, that this thing would come to pass: that he would die, and soon.

My father is so frail, Henry thought, full of sorrow. I'm leaving him so old and frail.

It should be me, Grandy told himself. He has years ahead of him. It should be me.

"Dad, I'm sorry. I should never have said those things."

"No," Grandy replied. "It is I who should apologize to you, Henry. For many things. I ask your forgiveness."

They embraced and parted. They did not say good-bye.

"You'll fight it, Henry." Ed's voice boomed out at him over the miles as he called, finally, to tell him the news. "I know you'll fight it. Don't give in, Henry. Our thoughts are with you. We'd come, right this minute, but there's an absolutely crucial meeting in Detroit that I can't miss." Ed's voice faded, then blossomed once more. "Marge says she'll come. If you want her."

For what? The thought of Marge lending them aid and comfort was so ludicrous that he laughed into the phone. Ed must think he was losing his mind.

"That's all right, Ed. Right now it's best if we're alone. I don't really want to see anyone just now. Just wanted to let you know."

The time had come to end the charade he'd been acting out. He told Burrell and it was much less difficult than telling someone he loved. "We'll do everything we can to make things easy for you, Henry. Full salary, all that. Modern medicine is a wonderful thing, Henry. They work miracles every day." Burrell's voice was hearty. "We'll hold your place open, Henry. As long as necessary." As Burrell spoke, reassuringly, his face became suffused with color. At the finish, he was scarlet. Looked as if he might be on the verge of another minor stroke like the one he'd had several years back.

The word had gotten out. People reacted differently. Some avoided looking at him, meeting his eye on the train, on the street. News of imminent death always gets around, he reflected, not without irony. Those who hear of another fallen comrade stop smoking for a day or two, bring their wives flowers for the first time in years, are kind to the elderly. Tip the blind man on Fifth Avenue.

"If I can do anything, Henry," they murmured with the best of intentions. "Let me know if I can help." If he were to say, "Well, yes, as a matter of fact, you can . . ." they just wouldn't be there. He was sure of that. On the other hand, how would he act if any one of them had been tapped on the shoulder instead of him?

His last day at the office, he told Jane about his cancer. She knew something was up—he could tell from her face—but he suspected that she thought he had another job offer, or problems at home, or a disagreement with Burrell. He had known it would be bad, telling Jane. And it was. She was shattered by the news, put her face in her hands and refused to bring them down, even when he said, "I've got to say good-bye now, Jane. I've got to leave." She stood there crying into her hands. "You've been a good secretary and a good friend, Jane. I thank you." She didn't give any indication she'd heard. He closed the door behind him gently, thinking that he would write her a letter from home.

When he got back to the house that evening, he found that some well-meaning fool in the drafting department, whom he hardly knew, had sent him a get-well card with a woebegone lion on its front. Inside, the lion beamed, rejuvenated. Keep Roaring! the card said. He tossed the card to John, who had brought him the mail. "Look at this," he said.

"Sheesh!" said John, succinctly, bending over ostensibly to tie his shoelace.

His father leaned back and crossed his legs. "You just never believe it's happening to you. Sometimes I forget, for as long as five, even ten minutes. When I sleep, I forget. Unless I dream. I never used to dream. Now I do." The room was silent. John could hear his father breathing. "The first minute of waking, I think, 'It's almost spring,' and I leap out of bed and sometimes get all the way to the kitchen without remembering."

A couple of days ago, this exchange between them would have been unthinkable. Now it only seemed easy, without strain.

"I know a kid whose mother tried to commit suicide," he said. "There's nothing wrong with her except she drinks too much and takes pills. My friend says he and his mother might try a suicide pact. I think he's joking, but I'm not sure. He talks a lot about committing suicide."

Asshole. Why'd you go and tell him that?

"What I wouldn't give for another year," his father said, as if what had just been said was perfectly relevant. "Another six months, even."

John had the feeling that a barrier had been crossed.

"I've been drawing plans here, John, a diagram, really, for my garden. I wonder if you'd look it over and tell me if there's anything I've forgotten."

He looked over his father's shoulder at the intricate plan he'd drawn up, what would be planted and where. "You left out the beans, didn't you?" he said. "I don't see beans anywhere."

"I knew there was something. Your mother would never forgive me if I forgot beans." The door opened and his mother stuck her head in. "Oh, it's you, John. I thought Dad had a visitor. What are you talking about?"

She sat down, frowning, her lips tucked up into a travesty of a smile.

"Death," his father said, "dying. Gardens, Ceil. I forgot the beans. John was telling me about a friend of his whose mother attempted suicide and the friend too talks about trying suicide. I said I would be glad of another six months."

Her hands, which had been fidgeting with a button, fell heavily into her lap.

His father got up, went over to her, and put his arm around her. "Just think. I might've fallen out of an airplane or been killed in a crash on the thruway. This way, I have a chance to say the things I might not have had a chance to say. This way I have a chance to mend my fences. It's hard, Ceil. I won't pretend it's not going to be hard. On you, on John, on all of us. I wish there was some way to make it easy."

"Nothing should ever be easy, Henry. Isn't that what you always say?"

"Is that what I always say? What an old windbag I'm getting to be. I'm going to order some manure today. You can spread it, can't you, John? We're going to have tomatoes coming out of our ears, given a little luck and plenty of sunshine. We never have enough tomatoes, do we, Ceil? This time I'm planting more than I ever have. You can even put some up." His mother and father held hands and laughed shakily. His mother hated to put things up.

"Come on." His father pulled her to her feet. "Come on, John, let's take a look around outside. The light is beautiful this time of day. If we had Les here, it'd be about perfect."

As if she'd heard her father speak, Leslie arrived home that evening, bags in hand.

"I'm home to stay," she announced. "The dean was very understanding. I told her about Daddy, said she could check with you, Mother, if she didn't believe me. She said she believed me and how sorry she was. My marks are good enough, so she said I didn't have to worry about making up credits. She said I could take my exams in the fall or whenever I go back to college. Everyone was very kind. I expected an argument, was all ready for one, and they were all so nice." Leslie turned away.

"So we're going to have you around all the time now," Henry said.

"I'm where I should be, Daddy," she told him.

"Yes," he agreed. "Yes, Leslie, you are where you should be."

When he and Les were alone, he said, "How's Emma?" He was proud of the effortless way he said her name. "What's she up to?"

"No good, I would imagine." Leslie lunged and got him in her famous shoulder pinch, with her thumb in that special little groove she knew how to hit just right, immobilizing him.

"Listen, John," she hissed, looking over her shoulder, making sure they were alone, "don't get me started. I don't have enough time to tell you about Emma. Who the hell does she think she is, coming to my house as my guest and seducing my little brother? Just who the hell does she think she is?"

Leslie, mad, was awesome.

"It was okay," he said meekly. "It wasn't all her fault."

"Bullshit." Leslie, who rarely swore, was on a rampage. "I know her modus operandi. I should've had my head examined, bringing her here. But it never occurred to me she'd pick on my kid brother."

He struggled gamely under Leslie's thumb. "I'm not a kid," he said.

"It was your first time, wasn't it?" Leslie's eyes dared him to lie to her.

"Sort of."

"There's no such thing as 'sort of' about the first time," she said. "Either it was or it wasn't." She took her thumb away and stood up straight, tossing her hair out of her eyes.

"Speaking of sex," he countered, "how's Varney?"

"He's gone," she said. "And even if this hadn't happened with Daddy, I wouldn't have gone with him. I decided you were right. I couldn't bug out on them. I had to finish what I started."

He was speechless. She had listened to him.

"How's Daddy? And Mother?" Leslie said.

"Well, he's all right. We're sort of friends, Les. I don't exactly know what's happening, but we're sort of becoming friends."

She turned and he saw her eyes were full of unshed tears. "Oh, Johnny," she said. "Oh, Johnny. I'm so glad."

27

His mother called Gleason to tell him of his father's illness. "I thought it was time they knew, John," she said.

He knew she was right, but dreaded their knowing.

"Dear boy." Mrs. Arthur's voice came at him, sepulchral, lachrymose. Smoothing her rambunctious hair, she said, "You have my—you have my deepest . . ." She choked up, unable to go on.

"Thanks," he hollered, and fled.

He found Keith in the lab, studying by himself for a science exam. "If you want, you can help me spread manure on Saturday," he offered.

"You've been spreading manure as long as I've known you," Keith said, looking up from his book.

"You're a regular laugh riot. You should get a better gag writer. It's for my father's garden. I hope you don't mind," he hurried on, "but when I was talking to my father I told him about your mother, about the suicide bit. I didn't mention your name, I only said 'a kid I know.'"

Keith looked pleased.

"That's all right," Keith said. "I don't care. Anyone

around here who wanted to could check the hospital records and find out she'd been in for a suicide attempt. It's no secret to anyone."

Keith put down his book.

"You know what my mother told me last night?" he said. "She told me the most important thing she'd ever done had been to try to commit suicide. She said it set her apart from other people and that it was the most memorable, would be the most memorable thing about her. That people would always remember she'd tried to commit suicide."

He was horrified, and didn't want to let Keith guess his feelings, so he stood there, head down, waiting for Keith to finish.

"I made up my mind there and then"—Keith's voice was so low he had to listen hard to hear him—"that there were going to be other things people would remember me for. Damned if I want to be remembered for trying to knock myself off. What a crock. I couldn't believe I'd heard her right. But that's what she said, and the worst part was that she sounded pretty pleased about it."

He thought of telling Keith what his father had said about doing a good job of dying, about not whimpering, but he wasn't up to it. Maybe some other time, when they were fully grown and in command of things. But not now.

"Keith's coming to help me with the manure, Dad."

"Good." His father peered over his glasses. "John, the money for your college is there. Your mother and I took care of that some years back. That is, if you don't start writing for Woody what's-his-name fresh out of high school." His father's eyes were kind. The fact was that he knew by now who Woody Allen was.

"Woody only wants guys with experience, Dad. It'd be a while before he'd take me on. But, thanks. It's good to know I can go if I can get in."

"You'll get in, John. No doubt about that." It looked as if there were to be no more diatribes, no more sessions about maturity, responsibility. There wasn't time.

"Daddy," Leslie bounced in, "I've been looking for you." She went to him, kissed him on both cheeks. "I love you," she told him severely, keeping his head in a tight grip. "You're a wonderful father. You know that, don't you?"

He watched his father's face flood with color. Les had the light touch, the right touch. Without being self-conscious, she said the important things straight out. Why couldn't he? Because he couldn't, that's all. He turned and, dragging his tail behind him, went out to await Keith and Mr. Tyler, purveyor of first-class fertilizer.

He and Keith whiled away the time by turning over the soil in the garden, getting rid of the rocks that seemed to grow there. Connecticut was famous for its rock crop. Mr. Tyler must have been delayed; didn't show until almost five.

"Sorry, lads. It's my busy season. Spread it in dawn's early light, lads. Gives the green things a better chance if the fertilizer's spread early." Mr. Tyler never referred to it as anything other than fertilizer. Though he resembled a linebacker for the Rams, Mr. Tyler had the sensibilities of a patrician.

"Don't forget to set your clocks ahead tonight, lads. We gain an hour's daylight, an extra hour of sunshine. A present from the Almighty." Mr. Tyler sent a reverent glance skyward, giving credit where credit was due. Also covering all the bases.

John had been trying not to dwell on the swift passage of days. Daylight savings time meant it was the last weekend of April. Spring was really here. His father was getting his wish.

There was a lot of fertilizer. He and Keith went to work. By dusk, they still hadn't finished. "Spend tonight here, why don't you?" he said to Keith. "That way we can get at it in dawn's early light, like the man said."

"I can't." Keith wiped his forehead. "I don't want to leave her overnight. It's better if I'm there. It keeps her mind off the bottle. I'll be over first thing, though, John."

He went on raking after Keith left, liking it out here; the smells of earth, of manure, the promise of warmth to come.

Leslie found him. "He looks awful, John," As usual, Les got right down to it. No beating about the bush for her. Hit the nail on the head. Nail everything to the wall.

Leslie shook her head. Even in the dim light, he felt the motion of Leslie's head, expressing bewilderment. "I thought he might beat this somehow," she said in a small, sad voice. "I'm always hearing about people being cured of cancer. One way or another. I kept thinking Daddy might be one of the lucky ones."

"No," he said. "He's one of the other kind."

"I can see it in his face. I couldn't before, but I can now." Leslie picked up Keith's discarded rake and began to work beside him.

"What will we do without him?" she said in a small voice.

"I don't know," he answered.

He and Keith worked all day Sunday. His father came out to supervise, offer tips. The sun was hot. It was a day worthy of full summer, a present from the Almighty. Les put on some shorts, found a nearly toothless rake somewhere, and worked alongside, singing old Beatles songs in a loud, enthusiastic voice. He saw Keith regarding her now and then, a bemused expression on his face.

His mother brought them a pitcher of iced tea and some plastic cups. His father sat in one of the canvas chairs, watching them, his face tilted up to the sun. His belt was pulled to its last notch and his pants and shirt billowed around him like a jib filled with wind. He dozed, and his mouth opened a little, making him look like a very old, very frail child.

"I think it's nice enough to cook outside tonight," his mother said. "I can make some potato salad, and Les brought a bottle of rare old Bardolino. We can have a picnic." She smiled at Keith in an open, friendly way, and Keith smiled back.

"You'll stay, won't you?" she asked Keith, who said he'd like to, very much.

"I'll cook the burgers, Dad, if you want." His father always cooked the burgers.

"If you promise to remember about dousing the fire when it gets too hot, John."

When at last they sat down, the sky was perfectly clear, almost without color, except for a band of pink that circled the horizon, as if just beyond it lay an all-night carnival; or a terrible fire raged, consuming acres of timber, herds of wildlife. There was no moon, and the stars showed off brilliantly.

"I don't think we've ever been able to eat out this early before," his father said.

When John was small, he'd asked where mosquitoes went in the winter. His father had told him mosquitoes holed up in a cave, hibernating, like bears, waiting for the first warm weather so they could come out and start biting people. He had believed his father and imagined a big cave, bulging with mosquitoes, lined up and waiting for the go-ahead from the head mosquito. On your mark, get set, GO!

Tonight, blessedly, there were not yet any mosquitoes.

He drank two glasses of wine and felt slightly tiddly. They all drank the Bardolino, which was as good as Les had said. Two spots of bright color decorated his father's face.

"How's my friend Emma?" his father asked Leslie.

"Oh, fine, Daddy. Sent you and Mother her best." Leslie refused to meet his eye.

His mother rested her elbow on the table, then set her chin inside the pocket made by her cupped hand.

"If you ask me," she said, taking a long sip of her wine, "that Emma is some tough little broad. That is my considered opinion."

"Ceil!" his father said, a look of amusement on his face. "Such language."

John saw Keith and Leslie smiling across the table at him.

Ma's really flying tonight, he told himself.

"Be a good boy, John," his mother said, "and get two glasses and the bottle of calvados for Dad and me. Leslie?"

"No thanks, Mother."

He rounded up the bottle and the glasses. Solemnly, he poured the brandy out, handing a glass to each of them in turn.

His father took a sip.

"Ceil, I think I'll go up now. I feel tired, and cold." His father rose in slow motion. They rose with him.

"Good night, everyone. Thanks, Keith, for all your help. It's been a fine evening, all around."

"I'll come with you, darling." Ceil took her husband's arm. Together, still in slow motion, they went upstairs.

When they'd gone, John picked up his father's unfinished brandy and drank it down, fast.

"That makes my eyes smart," he said, blinking.

That evening, as it turned out, marked the last time for a lot of things.

The last time they all sat around a table together. The last time his father felt well enough to be among them. The last time they would love life as much as they had before.

Ben called, several times a week, his voice reassuring, consoling.

Dr. Hall, it developed, was not without compassion, after all. They became friends, of a sort. He watched the doctor's face closely as he examined him, looking for signs first of puzzlement, then of astonishment, indicating the patient had confounded the medical experts, the patient was on the road to recovery.

With a longing so intense it was almost palpable, he imagined the day the doctor reared back and exclaimed, "You're cured! You're a well man!" and joy would illuminate the room.

John was a good and tireless companion, ready to run errands, read aloud, recite poetry if that was what his father wanted. Too late. He felt a surfeit of love clog his throat as he looked at his son. Too late. What had happened, why had he allowed this to happen? This was his son.

And Ceil was there. She was always there now, never distant as she had sometimes been in the past. He no longer had the energy to make love. His love for her was all in his eyes, his hands, whose strength was fading.

When he woke from one of his increasingly frequent naps, he found Leslie sitting beside his bed, reading, or sometimes just sitting quietly. He studied her, the planes in her face, the way her hair fell over her shoulders. Leslie would be all right. They would all be all right, in the long run. John would turn out to be a fine man. A responsible, loving man with a good heart and a good head. The children would take care of Ceil, as she had taken care of them. That, ideally, was how it should be. And very often wasn't.

They would pick up the threads of their lives and time would work its usual healing.

"I'm so tired," he said.

Leslie stirred, laid a hand against his cheek.

"Can I get you anything, Daddy?"

He shook his head with great effort. "If only I weren't so very tired."

Les seemed not to hear him. She brought him a glass of water and smoothed the sheets and put her face next to his. "I love you, Daddy," she whispered. "I love you."

Ceil made custards, floating island, chocolate pudding. No amount of sweetmeats could fatten him up. His flesh was melting away, his bones lay close to his skin.

"I've let you down, Ceil," he said. "All the things we planned to do when we had the money and the time, when the children were grown up and on their own, and now we'll do none of them. I'm sorry, Ceil. I'm sorry I've let you down."

She buried her face in his pillow. "Henry," she said. And although she wanted to close her eyes against the sight of his ravaged face, she kept them open, exerting her will so strongly that when he turned away at last, to sleep, she was nearly unable to close them then.

"This is for you, Dad." John laid a package on the bed. "Open it, why don't you?" Inside lay a medium-sized camouflage suit, the real McCoy, genuine army issue.

"You said you wanted one," John reminded him. "So I sent away for it." What John didn't say was that he'd paid for it with money earned shoveling snow, that it was meant as a birthday present. An early birthday present. With John's help, he put it on, over his pajamas.

A perfect fit, they both agreed.

"It's supposed to be loose," John explained. "You know the army."

"Yes." His father smiled. "One size fits all. Thank you, John." He raised his arms, laid them across John's shoulders. "I didn't realize how tall you'd grown. And still growing." John inched forward, so his father wouldn't have to reach so far. The arms encircled him, tightened. He's hugging me, John thought in amazement. He's actually hugging me. He hugged his father back and even through the heavy medication he could smell the much-loved scent of his father.

"It's the nicest costume I've ever had," his father said, releasing him at last. "I thank you for your thoughtfulness, John."

"That's okay, Dad. Glad you like it." His father looked pale and tired. "I better go," he said.

"John." His father's voice came clear, distinct. "I'm going to miss you."

His throat was very dry.

"Same here," he said.

28

In the late spring, with the lilacs in full bloom, his father died. At home, right on schedule, quietly, with no fuss, without pain. Mrs. Bickford, the day nurse, called them to his room.

"I think it's time," she said softly.

Any time might have been time. The day before his father had grabbed their hands and, for a minute, his grip was incredibly strong. He knew they were there, all of them, Mrs. Bickford said. She could tell.

His mother went downstairs, to call Grandy, to let him know. Grandy said, "I hoped for a miracle."

"You wouldn't have," his mother replied, "if you'd seen him."

His father had expressed a desire to be cremated and that no service of any kind be held. There was some tongue-clicking over this, but his wishes were observed to the letter. His mother kept busy answering letters of condolence, among them one from Emma Kendel.

"Dear Mrs. Hollander," the letter said. "I am so sorry. I remember the time I spent with you and your family as one of the happiest of my life. You were all so kind to me, especially Mr. Hollander. I will remember you and him always. Love to you and John, Emma."

His mother asked him to answer this letter as well as others she'd had from his friends. He thought about it but, in the end, he tore up Emma's letter and did nothing.

Keith wrote to all three of them:

Dear Mrs. Hollander, John, and Leslie:
    I would like to help you in any way I can. Please call on me for anything you need or want, and that includes spreading manure.

Your friend, Keith Madigan

His father had left a note addressed to him, which he kept folded into a neat little rectangle and transferred from pocket to pocket, as he changed clothes.

It said:

Dear John,

    You have been a source of great joy and pride to me. I only regret my inability to let you know this more often while I was still around. I have discussed this with Grandy and he blames this inability on himself. He told me he never allowed himself the luxury of being tender (his words) with me as a boy and felt it was his fault that I had, in my turn, done you the same injustice. I tell you this so that when you have a son, you will do better. I love you, John. Rest assured I will always love you.

                                            Dad

He read this letter for perhaps the fiftieth time and then tucked it away carefully, ready for the next read. He considered going down, maybe making himself a peanut butter on rye, turning on the stereo, dancing by himself for a while. But music, which had always cheered him, had ceased to do so. "I lose myself in music," Les had told him. "No matter how bad things are, I wallow in it. I don't know what I'd do without it."

He went instead to check the garden. The scent of lilacs was overpowering. The deadheads of the tulips and daffodils waved sadly at him, begging to be picked off, put out of their misery. He checked the pond for trout. There were none. He threw some stale bread on the water to see if anything would bite. The swans were gone. After a while, he went to his room.

Maybe a good book would help. He felt a strong urge to get into his camouflage suit. Then he thought better of it and went to his father's closet where his clothes were still hanging.

"I can't bear to get rid of them, John," his mother had told him. Every time she opened the door, she said, the odor of his father was so strong, so evocative, that she could pretend, briefly, that he was still there, just around the corner, coming up the walk. That nothing had happened. Nothing had changed. . . .

He put on an old jacket, one his father had owned for many years and, although he knew the jacket didn't fit, having tried it on many times, he loved it.

"Rest assured I will always love you," he said in a loud voice to the empty room. "Rest assured, Dad." Nobody else's father talked like that.

He buried his face in the sleeve and, for the first time, he cried.